I0586733

SUBURBAN ZOMBIE HIGH
FINAL CLASS
Jeremy Flagg

ISBN: 0-9989282-2-4

ISBN-13: 978-0-9989282-2-7

All characters appearing in this work are fictitious. Any resemblance to real persons, living, dead, or undead is purely coincidental.

Suburban Zombie High Series

Suburban Zombie High

Suburban Zombie High: The Reunion

Suburban Zombie High: Final Class

I dedicate this book to you, the reader. You know what, you're kind of awesome. You reached the end. Pat yourself on the back, give yourself a handshake, and know you have my gratitude. You'll always be a rockstar in my book.

I must acknowledge the support of many who without their help this book wouldn't exist. First I must thank the support of the Metrowest Writers, they have been my biggest cheerleaders. I must also acknowledge my students, you always remind me there is humor in life and somebody needs to write it down. Thank you to my editor, Suzanne Lahna. Most of all, I must acknowledge Joseph Vazquez and Alexa Wilcox for supplying me with plenty of quotes and outlandish behavior.

TUESDAY

"There's something here I tell you." The woman pointed to the complex equation on the computer screen.

The man stepped up to the monitor, adjusting the small square glasses hanging off the end of his pointy nose. "You know I don't understand any of this."

The woman threw her hands in the air. "I understand why Ms. Shelly preferred working at that God forsaken school. You're all a bunch of suits. None of you appreciate the science behind this project. Don't you see it?"

His face remained blank.

"Bryce had been trying to find a way to expand the serum to grant immortality. There isn't, except for a few rare cases--the serum will never grant this eternal youth you're hoping for."

The man removed his glasses, massaging the bridge of his nose. "So you're telling me that proceeding would be futile?"

She pointed at the screen again. "We found a way to bring back the dead. The possibilities are endless. Think about the military potential, the labor force that could be created. Your focus on cosmetics is limiting, sir."

He reached up and began to stroke his mustache. His firm had purchased the company earlier in the year, hoping to expand their portfolio. He was surprised by Provasive Beauty and how unorthodox their research methodologies were. He thought of the copious grants he would receive from the military, or better yet, overseas investors looking to create subservient armies loyal to their owners. Provasive was about to diversify its product line.

"Have you begun human trials?"

"Yes, sir. As of right now, we only have two successes. The young women seem to possess an anomaly that allows for a mutation of the virus that not only lets them survive, but creates an uncanny ability for regeneration."

"We need to find more commonalities. We'll need a much larger sampling," said the scientist.

"How many?" he asked.

"Potentially several thousand."

Mr. Lazarus continued to stroke his mustache as he pondered the situation at hand. When he had purchased the company, they were preparing to release the chemicals into the water supply to infect an entire town. He applauded them on their efforts, but they needed an experiment they had more potential to control. He didn't want their efforts being traced back to the company.

"Where would we get several thousand willing volunteers?"

She raised her eyebrow at the question. The trials had accidentally begun years ago, when Ms. Shelly exposed an entire high school to the virus. The woman was the first of the living dead they had encountered. There had been the mall, the museum, and her personal favorite, the Chipotle on the interstate. She was surprised how free burrito day made them more ferocious than her virus ever could.

"Well, we could just go back to where we started."

"You mean the school?"

"Two thousand specimens, ready to test. It would be an epic experiment, sir."

The man thought of the school just down the street from them. They were the snottiest, most entitled group of children he had ever experienced. If it hadn't been for the company, he and his family would have never moved to the town. He thought about those kids coming back from the dead and wrecking havoc.

"You have that sinister smile, sir."

"Make it so. Find as many of the immune as you can and let's get this underway."

"Yes, sir," she said. She watched as the man in the designer suit turned around and walked away from her lab area. The fluorescent light flickered as he exited her lab. She turned back to her computer and walked through the equation again, excited to watch the fruits of her labor be realized.

"It shall be exquisite"

She grabbed the small frame on her workbench and admired the photo inside--a woman with thick coke bottle glasses holding a test tube. Inside the tube was a deep green liquid that seemed to be radiating a soft green light. The woman in the photo seemed to be beside herself with glee. Her hair was a mangled mess, but she seemed oblivious to her gruesome looks.

The scientist put the frame down. "Ms. Shelly, you will be avenged."

The woman took off her lab coat and tossed it onto the table. She grabbed a tray of ointment-infused samples and started to walk out of the room. She paused and went back to her discarded lab jacket, grabbed her ID, and clipped it onto the chest of her blouse. "Fanny Shelly, you'd lose your head if it wasn't screwed on."

* * * * *

The methodic sound of the knife slamming down in rapid motion mixed with a popping and sizzling. He tossed the knife up in the air and caught it with one hand while he reached for the counter with his other. The blade spun in the air and he watched closely, projecting where it would land.

"Stop showing off," came a voice from the living room. She didn't have to see his face to know he was pouting. He always pouted when she told him to stop playing with his toys.

He hit the counter with his elbow, sliding the cutting board into the path of the knife. "Yes dear," he moaned. The knife stuck into the chopping block with an audible twang.

"I'm not taking you to the hospital again," she said.

"It was a flesh wound," he said, pulling a spatula out of the drawer.

"It was your big toe."

"It was still attached."

"By a tendon."

He pouted.

"Stop pouting," came the voice again.

With skill that revealed his hours spent in the kitchen, he slid a spatula under the omelet and tossed it in the air. The eggs flipped in a perfect fluid motion, landing in the center of the pan. "Dinner is just about ready."

"I can't eat."

He slid the omelet onto a plate and tossed on some bacon. "It's breakfast for dinner, who can say no to that?"

"This loser of a writer."

He rounded the corner into the living room and saw his beloved wife sitting on the couch, her laptop resting on the cushion next to her. He waved the plate just out of her reach. "I made bacon."

Her nostrils came to life at the mention of bacon. "I guess I could have a piece."

Cadence swallowed the bacon, barely chewing on the crispy morsels. He admired the way she used her canines to tear apart the thick pieces of pig flesh. "So what's wrong?"

He undid the tie on the apron and tossed it on the ottoman. Looking at her with bits of bacon grease already covering her shirt, he tried to stifle a laugh. "You have a bit of..." he bit his tongue and returned to his first question, "So what's wrong?"

"I'm stumped!" She threw her hands up in the air. She grabbed a pillow and stuffed her face into it, yelling. "I'm dried up. Done. Over with. I'm about to become a washed out writer." The blinking mouse on her monitor mocked her, a visual laugh from her laptop.

"Can you consider yourself washed out when you're the focus of an underground cult? Or if you've written seventeen best-selling zombie survival compediums ?"

His face went blank as he saw that she was not pleased with his nurturing tone. "Seventeen? You know what that is?" she asked, her face riddled with anguish.

"A prime number?"

She used her fork to grab bacon off his plate. "That, mister," she swallowed the bacon, "is not eighteen."

"Oh Jesus," he said, hanging his head.

"You know who had eighteen novels?"

Xander mouthed along with her rant.

"That is the number of best selling thriller novels that my heroine," she looked to the signed book sitting on the shelf, "Sydney Livery wrote. Not seventeen. Eighteen!"

"Yes, I know, you're all time hero and the woman you want to steal the record from. We've all heard the speech."

"And do you see the blank page?"

"So what's the problem?" he asked, gesturing to the computer.

"The problem is, I'm out of material. I've already had zombies on a ship, a spaceship, I even wrote that piece talking about an 80's television reunion eaten by zombies. I'm just out of ideas."

"You write some shitty stuff."

"Shut up," she said, "my fans love it."

"Your fans are sad adults. Why don't you return to what got you into writing?"

"You mean the high school?"

She put the food aside and curled up under his arm, trying to grab his last piece of bacon. He slapped her hand and shoved the fatty piece of meat in his mouth. "Yeah," he mumbled through his chewing, "It's what got you hooked on writing. It's either that, or go back to art."

She let out a deep breath. "I haven't been able to work on that in years," she said, looking to the two books sitting on the shelf, "I need inspiration."

"You always said you wanted to finish the story. Just begin working on the last book of the trilogy." He paused, "They're all the rage, right?"

She thought about it a moment, then shot up and began punching at her keyboard. She smiled at him. "You're right. I have the perfect first line."

Ten years ago, a thwarted apocalypse took place in a small suburban high school. A decade later there are new teachers and new students, an entirely new class. The final class.

A chill went down his spine as he read the opening. They both paused for a moment and looked around the living room, examining the shadows to make sure something creepy wasn't about to happen. She turned her head slowly until her eyes met his. She broke out into a shit-eating grin, "It's..."

His hand shot up, his fingers touching her lips. "Don't say it, Cadence Winters," he scolded her. He could see her grin spreading wider until he put his plate on the ottoman and stood. He shook his head, "I'm going to go make sure the guns have ammo."

As he rounded the corner, his wife squealed, "A finale!"

WEDNESDAY

Period 1

The small bridge crossed a babbling brook, splitting this section of the campus from the main building. The bridge was viewed as limbo, space considered school property but technically not. The smokers abused it. Here, they reigned supreme, masked in a cloud of cigarette exhaust, a constant haze of addiction.

"Kevin," yelled one kid, "yo' man, we need to talk."

Kevin cruised closer to the bridge, coasting effortlessly on his skateboard until he finally glided to a complete stop. The kid got off his board and kicked it up into the air, catching it with ease. "Make it fast man, I'm going to be late to class."

The small kid in all black looked around. Rob tried to be discreet as he took a step closer and leaned in, whispering, "Do you have," he gulped, "you know."

Kevin rolled his eyes at the wanna-be. "Uppers? Downers? What?"

Rob's face betrayed him, showing his confusion. "Uhm," he said, "what's good?"

Kevin put his hand on the kid's chest and gave him a firm push back. "You need to back up. This is not for you, man." Kevin had dealt with kids like this before. They were trying to fit in. They wanted a pill not to feel good, but a dose of cool in a small white tablet. This kid, a goth who tried too hard, was the perfect example. Kevin would call him a poser later, but for now, the kid was just a nuisance.

"What?" whined the kid.

"Dude, you sit out here day after day lighting up with

all the kids," Kevin said pointing to the cigarette in his hand, "but I've never seen you take a puff."

The kid scoffed, "You don't know me."

Several of the kids behind them began to chuckle. The small kid's face turned red. His near-white hair seemed to stand out even more with the red face and head to toe black clothing. "Never seen me smoke? Cause you're too busy going to class."

Kevin shrugged his shoulders and tried to move past the kid. "Whatev's man."

The small kid slowly lifted cigarette to his mouth, eyeing the Virginia Slim 120. The plumes of smoke billowed from his cigarette as his eyes crossed looking at the burning end of the stick. Closing his eyes, he put it to his lips and took a long deep drag.

"Ew," Kevin said with an amused look, "smoking is such a drag."

The kid spat out the smoke in a coughing fit as he tried to yell at the skateboarding punk. He fell to his knees, reached into his black pants, and pulled out an inhaler. Taking several hits from the small device, he looked to the group of twenty or so kids staring at him, and failed at hiding his embarrassment.

He stood up and took a deep breath. "For my emphysema," he said as he shoved the inhaler back in his pocket, took another cigarette out of a pack, and lit the end.

* * * * *

"What class do you have?"

The black girl turned around in her chair. "Me?" She stared at a small kid wearing sweatpants and glasses far too big for his head.

He took a step back as she scowled at him. He cleared his throat and spoke again. "Yeah, what class do you have?"

"What's it to you?"

He slid his hands into his pockets and looked down at the ground. Before he could speak, she took a deep breath and began again, "What I meant is, why do you want to know?"

He looked up at the girl, who was smiling at him now. "I saw you sitting at lunch by yourself yesterday," his cheeks turned red, "What I mean is..."

"You're new here, huh?"

He nodded, "Sorry for the abrasive start."

She held out her hand. "My name is Jess."

"David," he said, meekly shaking her hand.

"Nice to meet you David," she looked around at the vacant hall, "welcome to Boxford High School, one of the best schools in the state."

He pushed his glasses up on his nose. "Yeah, that's why my parents moved here. They heard the computer science program here was at the college level."

She inspected the strap over his shoulder connecting to a laptop bag. "I'm sure it is, not that I would know. But to answer your earlier question, I'm headed to," she paused and let the shiver work its way down her back, "to gym."

"Me too," he said.

"I hate gym," they said in unison.

She laughed, and he was taken back by how musical her voice was. "Do you know where we're going?" he asked.

She nodded. "Unfortunately."

She pointed down the hall. "I guess it's good that somebody else hates this class as much as me."

"You mean people like gym?"

She raised an eyebrow at him. "Oh boy," she began pushing him down the hall, "you're in for a shocker."

He started walking along and she fell in beside him. Her hair parted down the middle so it appeared that two giant poofy balls were hovering on her head. Wrapped around her neck was a thick pair of headphones with a cord that passed by her bright magenta hoodie and into one of the dozen zippers on her pants. He quickly directed his eyes forward as he noticed her looking back at him.

"How long have you been in Boxford?"

"Since yesterday," he replied.

"How are you liking it so far?"

He shrugged. "It's okay, I guess. The school looks brand new."

She nodded. "It's only ten years old. The old school got destroyed and then they built the new one."

"I guess that happens to old buildings."

She laughed. "No, I mean a group of students burned down the whole school."

"Really?"

She nodded. "Yeah, the school has some weird mysteries to it. Ask any of the adults and they get quiet really quick."

David went silent while he thought about that. "How long have you lived here?"

"Three years," she said. "When my foster parents adopted me, I moved out here going into my sophomore year."

"You're a senior?"

She nodded. "You?"

"Sophomore," he let out a deep sigh. "My parents refuse to let me skip grades. They say it's bad for my social skills. I should be a sophomore in college by now."

"Check you out, all sorts of smart."

They walked down the long hallway until they reached the double doors of the gym. She took a deep breath and opened the doors. "You can change in the lockerroom over there."

"I don't have clothes," he looked worried.

"Don't worry, I don't change either."

"Oh?"

"No chance in hell I'm participating with this psycho gym teacher."

"Jessica!" yelled a woman.

As the two of them rounded the bleachers, a small Asian woman wearing a karate uniform waited with her hands on her hips. David looked to his newfound friend. "That's the teacher?"

They continued walking towards the woman, "Yup." As they approached the angry looking little woman, Jessica bowed down low. "I was showing the new kid to class."

The little woman looked the kid up and down. "You look weak. You should drop class now."

Jessica hung her head down. "Be nice to him."

David looked shocked at Jessica's response to the teacher. He waited for her to be kicked out of class or sent to the principal's office.

"You didn't bring a change of clothes?"

Jessica shook her head. Before the teacher could reply, Jessica held up her hand. "We're going to sit over here," she took David's hand and started to walk away.

"Don't you walk away from me."

"Whatever," she said and added in a sarcastic manner, "mom."

* * * * *

Sam adjusted the microphone attached to his form-fitting plaid shirt. With a light tap on the on the receiver, he got a thumbs up from another kid wearing a headset. He sat at the anchor's desk in the TV studio, waiting for the camera light to turn red. He adjusted his thick black-rimmed glasses. "How long?" he asked in a disinterested voice.

"Fifteen seconds," cried out another student.

He looked to the empty seat next to him, turning about in his swivel chair to see if his co-anchor was anywhere to be found. He was nervous that he was doing this on his own, but secretly, he was ready for the limelight. He adjusted his tie and ran his hand through his neatly trimmed hair. He was ready to be the center of attention.

With seconds to spare, a kid flung the door open to the studio and hopped up into the anchor chair. As the other students counted down the seconds till the cameras would go live, the boy put his microphone on and gave a smart ass grin to his fellow anchor. "Don't worry, I've got this."

"Kevin," the hipster said, "you're such a..."

"Welcome to the Morning News. I'm your anchor Kevin Cowan."

The hipster quickly added, "And I'm Sam--"

"We have a packed show for you this morning. The principal will be coming down to join us and talk about the new anti-drug policy coming to Boxford. But before that, we have our weekly sports update for you all. Let's send it off to Billy."

As the red light above the camera went off the hipster turned to his co-anchor, the anger stirring in his eyes. "Are you fucking kidding me?"

"What could you possibly mean?"

20

"You know damned well what I mean! You don't do any of the work for the script, you show up late, and then you just steal the show."

"What can I say, I've got a way."

Sam clenched his jaw. "You've got a way all right, you pathetic skate-boarding freak."

"Says the Buddy Holly wannabe."

Sam began to clench his fists on the desk. Before he could open his mouth in reply, Kevin began again. "That was a great video. Can you believe it's been ten years since the football team won a playoff? Maybe this will be the big year."

"You don't say," Sam said, each word pushed through his grinding teeth.

"Now let's go to our weather woman and hear about the forecast for the rest of the week."

As the camera's red light switched off, Sam kicked Kevin. "You're such a douche bag you know that?"

"You're a trust fund baby, who the hell cares what you think?"

"Says the drug pushing punk," replied Sam with a smug sense of satisfaction.

Kevin slapped the glasses off Sam's face just before the red light came to life again. Kevin smiled at Sam's shocked expression. "You're right, those glasses did make you look like a poseur. I'm glad you came to your senses, Sam."

Kevin smiled as he turned to look into another camera. "We'll give you the daily updates, but first we're going to have an expose on the cafeteria situation. We'll hand it off to Liz."

As the light turned off, Sam threw a fist at Kevin's face. Kevin pushed the fist away before it could land, then braced his foot on his co-anchor's chair and kicked. The chair and its occupant sailed off the side of the small stage. "Have your dad write you a check to help you get over those hurt feelings."

Kevin's face quickly turned back into a smile as he looked at the camera. "Wow, that is an interesting origin story of the school's Magic Fish Stick Fridays Liz. Now onto our updates."

The cameras switched and Kevin changed the angle of his chair. He held up a collection of papers, tapping them on the desk in a well-rehearsed motion. "Last week, there was a debate for the position of Senior Class President. The verdict has come in and winning with an amazing 98% is Tina Sacarin. Today after school will be the first meeting for the senior class officers, quickly followed by a forum to allow all the former candidates a chance to bitch about losing."

He shifted papers.

"Our beloved ROTC instructor Drill Sergeant Williams has finally been sentenced. Due to his life sentence, he will be replaced as the ROTC instructor. Mr. William's replacement will be available after school for the first training session. From what I understand, the recruits will be shocked by the lifelike situations they will see in preparation for becoming canon fodder."

He shifted the papers one last time.

"Tomorrow will mark the annual rite of passage in which our parents come in to meet with teachers. Letters have been sent, voice mails have been left, and even a wave of text messages. The administrators are hopeful for 100% attendance. This will include not only parents but students. Administration has asked you make sure your parents remain sober before coming, as they do not want to see a slip-n-slide down A-Hall."

He turned to another camera and cleared his throat. "With that, I would like to turn it over to our Administrative Reporter Tina Sacarin. Congratulations Tina on ruling the senior class with an iron fist."

"Thanks Kevin," she said, giving him an over emphasized wink.

The blond in her tight white tank top held the microphone close to her luscious, lipstick-enhanced lips. She sat in a high chair as a gentleman casually leaned on a table next to her, attempting to be approachable and inviting. "I'm here with the principal," she said in a breathy voice, "to talk about the new drug policy."

She turned to face a man wearing a tailored suit and blue tie. "Mr. Rightoff, what is this new policy?"

He tried to reach for the microphone, but she pulled it away. Awkwardly leaning in, he spoke into the small black device. "Well, it has come to our attention the drug use is out of control at this school. To combat this situation we've instituted a zero tolerance policy."

"And what does this mean?" asked Tina.

"It means if we discover a student under the influence or distributing narcotics, you will be expelled."

"What about meds from your doctor?"

"Well, those don't count."

"What about Tylenol?"

"Well--"

"And what if drug use is part of my religious beliefs?"

"Well--"

"And what if my parents are giving me meds? Wouldn't your rule violate the sanctity of the child/parent relationship?"

"That's not what--"

The principal jumped as Tina slammed her hand down on the desk. "It seems that the administration hasn't fully grasped the consequences of their decision."

"Listen here, missy--"

She pulled the microphone back away from his mouth. "Well, it looks like this is another poor situation the administration has gotten themselves into. I'm sure our parents' lawyers will be contacting the school shortly to discuss this matter. For now, this is Tina Sacarin. Back to you Kevin."

Kevin waited for the small light on the top of the camera to turn red. As it came to life he flashed a toothy grin. "Thank you for joining us again this morning. You can catch repeats of our show every fifteen minutes until our next show on the public access station."

He gave a slight nod to the camera. As the light died down, the students behind the cameras and the teleprompter walked back towards the control room. The principal, huffing and puffing, stormed out of the studio grumbling swears under his breath.

As the door slammed behind the Mr. Rightoff, Sam sat up on the floor. "Kevin Cowan, I'm going to kill you."

Tina laughed. "Hard to collect money from your trust fund in jail."

Sam stood up, glaring at the large-chested girl. "Nobody asked you."

"Can you go away already? The socially acceptable are trying to have a conversation."

"Slut..." Sam mumbled as he followed the principal's path and slammed the door behind him.

Tina leaned over the anchor's desk, squeezing her arms

inward, accentuating her already large bosom. She took a moment to let Kevin take in the view. "Better be careful with your hobby. Sounds like the principal is on the hunt for you."

Kevin shrugged, brushing off the comment. "I'm not too worried."

"Of course you're not."

Kevin fought to keep his eyes on her face. He found his eyes slowly drifting downward, the studio lights showing a long shadow into her cleavage. He gulped as she smiled at his futile attempts to resist her womanly charms.

She reached out and touched his chin. "Going to the Dining Room tonight?"

He gulped. "Why would I go there?"

She stood up and batted her elongated eyelashes. "The music? The potential clients you could find?" She began to walk away from him, every step forcing her hips to sway side to side. "Oh, and I might be looking for you there."

"Uhm..." he choked.

Ring. Ring. Ring.

Period 2

"Are you serious?" groaned several of the students.

"We've done this assignment like three times already. Do you seriously think we need to do it again?" cried a cheerleader in the back row of the classroom.

"You're the devil," said a kid in the front row, his eyes drawn to tight slits.

The teacher took a ruler and slammed it down on her desk. The wooden stick exploded into a flurry of splinters. She had a moment where her eyes went wide as the shards flew across the room. Composing herself, she tossed the ruler aside. "You've done this assignment so many times because none of you seem to have it right yet."

"This is creative writing, not Nazi camp 101."

"First off," said the teacher, straightening out her tight pencil skirt, "that's the stupidest statement ever."

"Hey--"

The teacher held up her hand, quieting the student. The teacher pulled the small reading glasses from her face in an overly dramatic gesture. She rubbed her eyes as she continued to hold her hand up. Finally, she put the glasses back on. "Stupidest," she said again.

"The reason you keep doing this assignment is because you are learning a valuable process. You can bring your stories to life on the page, but it's the editing that will take you to the next step. So we're going to have a bit of a write-in where we come up with new ideas and see how they compare to our first. Then we'll break up for peer critiques."

"Yeah, I get that--"

The teacher made a sign across her throat to cut the talking. Her other hand reached around on her desk looking for the splintered ruler. If he opened his mouth, she was pretty sure she could stab him before she had to hear his nasally voice again.

"If we can get through the rest of class without you complaining, I'll bring Starbucks for everybody tomorrow."

Several of the people in the classroom smiled in response. There was complete silence in the class until one girl graciously said, "Wow, that's a lot of coffee."

The teacher nodded, "I know a girl who works there."

She obtained rockstar status. She was the divine presence in the room as long as she offered to bribe them. This gig started a few months prior and she was already learning how to manipulate and control teenagers. When threats of violence wouldn't work, food and free coffee would. She stifled a chuckle, and most teachers went to school for this? It was a piece of cake.

"Okay, so for this assignment we are going to take a look at confining your novels to a set space and within a set amount of time. Some of you have decided you're the Tolkiens of the new generation and want to write long, exasperated epic novels. However, what if you were given the restriction of forty-eight hours? What if you could only write about the actions happening within a single room? What would drive your story? How would your characters handle this confined space?"

Her students stared, captivated at her words. Occasionally, she managed to grasp their attention. Her creative writing course was a new class at the high school. The woman who should have been teaching the course had won the lottery and decided to give notice.

One of the small children in the back of the room raised their hands slowly, carefully, worried that they would invoke the teacher's wrath. The woman nodded in the direction of the kid and they finally asked, "Do we have any restriction on genre or motivation?"

The teacher smiled. "What if your characters are trapped in a warehouse? While they're contemplating their escape," all the smiles faded, "they're met with a zombie outbreak."

The class groaned in unison.

"What?" asked the teacher.

"Mrs. Winters," raised the hand of a small boy in all black, "do we have to include zombies again?"

"Again?" asked the teacher.

Another girl began speaking, "Seriously. I get it. You're the all powerful and mighty Mrs. Winters, seventeen best-selling novels. I also get that it's been three years since your last novel. But requiring us to write this drivel over and over again? What do you hope to accomplish?"

Cadi threw her hands up in the air. "First off, you bleach blonde sac of estrogen," the whole class gasped. "I am in the midst of preparing for my eighteenth novel. So you can bite me. Second, besides teaching you some decent literally skills, you never know when an in-depth look at the zombie culture could save your life."

All the students in the room froze at the comment. They had suspected there was something wrong with the writer ever since she began teaching at Boxford. Her obsession with the living dead made them wonder if she was still sane. She was mocked by the blondes, and hailed as a champion amongst the goths. Overall, the classroom still found it best to freeze during her outbursts.

She growled, "If zombies show up today, I'm going to

trip every one of you little bastards."

There was an audible intake of breath from each of the students.

"Like you haven't heard worse."

"Jesus Christ," one of the kids said out loud.

"The original zombie," Cadence said without batting an eyelash.

"What?"

"He dies, come backs to life, tortures us all for a few thousand years."

One of the small girls on the side of the room raised her hands. "Uhm, can I go to the nurse? I think I'm going to be sick."

Cadence's eyes went wide, a crazed look of glee spreading over her face. She reached to the small of her back, feeling the gun tucked away underneath her blazer. She walked slowly to the girl and looked at her complexion and slowly reached out to touch her forehead. "You don't look sick."

"It's a headache," the girl said pushing away from Cadence.

The girl didn't wait for Cadence to say anything. She grabbed her notebook and backpack and slid past Cadence and turned in the doorway. "You are going to hear about this tonight. My father is a lawyer."

Cadence shook her head. "Your father is not a lawyer."

"Uhm," the girl hesitated, "he works in a law office."

"Your father is a janitor."

The girl screamed as she went running out of the room. "I hate you!"

"You and half the rest of the world," Cadence said out the door at the stormy teen.

Cadence adjusted her blazer, and looked to the shocked faces of her classroom. "Seriously, of all the things I've said that's what shocks you?"

They laughed at her.

"Now get writing," she sat down at her computer. "While you're working, I think I might join you."

As she flipped open her laptop, she examined the classroom. "Erica, can you go see if she's alright? If she dies at the nurse's office, do you know what to do?"

"Head shots only," mumbled Erica as she walked out the door.

"Good girl! I knew there was a reason you were getting an A in this class!"

Cadence watched as her minions wrote in their creative writing journals. She was always inspired watching them hard at work, conjuring the next great horror masterpiece. She could only hope that the loud-mouthed brat died at the nurse and an outbreak happened.

Cadence stared at the blank screen again as the cursor blinked. She tried to come up with something, but every line she wrote sounded like a bad cliché. She hoped something invoked the true spirit of zombies. As of right now, she knew exactly where she wanted it to take place, she even knew her characters, but for some reason her muse abandoned her.

She switched screens to the Power Point presentation she had been working on. Tomorrow was parents' night, and she wasn't looking forward to dealing with the hell spawns' creators. It was one thing to yell or threaten a teen, but their parents tended to be less about spitfire and more about legal battles. Nobody was ever inspired by a legal battle. No, she needed a serious student beat down to get her blood going.

She watched as the program loaded and finally the

screen popped up. Her presentation was labeled, "The Writer Within." Cadence watched the following slides and quickly realized she had just reused her zombie apocalypse Power Point Presentation. The next slide talked about infection, then about spreading the virus, and ultimately on tactics to survive.

She looked out to the kids writing. They had no chance of survival. With the way they relied on their cell phones and their computers to keep themselves connected, they would die within minutes. She hoped after making them write non-stop about the impending zombie invasion they would stand a chance. She knew better. There was no chance for the final class of Boxford High School.

* * * * *

He watched as one of the students had her eyes pointed toward her lap. He walked over and, nonchalantly as possible, snatched the cell phone out the student's hand. "What do we have here?"

He swiped his thumb across the screen revealing the last text received. "Mrs. Winters is a psychopath."

He raised an eyebrow in admitted defeat and nodded in agreement. "You know," he said, "sometimes I can't argue with that."

"I'm so sorry," said the girl as she slouched down at her desk.

"Am I going to need to talk to your mother?"

He leaned in close the young woman. "You know, if I have to tell your mom that you're slacking in class, she's going to kick my ass."

Jessica nodded. "Sorry about that Mr. Winters."

"You and me both."

One of the kids next to the girl blurted out, "You know Mrs. Li?"

Jessica put her hands over her face and slumped further down into her seat. Xander stood and looked to the room, a group of students doing everything in their power to distract him from actually doing work. He decided to indulge their procrastination.

"Yes," he said walking to the front of the classroom. "I went to school with Mrs. Li and with Mrs. Winters."

"That must have been eons ago."

"Yes, eons," he laughed. "Mrs. Winters was an aspiring artist who was struggling to find her voice and Mrs. Li," he paused. What exactly could he say about the tiny Asian that wouldn't instantly have him fired from his job? "She was a bit angry."

"Was?" asked Jessica.

Xander kind of shrugged at the question. "We all went to school at Boxford High as well."

He looked around the room and recalled the moment when he finally had it with the Teacher. It had been in this very classroom. He had been thrown out for challenging the teacher and his discussion of the plague. There was some irony in the fact Xander had taken over the exact class he had been removed from. It never crossed his mind he might someday be the new "Teacher." Thankfully, students knew his name; it would help keep him alive in the movie version of the zombie apocalypse.

"So how did you end up teaching here?" asked another student.

It was a good question. The short answer was Xander needed something to kill time. The long answer was he and a group of former Boxford students were working with an elite strike force to prevent the genocide of mankind.

"My love for learning?"

Thankfully, the outbreaks had slowed over the last six months; now it was Angelica and Min's husband Hank working to uncover the source of the outbreaks. He missed the field. There was something satisfying about carrying that much ammunition on your body. He was more annoyed than anything; six months and no leads. Ever since the attack at the David Lake Mall, he had been one of the elite commando's. Now he was sitting in front of a group of hormonal teenagers.

"I would rather take my chances with zombies," he mumbled.

He flipped the lights off and turned on his overhead projector. His computer projected an image of a walking cadaver with its neck nearly missing.

"Ewww," came several voices.

"Today in your favorite Pop Culture Class, we're going to talk about the modern incarnation of the zombie."

"You are so married to Mrs. Winters," said another voice.

"Yeah," he said, "she's rubbed off a bit. But it's an interesting topic, and with the random naked man in Florida eating the face off another, it's only appropriate we talk about zombies in popular media."

"Dude, did you see it? It was a naked man, eating the face off another guy."

Xander looked around about to spit out a retort when he caught himself. It wasn't funny cracking gay jokes if Victor wasn't around to confirm the stereotype. Thankfully, a couple of snickering students made him smile. "Yup, and that'll be our lead into zombies in cinema. What's your favorite zombie movie?"

"Resident Evil."

He nodded. "Good choice. It teaches that any woman in stiletto's can survive the zombie onslaught."

"Dawn of the Dead."

"Original or remake?"

"What?"

He shook his head. "Was it kind of new?"

"Yeah."

Xander smiled. "That's one of my favorites. Anybody else?"

"28 Days Later!"

"Aha," he exclaimed. "What's the problem with this movie?"

Not a single student replied to his bait. "Okay, so let's discuss what actually makes a modern day zombie and discuss some of the variations."

He walked across the rows of desks, eyeing each of the students. The group of upperclassmen were avoiding eye contact with him, determined to not speak so early in the morning. He stopped at a student's desk and pointed to the sleepy teen. "Do you remember how the zombies were made in 28 Days Later?"

The kid thought for a moment, trying to recall a movie that was made when he was in elementary school. "Wasn't it something from the monkeys? Like a virus?"

Xander pointed at the kid, getting excited over the answer. "That's one of the most popular methods of zombie origins. Somehow a virus is made, either through accident or on purpose, and it gets out. Sometimes it's the government, other times it's an evil genius. But once it gets out, it quickly gets out of control. Now, did the people in 28 Days Later die?"

The kid shrugged. Xander waited for anybody else in the audience to raise their hand. He raised his eyebrows, gesturing to the class in a sweeping motion. The silence became awkward, until Jessica finally answered. "No, they caught it while they were alive, nobody died."

"Now we have a debate brewing. So how are they fundamentally different than other popular forms of zombie?"

"Real zombies catch the virus and then die. Then they come back to life."

Xander pointed to the student cheering him on. "You might survive the zombie apocalypse."

The kid gave an awkward smile. "Uh, thanks, I think."

"So we know that zombies are most often reanimated by the virus. However, in this movie the people who catch the virus are consumed with an uncontrollable rage. But at the end of the movie, because they haven't been able to eat, they wither and die. In popular zombie culture, zombies don't die from lack of human necessity. They simply wander until they find food."

"So is it a zombie movie?"

Xander pointed to some writing on the board. "That's what your homework is going to be. You need to write a one-page opinion paper about this. If they have all the same attributes of a zombie, but they are still alive, are they still in-fact a zombie?"

The students flipped open their notebooks and scribbled down the notes on the board. He waited until they were done. "Okay, we're going to talk about zombies, how they're made, and the clichés that appear in modern film. I think later this week we'll watch a movie that makes fun of this called, 'Zombieland.'"

"I love that movie!" cried one kid.

"Okay, let's get started--"

"Excuse me Mr. Winters," one kid asked, "I forgot to ask, did you have any of the same teachers we do?"

He laughed. The students were naïve when it came to the school. They were naïve when it came to anything. He once had been the same, he could only hope they never experience what he had.

"The librarian."

"Mrs. V?"

He nodded. "Yup, she was our crazy librarian back then too. She took a few years off after the school went up in flames. But she came back. How could she say no to you guys? She's never been happier..."

* * * * *

"I hope you all die a horrible little death you spawns of Satan!" screamed Mrs. V. at the top of her lungs.

She darted through the stacks towards the back of the library. A faint cracking filled the room, assaulting her ears like nails on a chalkboard. She paused through the maze of books and waited for it to happen again. As the sound repeated, she darted through a set of bookcases, coming out the other side to see a student holding a book flat on the table.

She cringed as the young blonde girl lifted the book and bent it backward, breaking the spine. Mrs. V. thrusted a finger toward the teen in an accusing manner. "What do you think you're doing?"

"What?" asked the student as Mrs. V snatched the book from her hands.

"You're killing that poor book."

"It's just a book," said the young girl.

Mrs. V. took out a chair and sat down next to the girl. As the girl reached for the book again the librarian slapped her hands. "How would you feel if I bent you backwards and cracked your spine?"

"I'm a gymnast, I can bend every which way."

Mrs. V. shook her head. "That's not the point Ms. Sacarin. These books are meant to last forever. They're not going to make it very long if you keep breaking the spines. The pages are going to fall out."

"Oh," Tina replied, "I'm sorry."

Mrs. V. stood and smiled at the sweet blonde book killer. "It's okay, just try and be gentler with them."

As the librarian began to walk away, she turned back to the gymnast. "Did I hear an accent in your voice?"

"I don't think so," she said, "I was born in Boxford."

"It sounds a bit more exotic," Mrs. V. paused and rifled through the rolodex of information in her head. "Mandarin? Have you spent time in Beijing?"

Tina's jaw hung open at the statement.

Mrs. V. returned to the seat next to the girl, suspicious of what the answer could possibly be. There had been reports the last virus outbreak involved an anonymous phone call from a woman speaking Chinese. "How do you know Chinese?"

"I lived in China for four years. I went over to watch the Olympics after I didn't make it for the American gymnastics team. Once I was over there, I decided to stay and study with some of their teachers."

"Interesting. And what brought you back?"

"I wanted to finish out my senior year in America. I

figure I can go to school here while I keep training. Eventually I want to become a neurosurgeon. There aren't a lot of opportunities for women in Asia."

"Neurosciences?"

"What? I can't be smart?"

Mrs. V. smiled at the young lady. "I wish more students were that ambitious."

"Oh," Tina replied, "It's not ambition. It's just a matter of time."

"You remind me of a cocky cheerleader I once knew." Mrs. V. thought of the girl who had sat in this very library only ten years ago. The world was a quieter place since Olivia died. She hated to admit it, but she missed the girl.

"Lose touch?"

"She passed away after a knife fight."

Tina's face showed she was appalled at the thought.

"I'm kidding," said the librarian, "she passed away after a nasty fall."

"That sucks," Tina said.

"Yeah it does. Well," she changed the subject, "welcome back to the United States, hope you find a great opportunity after school."

"Oh I will," she said. "I just got a secretary job at one of the research facilities near town. I'm excited. It's just pushing envelopes, but you never know, it could be the recommendation that gets me into Harvard!"

Mrs. V. raised her eye as she walked away. She was constantly leery of students now. She thought working with the Special Forces would have better equipped her for the struggles of a high school employee. What she had discovered was that she would rather fight terrorists, the supernatural, and stop plots for world domination any day.

High school students were more ruthless than any villain she had faced.

Yet.

Ring. Ring. Ring.

Period 3

Jessica worked her way down the hallway, pressed against the wall. The push and pull from the hoard of bodies attempting to get to class tossed her about. She braced herself as she was shoved against the wall, her cheek firmly planted against a locker. She decided to wait until the crowd died down. The underclassmen maneuvered the halls with their rolling backpacks, while she watched in amusement. Jessica was thankful the only thing she had in her hands was a notebook and pen.

Hand braced against the locker, she pushed off from the wall across lanes of speeding students until she got to the railing overlooking the quad. She always enjoyed the view from up here, the sunlight pouring in through the giant skylights and the quick paced movements of the small people below her.

Jessica slipped on her massive headset and adjusted it until it fit snug against her ears. She reached down to her form-fitting black gloves and pushed the back of her left hand. After waiting a moment, music started to flow into her ears. Touching a couple more spots on her glove, the music switched, and a deep bass drowned out her classmates.

She leaned over the railing to see a group of students beginning to congregate in the quad. It was the usual collection of burnouts, geeks, and card game enthusiasts. Jessica wasn't close to any of them, but since she had been at Boxford she learned to co-exist in the world of teen cliques. For the most part she was seen as an outsider, the adopted daughter of a crazy Asian teacher who constantly threatened to kill students.

She let out a tired sigh.

Below, the notorious anchor Kevin Cowan spun around on his skateboard, showing off to a collection of his minions. She watched as he stopped moving on his skateboard and looked around the quad. She had no doubt what was going to happen next.

The skateboarder's hand shot out and grabbed some money from one of his comrades. Kevin leaned in with one arm and gave the guy a "bro-hug." As he patted the other kid on the back, she watched his hand slide into the other kid's jacket. He drew back and with the skill of a practiced drug dealer, acted like nothing had happened.

"You're such an ass," she mumbled. She had been around plenty of drugs at the raves she used to attend, but she had always considered herself above it. In a way, she didn't mind the people who did them; the dealers though, for some reason they bothered her. It might simply be the smug way they conducted themselves. Or it could be that she had this image he went home and brewed meth in his garage and ran a prostitution ring. Yeah, that was exactly the problem--he was only days away from being a pimp.

The only saving grace to Kevin and his drug dealing ways was the rivalry between him and the obnoxious hipster, Sam. She didn't care for Kevin, but Sam was downright haughty. Every opportunity the high and mighty Sam got, he would try and stand on a pedestal and throw stones. He went out of his way to intrude on her conversations during chemistry and explain how everything she wrote during the lab was wrong. Of course her lab was wrong. Unlike him, she couldn't hire a tutor who worked as a chemist at some prestigious lab. The kid was an ass.

She laughed when she saw Sam's eyes trying to shoot lasers at Kevin. The best part, the rivalry was known by the whole school; it constantly spilled onto the television when they co-hosted the morning news. She made a mental note to swing by the café and watch the morning show. Hopefully they finally got over their battle of testosterone and made out. At least that would explain a few things.

She found herself tapping her foot to the loud bass thumping its way into her headset. Free periods were what every senior dreamed of. She wouldn't pass it up. It gave her a chance to decompress in the middle of the day, and every now and then she would get around to doing some homework. Mostly, she just wanted to listen to music by local DJ's and dream about dancing in the clubs. For now, crazy Asian mother refused to let her out after dark. The woman would mutter something about the scary things in the night.

Leaning over the railing, she noticed her new friend David sitting next to Sam. Jessica waved her arms furiously, trying to get his attention. She watched in horror as Sam broke his gaze away from Kevin and turned towards the geeky new kid. She knew it would only take one statement for Sam to somehow destroy what little self-esteem David had accrued today.

Sam opened his mouth in slow motion. She knew from the look on his face it was going to be anything but nice. She didn't want to tarnish her reputation of being stand offish, but she had to interrupt the crime against humanity unfolding beneath her.

Jessica dashed to the spiral staircase leading to the quad. She pulled off her headset as she hit the ground, and jumped over a half wall in a fluid movement. As her feet touched down, she moved through the crowd of students to where David was sitting. She could already hear Sam beginning to talk about his ability to walk on water.

"That's why you'll never really fit in at a school like Boxford," Sam said, staring down his nose at David, refusing to blink until the insult fully set in.

David's eyes were wide with disbelief at the audacity of his classmate. "Kids here can't possibly be that mean."

"They're not in general," Sam said, still staring down his newly discovered arch nemesis, "but you're not exactly handsome, rich, or from a well-established family."

"How would you know?"

Sam eyed David, giving his clothing the once over. "How could you not know?"

Jessica plopped down in a chair between the two boys. "David, come with me," she looked at Sam, "nobody wants to listen to this douche bag talk about how awesome he is."

David gestured to the boy. "He seems to want to hear how awesome he is all the time."

Jessica laughed as she pulled David away. "Sam, I think God is calling, he wants his job back."

As she turned around, she slammed into another student, knocking a girl backward. The girl, instead of falling onto her ass, arched her back, hands planted on the ground, and with a kick she flipped backwards. As her feet touched down to the ground she crouched low, eyeing her assailant.

"Sorry," Jessica said honestly.

Before she could mutter another apology, the gymnast reached up to slap Jessica across the face. "Watch where you're going, bitch."

In the second it took the hand to reach out, Jessica's

brain had already assessed the situation. Tina Saccharin, known cheerleader, somewhat of a bitch. Her abilities were Olympic level. She was kind of like a comic book character with her super moves and big breasts. Jessica grabbed the girl's wrist and without hesitating, used her own weight to pull the girl over her shoulder and chuck her across the quad.

"Holy shit," David said, taking a step back from his friend.

The cheerleader hit the ground in a roll and jumped up. "Who the fuck do you think you are, black girl?"

"Really? You're going to play the race card, blondie?"

"Tina and Jessica are in a fight!" cried one of the students in the quad.

David whispered to an angry Jessica. "You're going to get in trouble."

"Dye job Barbie started this shit," she snarled.

Tina growled at the girl, cranking her head so her neck cracked. "Bring it, Amazon."

Jessica pushed David away as a crowd of students gathered in a circle around the two girls. The chanting for blood grew louder and louder. Jessica had a split second to wonder what school would allow its students to congregate without adult supervision.

Before she could answer the question, Tina's fist came directly at her face. Jessica brought up her arm, deflecting the blow. She wrapped her arm around Tina's, brought her in close, and threw her knee up towards the girl's perfectly chiseled abs.

Tina spun around Jessica so they were back to back and kicked with the heel of her foot. Jessica felt her knee give as she fell to the ground. Before she could spin around, she sensed the fist heading toward her spine. She absorbed the blow, somersaulting forward, removing the majority of the impact.

As she turned around, a knee flew toward her face. Her hands slapped the white girl's leg back to the ground. The cheerleader was fast. Jessica knew she was reacting too slowly, the half second delay would leave her open for easy hits. She used her forearm to block a sidekick from the cheerleader.

She had heard rumors Tina had been overseas for years. She assumed the girl had been studying gymnastics, but what's to say that she wasn't part of a government program where she trained to be a super soldier. She couldn't help but grin at the influence her foster mother's conspiracies had over her.

"Afro Pom Pom want some more of this?" Tina said taking a step back. She beckoned Jessica, taunting her forward. "Looks like the mean streets didn't teach you a thing."

"I was born in Vermont, you poor excuse for trailer trash."

The crowd silenced at the mention of the trailer park. Boxford was well known as a rich community where the elite and wealthy sent their children to school. Amongst all those mini mansions was a small trailer park, and everybody knew Tina lived there. She had beaten all odds to become the homecoming queen and the president of the senior class. Jessica had pressed the one button capable of sending Tina into a rage. The last time a student had used the word trailer in front of Tina, she had tried to snap his neck, and he was only talking about a movie trailer.

Jessica tried to sweep her leg across the floor, but Tina

easily jumped and snapped her right foot outward. The toe of her shoes caught Jessica by the chin, launching her backward. She couldn't react fast enough. Her body smacked against the ground and slid to a stop. Before she sat up, Tina was on her, a fist slamming into the side of her face. "I'm going to kill you, whore!"

"Stop it!" David yelled. He charged in and grabbed Tina's fist. Before he could figure out his next course of action, she pulled her hand away and slammed him in the chest with the flat of her palm.

Jessica struggled under Tina's weight. She brought up her legs, snagging Tina's neck and dragging her to the ground.

"Tina is going to punch her lights out," came several voices.

Tina tried to get free, but years of dancing had given Jessica solid legs. Jessica reached to the headset around her neck. While she squeezed her leg muscles, holding Tina in place, Jessica adjusted the headset until it covered her ears. With the flick of a gloved hand, the music came to life.

"Okay bitch," she muttered, "game is on."

Tina raised a foot up off the ground and attempted to slam it into Jessica's face. Jessica caught it with two hands and twisted the girl's leg, sending her into a spin along the floor. "Black girl rage is here."

The crowd took several steps back as Jessica flipped onto her feet. Jessica flexed her muscles, and the crowd took another step away from the girl. They all turned to Tina still lying on the ground.

"Black girl think she has some moves," hissed Tina. Jessica did a backwards roll onto her feet. The cheerleader didn't look impressed. "This ain't the Bronx, sweetheart."

Jessica closed her eyes and listened as the song came to a crescendo. The charge of the music flowed through her body. Before she opened her eyes, the air vibrated as Tina's fist threatened to strike her face. Jessica reached out, grabbed the girl's fist, and spun around so they were back to back again. Unlike the previous time, Jessica knocked Tina's heel back to the ground. Jessica reached back, grabbing Tina's shoulders, flipping her. The two girls were face to face, Tina's eyes went wide at the strength in the black girl's arms.

Tina's mouth dropped in shock. With trained precision, she knocked Jessica's arms out wide and crouched down low as she shoved the flat of her palm out toward the black girl's sternum. Jessica grabbed the hand and rolled backwards, taking Tina with her. As the white girl reached the height of the roll, Jessica kicked out hard with both feet, launching Tina into the crowd.

Jessica's movements were fluid as she came back to her feet. The sound of Tina's feet gave away her charge. Jessica started in a jog forward. As she reached the small half wall that surrounded the quad, she stepped up and pushed backwards in a large arcing flip. Her hands braced against Tina's shoulders as she performd a handstand directly over the girl.

Jessica could see the faces of the crowd as she finished her descent, landing on one knee. She spun around in a sweep motion, knocking Tina off her feet. In what seemed like supernatural speed, Jessica jumped up, took the falling Tina, and slammed her onto the ground.

The whole quad shivered as they heard the thud. Several students looked away at the brutality of the chick fight.

Jessica brought her knee down on Tina's throat. "Say another stupid thing, whitey," she whispered to her, "and I

47

will kill you Vermont style."

"But how," Tina said, her eyes pleading with Jessica.

"My mom is a T'ai Chi master."

The whole quad was quiet as Jessica stood. She pointed at Sam. "Careful, you're next on my list."

Sam's face turned white.

The black girl turned to the geeky kid she had come to save. "Told you I got yo' back."

As Jessica and David walked away from the crowd, the group gathered around Tina to see a drops of blood around her lip. One of the boys turned to his friend and finally asked, "Dude, I thought when chicks fought they got naked."

"Only when your mom does it."

The kid nodded in agreement. "True 'dat."

* * * * *

"Are you seriously eating a cheese burger right now?"

"Why the hell would I wait till we were done?"

Angelica turned to the large man in seat next to him. "Uhm, do we have to go over this whole vegetarian thing again?"

"Oh yeah," Hank said, "that."

Angelica shook her head in disbelief. "I don't think I can do this much longer."

"You ain't no walk in the park either."

She shot him a look that could kill. "I meant, I can't sit here and wait for something to happen."

"Oh, that." He smiled at her with a mouth full of burger.

"We have the intel. We have verification there is something going on here. I think we should just bust in and take them all out." She pulled off her headset and threw it onto the table in front of her, covered in computer monitors.

"You realize you have anger issues."

"You have a hygiene issue," she replied, "and there's nothing angry about it. We just need to get in there. We can sneak in and then we can get the intel we need. If we're confronted with hostiles, we can just respond with force as we always do."

He turned to look out the van door with his binoculars. "You do realize your intel says that there is a biological weapon being housed in a daycare right?" He eyed the sign in the front yard, a rainbow leading to a cheerful sun with arms hugging itself.

"I know," she said, "it's diabolical."

He shook his head, refusing to let her lack of humanity get to him. This had become their reality. When he had met this woman, he had been a mall security cop. Five years later, he was staking out a daycare in hope for corporate espionage or a zombie outbreak.

It hadn't been this way all the time. For the first year after he joined this outfit, he had been one of the gun-toting grunts of the operation. Hank, Min, Cadence, Xander, and Victor had become whose sole purpose was to ferret out potential viral outbreaks. It had been a glorious job; he finally felt he had a purpose. He was protecting America, and even more than that, he was protecting mankind. The outbreaks had started randomly, another small mall in New Hampshire, a telemarketing company in Ohio, then it got out of control. The outbreaks were no longer testing grounds for the serum that Bryce and Mrs. Shelly had concocted; it was warfare.

During a containment situation at a museum in Boston, they had been forced to eradicate a large number of patrons.

They managed to contain the outbreak, but he had walked out of the fight with cuts down his arm that made him think it was his final battle. Min had dragged him into a storage closet while they waited for reinforcements. She kept a gun pointed to his head the entire time.

He remembered pleading with her at first. He was willing to die with dignity, but he wasn't ready to be shot in the head. It seemed as if Min was more than willing to do the deed before it was time. When he finally asked her to put down the gun in a calm voice, she responded with, "If somebody is going to kill you, it's going to me."

It was love.

The walking dead scratched at the door, nails breaking, trying to get at their next meal. They could only pray the door would buy them enough time for the others to rescue them. While her arm began to shake, he finally asked her, "Marry me?"

"But you're white."

He raised an eyebrow at her. He had been doing this for weeks, giving her perplexed looks, while their odd courtship unfolded. He had asked her to tea and she almost broke his hand for not asking properly. Then over dinner he almost had a fork through the hand as he offended her with his inability to use chopsticks.

He started to laugh. She would ultimately return the confused look. "You crazy?"

"You're not too worried about me dying if that's your biggest argument."

She thought about it for a moment and holstered her gun. She turned around, opened the door and began hacking her way through a hoard of zombies. He could only see the occasional body part flying past the door as she pulled out her boot knife, her katana, her travel blade, and then her switch blade. Once the commotion ended, she walked back into the closet, her face soaked in what he hoped was only blood.

"Don't die and I say yes."

He smiled and held out his hand as she helped him to his feet. "Deal."

They were married the next week by Mrs. V, and shortly after they adopted a young girl to come live with them. It wasn't the family he had originally planned on, but he was a kept man and he was okay with that.

"Oh sweet Jesus, you're thinking about her again aren't you?"

He looked at Angelica with a grunt. "Uhm," he said as he grabbed his phone. He flipped the screen and it was a picture of Min with a sword ready to stab him in the chest. It was a honeymoon he would never forget. With a few quick strokes, he sent his beloved a text message. "Sorry, I just wanted to send a quick text."

"You two make me sick."

"You're just annoyed the only man you've had a thing for in years was Victor."

"And we both have the same taste in men," she said with a slight pout.

"Ones with penises."

She punched him in the shoulder. "Have you been able to get in touch with any of the others? Any backup?"

"They're all still at the school. Tomorrow is parent/ teacher meetings and Mrs. V has a feeling something is going to go down."

Angelica checked the gun on her thigh. "All because Cadence had a moment? Just because that bitch has some inspiration for a novel, we go into red alert. What about the B squad?"

He shook his head. "You act like the department still has a budget."

She crawled into the back of the van, pulled a gun off the rack, and slung it around her shoulders. "We're going in."

"You're about to storm a daycare," he tried to reason with her.

"They have to grow up some time."

"They're four!"

"I was shooting my first gun by then."

"I question your sanity."

She tossed him a hand gun. "Fine, if it makes you feel better I'll leave the assault rifle here," she said putting it back on the rack. She took two more handguns and tucked them into her shoulder holsters, then a third into the small of her back. "Happy?"

"Sure."

She got out of the van, slipped on her black sunglasses, and clicked a button on the side of the frames. "Stay here."

"I'm not letting you go in there alone."

"I need somebody to work the coms. There's no way I'm going in there without tech back up. It'd be Sparker's Furniture outlet all over again."

He thought back to the handful of them, covered in zombie remains standing in a master control room. The computer should have locked all the doors to the store and keep them safe. None of them were thrilled at the busy icon spinning on the computer screen with nobody to call for help. Hank jumped into the back of the van and sat at the computer screen. "Try not to kill any children."

"No promises."

Ring. Ring. Ring.

Angelica looked at the burly man. "Seriously? You're phone?"

Period 4

"Thanks Lauren," Cadi said as she took a swig of the coffee warming both of her hands.

"No problem," the thin black woman said with a twitch.

Cadence stopped to examine the former barista. Lauren had been working all morning, which meant she had had no less than twenty cups of coffee sludging through her veins. While Lauren still managed to scare her at times, the woman was a good person overall. In the last few years, they'd become friends, mostly for the coffee benefits.

"How's the new store doing?"

Lauren reached around and hugged herself in a nervous manner. "Well. It's been good. The new hires are nice. However, they're slow. I mean really slow. You'd think they'd pick up the pace. I mean like really."

Cadence was always amazed at how fast the girl spoke and how long it took her to translate the coffee-speak. Once she finished translating, she responded, "I can imagine not many people keep up with you. Let's be honest, you're a bit of a coffee addict."

Lauren's eyes widened, unsure at how she should react to the allegation. "What!"

"In five years I've never said that?"

"Why would you say that? You've never said that. Not in five years."

"Damn," Cadence said, "maybe I'm getting nicer without Olivia and Dione around with their bitchy auras."

"Are you going to go do that thing you do?" asked Lauren. The black girl looked down at Cadence and saw her eyes staring off into space. Lauren waved her hand in front of the girl's eyes. "Yeah, that thing." She reached down and stole a swig of Cadence's coffee.

Cadence remembered the moment in the mall when Dione stopped being a crazed bitch and sacrificed herself to save the entire group. Dione had gone out of her way to protect them from an explosion, determined to take out the bad guy with her. It still seemed impossible, not that she died, but that she sacrificed herself for somebody else. It was also a bit hard to swallow she would do anything that would threaten to chip one of her acrylic nails. Cadence had hoped it was like the movies, and Dione would emerge unscathed from somewhere at the end of the scene. But alas, she never emerged, they found parts of her singed weave amongst the heaps of dead bodies.

Olivia had been a similar situation. The cheerleader sacrificed herself to save them from that evil bitch Sonya. Cadence wanted to be sad that the Patriots' cheerleader had died, but she had always assumed Olivia would die a horrible death. It was more surprising it wasn't at the hands of a jealous wife. She was shocked Olivia died by her own free will. Cadence lost the betting pool with that one.

To this day, she struggled with them being gone. Dione had been right all along, there could only be one black girl at a time. Two black women in one conspiracy was too much. She thought about Victor, were two gay men too much? If another gay man showed up, would he bite the bullet? *Nah,* she thought, *you can never have too much gay.*

"And she's coming back," Lauren smiled at Cadence's blank face, "now."

"What?"

"Every time you mention Dione and Olivia, you go into

a flash back. To be quite honest, I'm glad Dione's gone. She was always a bitch to me. That," Lauren thought for a moment, "and there can only be one black woman during the apocalypse."

Cadi looked up at the girl, convinced she heard Dione's voice come from the barista. She shrugged, shaking off the ghosts. "It must be a black chick thing."

Lauren brushed off the racist comment. "So, do you want me back here before the end of the day?"

"Yes please." Cadence straightened up her desk. Lauren grabbed her bag and walked out the door, most likely heading to her car for the secret stash of coffee in the trunk she believed nobody knew about.

As Cadence lifted her cup to her lips, she realized it was empty. She groaned loudly.

"What?" Lauren yelled back down the hallway. "You spaced out for a whole thirty seconds."

* * * * *

Mrs. V. surveyed the library. With the stacks empty, she could finally breathe for a moment. She lived for fourth period. The one time of the day she shut down the library. Now, for an early lunch. There were no screaming students, no destroying of text books, and no desecraters of periodicals. For the next fifty-five minutes, she could slam a can of Red Bull and get to her real mission.

She walked into her office and shut the door, drawing the blinds to a close. With a slight turn of the crank, the blinds sheltered her from the rest of the school. She quickly walked over to the mini-fridge and popped open the door, reaching past the hand gun to a Red Bull located in the back. She was getting closer to admitting she felt her age. At one point she had been able to out run the kids, now, she needed to supplement her energy with caffeine just to make it through the day.

She popped the cap and took a swig of the vile liquid. Sitting down at her desk, she looked at her unread emails.

"Porn," click, "Porn," click, "Viagra," click, "Porn sponsored by Viagra," click. She moved them to the trash bin and then opened the only actual email.

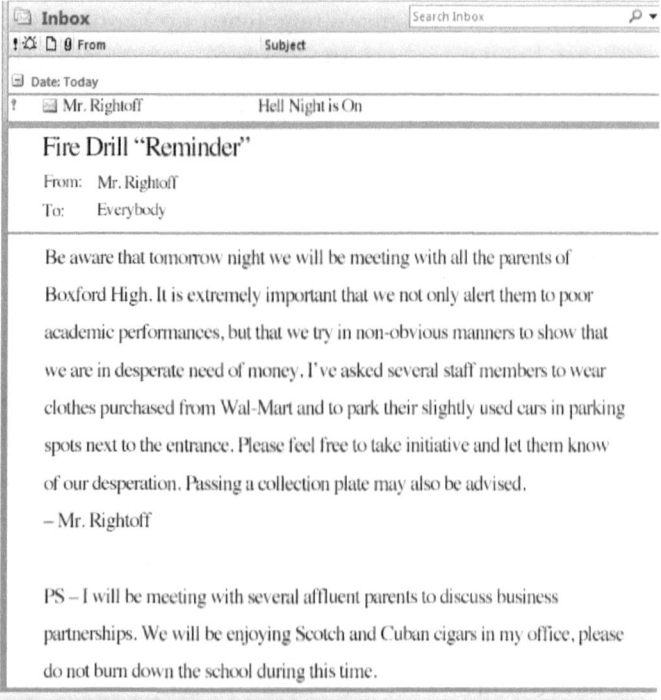

"You're such a tool," Mrs. V. said as she moved the message to her trash folder. She took another long swig of Red Bull and as she finished the disgusting concoction, she clenched her hand, crushing the can. As it hit the trashcan, she pulled out her industrial sized laptop.

The librarian flipped open the government machine and a small green dot blinked in the middle of the screen. She leaned in to the massive machine and a red light scanned her eye through her glasses. Her thumb pressed on the side of the keyboard and the blinking green cursor typed out, "Welcome Mrs. V."

She clicked several buttons and began typing. Lines of code flew across the page as she continued to type at breakneck speeds. The word "secure," "security" and "authorization," were seen several times as she reached a blank screen with just the green cursor again.

"Okay," she said as she cracked her knuckles, "let's see what new information we have."

V: Are you there?

She waited for several moments before she repeated the message. She started to understand the way Lauren felt. The caffeine coursing through her veins made her jittery.

Delaware: Here

V: Any new intel?

Delaware: I still don't understand who you are.

V: My identity must be protected.

Delaware: Pedophiles say that.

Mrs. V. dropped her head. "The little bastard," she paused, "you're not an adult are you?"

V: I've hacked the FBI and CIA databases. There has been no chatter.

Delaware: Yeah me too.

She raised an eyebrow at her liaison's abilities.

V: You hacked the FBI?

Delaware: Homework was done early.

"You are a kid," she said with a grin.

V: Last we heard, there was going to be an encounter.

Delaware: Terrorists?

V: Worst.

Delaware: Sure, whatevs.

She stared at the little green blinking dot. Somehow, this little brat managed to hack into her communications a month ago. He had explained how to secure the channel so it couldn't be picked up foreign interests. Mrs. V was worried she was being snooped on by the same people she hunted. Whoever was behind the zombie outbreaks had deep pockets, and it'd be ironic to find out she was the one giving away the plan.

Delaware: You didn't check Facebook.

V: What?

Delaware: Or twitter.

V: What's that?

Delaware: You're not very good at this are you?

She gave a low growl as her hands tightened into fists. "I might have to squeeze your pubescent neck at this rate." While she was annoyed, she had to admit she was apparently missing something. The hacker had a knack for holding information over her head. It was only because of him, she had managed to land Cadence and Min jobs at the high school. The informant had mentioned that the source of "distress" was somewhere in these halls.

Delaware: Twitter blowing up #zombieapocalypse

V: What?

Delaware: You can hack the CIA, but you don't know what twitter is?

Delaware: You need to read more periodicals.

Delaware: Whatever is happening is going down tomorrow night.

Delaware: Also #quadbitchfight is trending at the high school.

She stopped to gawk at the screen. It was the first time the hacker had given her any information indicating who they might be. She had assumed it was a government informant or a scorned employee. No, her informant had been a teenager all along. She stared at the computer in disbelief.

"We've been suckered."

Delaware: Have to run, teacher is checking homework.

She leaned back from the computer and continued staring at the blinking cursor. The woman wanted to believe the information was reliable, but if she had learned anything, the little bastards of this school couldn't be trusted. Every morning she saw the mouth breathers in the hallway sipping their coffees, and she thought, they're about as smart as zombies.

She moved back to her desktop and opened an internet browser and typed "twitter" into the search bar. A few clicks later she was amazed to see how much useless trash congested the internet. She stopped long enough to admire a picture of a cute kitten sprawled out on its back.

She looked about the page and saw the #zombieapocalypse tag. Clicking, she saw pictures of teenagers drooling on themselves during school. Their hoodies were pulled close over their heads and they were attempting to hide behind books so they could sleep. She stopped at one photo and saw one of the girls sleeping in class. She recognized the degenerate, but it was the small vial of makeup sitting on the desk that caught her attention.

"Holy shit," she said.

She grabbed her cell phone and quickly sent a text

message to Cadi. "It's happening."

She waited for a moment and groaned as Cadence replied with, "Woohoo!"

Period 5

Her brow furrowed as she saw three teachers sitting at the only gray table in the room, laughing over a joke she missed. She waited for them to acknowledge her presence, and when she realized they weren't paying her any mind, her face scrunched up in annoyance.

"Ahem," she coughed loudly.

"Oh," said one of the women, acting surprised. "Mrs. V, it's great to see you. That window display you did last month on banned books in America was just awesome."

"The one before that," chimed in another guy, "a month long tribute to the Anarchist Cookbook," he paused, "that was special as well."

"I guess knowing your napalm ingredient ratios is helpful," said the third.

Before Mrs. V could comment on the sideways compliment, Cadence burst into the room. Cadi tried not to snarl when she saw the mundane trio of beige wearing teachers sitting at the table. "Freaks and geeks, get the hell out. The real adults have to have a meeting."

"Who the hell..."

Cadence lifted her skirt showing off the gun attached to her thigh. "I have six bullets and I'm just itching to shoot something."

Mrs. V rolled her eyes while hanging her head down in shame. She stepped out of the way as the three teachers ran from the room. As they bolted down the corridor, the librarian glanced back at Cadence. "Really? Shooting co-workers?"

"They're math teachers," she said.

Xander rounded the corner, smiling at his disgruntled wife. "Yeah, I can understand wanting them dead."

Cadence flattened out the front of her skirt, hiding her holster again. "What's this about Mrs. V? Is it what I think it is?"

Mrs. V watched as the writer kept scoping out the hallways, appearing far too excited for the situation. "Uhm, no," she saw the disappointment, "sorry, it's not the zombie apocalypse."

"Are you sure?"

Mrs. V. walked into the room and took a chair. "Do you see me with an assault rifle?"

Cadence pouted at the bad good news. "You could have it hidden."

"She's been like this all day," Xander admitted. "On the drive to work today, I think she was aiming for students. She was, and I quote," he made air quotes, "'making sure the little bastards stayed dead.'"

"It was a valid science experiment," she said.

Mrs. V waited for the girl's zeal to subside, "I haven't heard from Angelica and Hank in hours. I'm starting to get worried."

Cadence's pout continued. "Ugh, military stuff," she whined. "That doesn't help my novel at all."

Xander ignored her. "Could they be in the middle of something?"

"The last mission notes that came in had them watching a daycare. They had a tip from an anonymous online poster."

"You're online boyfriend?" Cadence asked.

"Stop acting like Dione," Mrs. V. chided her, "and yes, it

was our online source."

"Any closer to figuring out who they are?"

She nodded, "Not only do I have an idea, but they're closer than we think," she waited for them to lean in a little. "I think they're a student at the school."

Xander shook his head in disbelief, "You mean we've been chasing tips from a high school student?"

"Mrs. V, we're going to start calling you Mrs. Robinson," laughed Cadence.

"You don't even get the reference," Mrs. V scolded her, "and yes, I'm convinced it's a student. Whoever it is, they're unbelievably tech savvy. I mean, they managed to hack both the FBI and CIA for some of their intel."

"Seriously? I can't even get my students to put names on their papers."

Cadence nodded in agreement, "And what's to say anything they're saying has any validity? I'm not knocking a high school student, but really, it wouldn't surprise me if they were pulling your leg. What student is going to be aware of the impending zombie invasion?"

Xander shot her a look. "Really? You mean after we've had weekly after school discussions with the Zombie Survival club? Or you constantly forcing them to learn about viable escape routes, cliché methods of survival, and protocols for documenting?"

Cadence nodded. "Don't forget your history of zombie media, and somehow working reliable firearms and alternative decapitation tools into your midyear essay."

All three of them stopped and looked at each other. Xander laughed and broke the ice. "If any of this shit was on the SAT's, we'd be the best teachers ever."

"Mrs. V can hack their computers. We could make that

the entire test."

Mrs. V. smiled. "True. Also, we might want to think about keeping a lower profile. We might be turning the graduating class into a bunch of murderous little wretches."

"They were like that far before we got to the school," Cadence laughed.

"True 'dat," Mrs. V added.

A collective sigh filled the room at the Librarian's ability to make even the trendiest dialogue uncool.

"It might have been a bit much when we forced the nurse to take that online course about infectious diseases."

Xander snickered. "Or when you forced her to learn about proper bite mark indentations and how to spot deviations from the norm."

Mrs. V stopped laughing. "To think, somebody let us teach at a school."

"It could've been worse. Remember the last school we were at burned down," Xander added.

"Let's hope it does again," Cadence said with a smile.

"White people!"

They all turned to the doorway where a small Asian stared back at them. Her angry face hadn't dimmed with time. They all knew she had gotten softer since marrying Hank, but nobody had the guts to tell her. They waited for her to add something to the conversation.

"Sorry 'bout the time," she said, "Jessica had a fight with another girl."

"That was Jessica?" asked Xander.

"You don't listen so well," Min said. "She and another girl had a fight in the quad. Apparently it was over a boy."

"She takes after her mother," Cadence said. "Don't let that mocha-colored skin tell you anything; she's Min's through and through."

"Brown Rice," Min smiled.

Xander laughed. "Is she okay?"

"She's my daughter," Min said flatly, "of course she kicks other girl's ass. She schooled that bitch, Tina Sacarin."

Mrs. V's eyes lit up. "Good, the book-breaking little bitch deserved it."

They all froze, gawking at the elder woman. She shot them all a look. "People who break books deserve to have their spines snapped."

"Whoa," Cadence said putting up her hand. "A little teenager angst, woman?"

"So why are we here?" asked Xander.

Mrs. V sat down next to Xander. "I'm hoping Angelica and Hank check in soon. The informant told me something was going down tonight. I'm worried that something may have already happened, and that's why they haven't reported."

"When were they supposed to check in next?" asked Xander.

The loud sound of a screaming Asian woman shrieked from Min's pocket. They all rolled their eyes as she grumbled about white people. She pulled out her cell phone, punched a few keys, and let out an exasperated sigh. "It's Hank, he texted to say how much he loves me."

"Gross," Cadence said.

"Shut up Emo girl!" Min shouted at her. "He's my piece of man candy."

"Grosser," Xander added.

The scream sounded again. "He said he has a present for me," she said. She held the phone out for Xander to read the message.

"No," he grabbed the phone, "he says a present for us, as in all of us."

Min grabbed back her phone and shoved it in her pocket. "Can't be anything good then. Hank wouldn't be buying a sexy electrician uniform for all of us."

They moaned in unison. Mrs. V shook her head. "That image is going to be with me all day long."

"Shut up woman," Min said. "Where's Victor? He appreciates my man love."

"He'll be here later. He's running some errands before his class," Cadence said flipping through her text messages. "I am so excited to watch him with the students."

"Think he'll be crazy?" asked Xander.

"Crazy, military, and fabulously gay," Cadence said. "This is going to be magical."

"Those poor kids," Xander said.

Mrs. V started to head to the door. "I guess there's no reason to meet. We keep up the watch and look for anything out of place. I'm going to scan security tapes and see if I can narrow down who our informant is. Maybe he knows more than he's letting on," she paused. "Otherwise we don't have anything."

"Wait," Cadence yelled.

They froze. They could tell by the vacant look on her face that she was piecing together a conspiracy. One of the more lovely traits she inherited from Xander, her ability to turn anything into the upcoming apocalypse.

"Victor is teaching later."

"Yes," Xander said, "we just had this discussion."

"White girl not feeling okay?"

"Lauren is coming by before parent's night to bring me coffee for the parents."

Mrs. V raised her eyebrow. "Cadence, dear, where the hell are you going with this?"

"We're all going to be in the school? At the same time?"

Min threw her arms up. "If there was an apocalypse every time you had a weird hunch, we'd die daily."

"First the school," Cadence continued, "then again when we all got together at the Mall. Now we're going to all be in the same place again." She looked to each of them, "Don't you see what this means?"

"You crazy."

"Seconded," added Mrs. V.

"Bastard," she said as Xander started to raise his hand as well.

"Every time we're all in the same place. It happens. And with the weird feeling of dread and anger last night, I'm sure this has to be it."

"Cadence," Xander said calmly, "we're not all in the same place. Hank and Angie are away on an operation. I hate to burst your bubble of doom, but I think we'll all be safe for another day."

"Wait for it," Cadence said in an ominous tone.

They all looked up to the speaker that normally sounded the end of the period. She waived her arms, "Not that."

"What?" Mrs. V asked.

The screaming Asian voice came from Min's pocket. Min grabbed her cellphone and looked at the text message. She started swearing and stomping her feet.

"What is it now?" asked Xander.

"Wait for it," Cadence said again.

Min thrust the phone into Xander's chest and stormed away. "She'll never shut up now."

Mrs. V.'s eyebrow raised. "Jesus, just tell me."

He held the phone up for her to see. The text message read, "On way home. Have surprise. Will meet you at Parent's Night."

Cadence just smiled. "We're all gonna die."

Mrs. V. threw up her arms and walked out of the room. Xander gave his wife a disapproving glance. "You could try not to be so happy about our impending doom."

"It's not like I'm singing about it," she said as they walked out.

"I can hear you humming."

She gave him an innocent smile. "I have no idea what you're talking about sir."

Hmmmmm. Hmmmmm. Hmmmmm. "Gonna die."

* * * * *

"You know you can't burn holes through the side of his head," Jessica said to the kid dressed in all black. "I know you'd like to, but nope, no laser beams."

"Shut up," Rob said, resuming his deathly stare at Kevin. He focused his eyes on the boy, squinting and grinding his jaw until his head shook.

"You're not exactly an evil genius."

"I hate you," he said quietly to both Jessica and his arch-nemesis.

"You going to take that from him?" Sam taunted from behind.

Jessica turned around at the lab bench to shoot Sam a dirty look. "I think I'll live."

"My life will not be complete until he's dead." Rob said to nobody in particular.

She looked at him, slightly concerned there was something wrong with the goth. "Dude, if you keep this up,

I'm going to ask to switch lab partners. Your creep factor is higher than normal."

"I hope you die," he mumbled never taking his eyes off the drug-pushing Kevin.

She examined the small kid. His face was a pasty white, paler than normal, and she could only imagine there was some sort of powder making it this level of white. His greasy slicked hair, dyed black over and over again, hung down into one of his eyes. She cringed at the amount of metal chains and pins on his shirt. Her eyes landed on the giant sharpie'd x's on top of his hands.

"You realize life would be happier if you weren't," she paused, "how do you say, such a creepy whiney, pissy little bitch of a boy?"

"Burn, girl," said Sam from behind her.

She spun around growl at the annoying hipster. "Look," she said wagging her finger at him, "if I wanted the opinion of some tight-jeaned androgynous little rich boy with an affinity for plaid and no hope of ever procreating, I'd call you by your name. Until then, keep your punk ass mouth shut."

He froze.

"Good, we understand one another" she paused. "Open your mouth again and I'm gonna get all black on your ass."

"Yes ma'am," he said quietly.

She turned around and stared down at the papers sitting on the table in front of her. The teen picked up a bag of ice and pressed it against her jaw. The ache had set in from the unbelievably invigorating fight she had last period. She was thrilled somebody had the opportunity to put Tina in her place.

"I'm becoming my mother," she mumbled to herself,

slumping down in her seat from the weight of her epiphany.

She felt a familiar vibration come from her pocket. Reaching in, she grabbed her phone and looked for the teacher. Once the coast was clear she checked the text message. It was David. She had to admit, she liked the little geek. She was all too familiar with being the new student, and she was happy to show him the ropes while he adjusted.

Tonight?

Yes tonight. It's @ the warehouse on the far side of town.

I don't know if my parents will let m stay out that late.

You're a good boy huh?

Yean, kinda. :)

You in?

A rave? I don't know.

What if I threaten to kick your ass?

Angry black woman syndrome.

She laughed out loud and everybody lifted their head from the classwork to stare at her. "You got a problem?" They quickly returned to their lab reports. She sent him a message.

Meet me right after school.

Front lobby.

Deal.

She looked at Rob again. She almost felt bad for the little goth. He wasn't a bad kid, he was just a bit confused about how to grapple with reality. "How much makeup do you own? Like, a little mascara, or like the whole makeup counter?"

He looked offended.

"Seriously, going to be offended because I asked you about the eyeliner, black nail polish, and the dyed hair?"

"My hair is not dyed," he hissed at her.

"I can see your roots."

He touched his hair and raised his hand. "Can I go to the bathroom. It's an emergency."

Before the teacher could reply, he bolted for the door. She hoped nobody heard her insult the Lord of Darkness. "I was kidding," she said quietly to herself.

She took a deep breath and shuffled the papers in front of her. The equations began to blur and she was convinced the teacher never taught them how to do this. Opening her massive text book, she looked for similar problems to help her along. She realized that there were no equations in the chapter even remotely close. "Uhm, when did we learn this?"

The teacher, a tall skinny man, gave her a defeated shake of the head. He looked around the room for somebody to help her. "Kevin," he pointed back to the vacant seat next to Jessica. "Go back there and show her how to do her work."

Kevin turned around and gave the black girl an exasperated look. He couldn't help but smile when he noticed the student sitting behind her was Sam, his favorite co-anchor. He grabbed his books and moved back several tables, the smile spreading further across his face.

Jessica followed Kevin's gaze to Sam. When she realized the hipster was giving the same death stare as the goth, she laughed. She eyed the kid with his thick black-rimmed glasses as his face turned red with anger. "Oh burn," she whispered loudly.

"Going to kick the crap out of him next?" asked Kevin.

"Maybe I will," she said defensively, "what's it to you."

"You know, Tina is wicked piss," he said.

"Bitch got a problem with me, I'll finish what I started." She could feel her blood boiling; she tried to take calming breaths to subside the building rage.

"I mean, somebody had to do it. She was always a little too perfect for me," he admitted, "too smart, too pretty," Jessica was sure he drooled a little, "perfect hair, perfect skin, and those ample breasts. And she's a gymnast, so you know she's flexible."

"Okay, I'm not sure if you're a creeper or a complete man whore."

He shrugged.

"Why do you do that?"

"What? Shrug my shoulders?"

"You go from agitating everybody around you and then you just go back to not caring. If you weren't so nonchalant about it, I'd hit you."

"Did you just use nonchalant in a sentence."

"S.A.T. vocab word."

He nodded. "There's no point in getting worked up over everything. Not all of us can suffer from Angry Black Woman Syndrome..."

She raised an eyebrow. "How did you--"

"Even the teacher's say it about you," he admitted. "You really need to learn to calm down. You'd be pretty cool shit if people weren't convinced you were going to beat the crap out of them. You know, you're not your mother."

Suddenly, she felt bad. There was always going to be some anger about being adopted and moving to a new place. She didn't like all of it. But it did give her opportunities she wouldn't...

"What the hell. You did it again. We're talking about you, not me."

He smirked. "Can't blame a guy for trying."

"You're an ass."

"You're a bitch," he replied in a matter of fact tone. He stuck his tongue out at the hipster trying to drill a hole in the side of his head with his deathly glare, "and he's a punk. But what's your point?"

She snickered at the comment. "Right on both accounts," she grabbed her phone, "I should tweet that."

He watched as she punched the keys on her phone. "I don't let crap get to me. It drives people crazy. I guess it's my Zen approach to life."

"I guess that works."

"Besides, there are bigger things to worry about."

"Like your side business?"

"What are you talking about?"

"Going to act like everybody in the school doesn't know you're a pharmacist."

He searched the room to find the teacher correcting papers at the front of the classroom. He looked back at Jessica, holding his finger up to shush her. "Keep your mouth quiet."

"Not so Zen, huh?"

He turned back to his paper. "We should probably do our--"

"Oh hells no. You're going to answer me," she shut the book. "Does Zen come in a pill?"

"It's not what you think."

"Dude," she said, "I've seen you at the Dining Room, and I've seen you swapping bills with your buddies. We all know about you. I'm pretty convinced the rumor that the principal buys his weed off you is true."

"Really?" he asked in disbelief.

"Seriously."

"I mean, really, he smokes weed? I wonder if he'd endorse my business."

"You're an ass."

He took a deep breath and let it out slow. "How about we teach you something useful?"

She slid the book into her backpack and pointed her finger up in the air and waited a second. "Gotta go."

Ring. Ring. Ring.

Period 6

"Have you tried it? Her mom is a sales rep for the company."

"Of course she is.

"True, of course her father is also the owner of the company."

"That rich bitch."

"Yes she is, but her skin is so smooth. It's as smooth as a baby's bottom."

"Ew, that's kind of gross."

"Don't hate."

* * * * *

"Are you serious Mrs. Li?"

"What do you mean, am I serious? Always serious."

The small Asian woman paced back and forth. She paused every few moments to look at one of the kids standing in a row in front of her. She was still barefoot, wearing her gi, throwing threatening glances at each of the students.

"When in the hell are we ever going to have to climb a rock wall?"

Min's back straightened, a sneer working its way across her face. She raised her arms, as if to pay a tribute to the rock wall gods. Years ago, it had been a poor school's attempt at a rock wall. Rock looking shapes had been drilled into the gym wall, working their way up to a wooden platform. Now it was a professional rock wall used by trainers. She had managed to work it into her budget this year. The tiny Asian refused to let another rock wall almost get her killed during the zombie apocalypse.

"You never know, rice patty," she said, "you might be chased by something and the only way to escape is up."

"Chased by something?"

"What the hell," cried another girl, "another zombie lecture?"

"I mean suicide bombing Asians."

"Oh," said the corrected girl.

Min paused, waiting for another outbreak from her students. "Now, who goes first?" She searched for a worthy contender. She worked down the line, until she saw a young lady with a bruised eye and a fat lip. "I think you should go."

The girl paused to digest the information. The girl let out a low groan as she followed the line of blocks up the rock wall. "You only want me to go first because I beat the piss out of your daughter."

Min let the vicious smile show. "Yup."

Tina tried to pout, but every time she tried, her lip quivered from the pain. She looked from the small Asian woman to the giant wall. As Min held out the safety harness, Tina slapped her hand away. "For wusses."

"You can't climb without the gear..."

Tina took several fast steps to the wall and jumped up to the first handhold. She effortlessly pulled herself upwards, and then grabbed onto another of the protruding blocks. She placed her foot on another brick and slowly spidered herself up the wall.

"Holy shit," one of the boys said.

"She's crazy," another commented.

Tina made sure her grip was firmly planted, and with one of her legs she worked it into a position the average human could never achieve. She pushed off with her hand

and for a moment she hovered in the air and all the students gasped at her impending plummet to the ground. She spun around until her back was against the wall and her hands were all firmly secured.

"She's going up the hard way."

Min hated to admit it, but the girl was gifted. "A worthy opponent."

"What?"

Min shot the kid an icy stare. "Respect your adversary."

Tina had managed to get her stomach to the wall again. Her legs were dangling, crossed at the ankle as she used her upper body strength to pull herself up the wall one grip at a time. She finally reached the third story where the rock jutted out and the climb turned horizontal.

"She'll never make it."

Min watched in amazement. She had wanted to humiliate the girl. She wasn't the typical mom, but nobody laid a hand on her daughter without consequences. She wanted the young girl who started the fight to suffer. As the gymnast showed off her rippling muscles, Min realized she was beginning to respect the young warrior. Jessica was the reluctant child, always hesitant to fight, use weapons, or take down a bitch. Tina however, might not be so different than the small Asian.

"The chi is strong with her."

"Mrs. Li, you know you say some weird shit?"

With a swift movement, Min chopped him in the throat, knocking the wind from his mouth. "Mind your elders."

"I hate when I have to sweat," Tina shouted at the top of the wall. "This isn't so hard! I swear this class is full of wimps. I could kick all their asses."

She glanced below to the students with upturned heads.

Tina swung out onto a horizontal ledge, her legs hanging freely. She began a rocking motion with her body and worked out to the tip of the ledge. She could feel the sweat beginning to build on her brow. It would be easy enough to spin around and grab the ledge and pull herself up. It would be easy, so that wasn't an option.

"Suck it bitches," she said to the crowd below.

She pulled her foot up to one of the grips and wedged her toes into the crevice. Lowering herself, she hung upside down from the rock. Every motion brought a gasp from the crowd. She couldn't help but raise the drama for the audience, giving them a show.

She hung motionless in the air with only one foot holding on. She took several deep breaths and visualized the movements her body would have to take. She let her muscles tense as necessary and she watched herself achieve victory. She could feel her vision narrow, either from her extreme focus or the blood rushing to her head.

Min's eyes went wide as an electricity crackled in the air. Her grandfather would talk about sensing another person's energy, but she chalked that up to the ramblings of an old Asian man. Squinting, she could see something different about Tina, something she hadn't seen in her lifetime. "Another chi master," she gasped.

The gymnast began swinging her body back and forth with her arms outstretched. As she reached her ascent, she pushed off with her toe. The class below watched as she flew from the rock. They began backing away to avoid the bloody mess about to occur.

At the last moment, Tina grabbed the ledge with her fingertips. She used her momentum to turn around until she was doing a perfect handstand on the ledge. Every muscle in her body worked together to hold her upright. She let her legs down onto the flat of the ledge, arching her back until both her hands and feet were touching. With a well-rehearsed grace, she stood upright, her arms stretched out for a perfect dismount.

She took a deep breath and smiled. She was the best. "Olympics, here I come," she mumbled to herself. She turned around and looked down to the audience, their mouths hanging open. "Suck it, you dumb ass punks."

Min began to applaud the young woman. Tina was shocked at the response and gave a slight nod to the gym teacher. She stood up and wiped the sweat from her brow and looked around. She could see that the wall didn't have any easy way to get down.

"Who the hell makes a rock wall that doesn't lead to an exit?"

* * * * *

"We have a new teacher?" asked Jessica.

"This is my second day here," David said with a shrug.

"The substitute we had before was called Five-Finger-Frank. He was kind of a legend here."

David raised his eyebrow. "Elaborate?"

Littered around the massive wood shop were various woodcutting machines. In one corner, a planer, in another a table saw, and various jigsaws positioned around the room. She pointed in the corner. "That's where he lost his thumb," she continued to another machine, "he lost his ring finger there," and then to another, "I think that's where he lost a pinky. And finally that's where he lost his other ring finger."

David's face showed his horror. "Wait," he said, "that's only four fingers."

"Yeah," Jessica nodded, "he had some sort of incident with a plastic butter knife too."

"And he still taught here?"

"He loved it here," she said. "You'd think he woke up every morning thinking, 'I can't wait to lose another finger today.' He was a bit crazy I think. Maybe too many varnish fumes."

"I'm not looking forward to it."

"Why not? It's a good class. Not a whole lot of people in it."

"My idea of working with my hands involves a keyboard," he said, wiggling his fingers in front of his face.

"I'm sure it only hurts when you lose the first one," she smiled.

David tried to muster a smile at her playful banter. It was only his second day at school, and he already felt lucky to be friends with the senior girl. His last school had been miserable. He had been in all advanced placement classes, but those kids were crazy intense. He was smart, but unlike his peers, he also enjoyed human interaction that didn't involve clawing his way to the top.

He waited patiently as the other students milled into the room and dropped their backpacks along the far wall. They were all looking at each other, waiting to see who would speak up about the obviously missing teacher.

"Think he cut off another finger?"

"A hand perhaps?"

"I'm betting on a nail to the forehead."

"Would you be shocked if it was all three?" came a voice from behind them.

All the students turned and David raised an eyebrow at the man standing in the doorway. He wasn't exactly what he expected from a typical shop teacher. Where he expected a man in an apron covered in saw dust, there was a clean shaven man wearing camo clothing.

"Victor?"

David didn't hide his surprise. "You know him?"

"He's a friend of my mom's."

"That's Mr. Spear to you ,Jessica," Victor said with a wink.

"What are you doing here, Mr. Spear?"

He nodded to the young black woman. "I'm the substitute while your teacher is having his arm reattached to his body."

"Did you say your mom was also friends with Mrs. and Mr. Winters?" asked David.

Jessica nodded.

"Don't you think it's weird that all your mom's friends work here?" asked David.

Jessica paused for a moment at the thought. It was a bit weird everybody that came over to her house for dinner was now working at the school. They would sit around the outdoor fireplace and talk for hours. She never thought it was odd, but she did notice the major age difference between most of them and Mrs. V.

"Now that you mention it," she thought, "it is a bit suspect."

There were others that would show up from time to time. There was the red hair woman and the barista from Starbucks. But something about the group of them currently employed at the school made her think there was some connection she wasn't able to place yet.

"Something wrong?"

She looked at David. "Yeah, there's something wrong

alright. I just haven't figured out what."

"Maybe they're all here for a reason," he suggested. "Like they were handpicked or something?"

She nodded, "Yeah, I think..."

"Quiet down over there," Vic shouted to the two of them. "I've gone over your assignments and I think other than the obvious lack of attention to safety, your shop teacher was pretty good at his job." Victor started marching back and forth, his hands clasped behind his back.

"Five-Finger-Frank would want you to keep on working. So let's get the attendance done, and then we'll talk about getting to work."

Vic looked down at his clipboard and began working his way through the names. As he finished the roll call, he watched as one kid stepped forward toward the machines. "Did I say you could move, cadet?"

"But..."

Vic raised his voice. "You'll begin working when I tell you to begin work."

"What?"

"Are you talking back, cadet?"

David was about to ask what was going on, but Jessica grabbed his hand and shook her head. She signaled with her eyes that it wasn't a time to talk up. She was well aware of his legendary rants. He was mostly talk, but there were times she thought he was going to snap. The last time had been when Vic accidentally broke a wine glass. Jessica thought the man would burn the house down..

Vic walked up to the disobedient student and towered over him. "I'll let it slide this time," he said, pushing his finger into the kid's chest. "Next time you'll be running laps around the gym."

"I'm not one of your..."

Before the kid could finish Vic kicked the student's legs, knocking him over. The marine quickly grabbed his victim with one hand and dropped him onto his stomach. "Now push!" he yelled.

The kid reached out and began doing pushups.

"Count them out," Vic ordered.

"One...Two...Three..."

Vic stood and looked at the shocked expressions on the rest of the student's faces. "Does anybody have anything else to add?"

They all shook their heads in unison.

"That's what I thought."

He checked off the last name from his clipboard and gave the group of kids a nod. "Get to work, cadets."

They didn't budge, scared to step out of the line. The class waited until Jessica finally stepped forward and grabbed a pair of safety goggles. One by one they started working, grabbing various pieces of lumber.

David stood next to his friend and looked back at the marine who had one foot on the struggling student. "Holy shit, that was intense."

"Yeah, he gets like that when he's had one too many Sour Apple Martinis," she shivered. "He's harmless I swear, but he barks plenty loud."

"Your mom hangs out with these people?"

Jessica nodded to him as she reached for her project. She pointed at the sad looking piece meal of lumber. "I'm building this for mom's Christmas present, and you think he's crazy?"

He stopped to look at her project. David tried to figure out what it was and finally said, "It looks really..."

"Don't lie," she said, "you have no idea what it is."

He gave an uncomfortable laugh. "Yeah, no idea."

"Nice weapon rack, Jess," Victor complimented, standing a few feet from them. "I think that'll hold your mom's sword collection quite nicely. Have you thought about making another one for her spears?"

David watched as the marine casually walked by their work station. "He's serious isn't he?"

"Like a heart attack."

"Weapon rack?"

"You think that's crazy, I was thinking of making Mr. and Mrs. Winters a gun rack for their living room."

"I'm seeing a pattern," David admitted.

"You think? I live with a bunch of crazy people. You thought my foster mother was out of it? She's probably the sane one."

"I'm starting to see that."

"Now you see why I go out dancing whenever I can. At least there I don't have to worry about the adults, and let's be honest, I use that term loosely. With my luck, I'm going to get stabbed accidentally."

"Or shot."

"Or blown up."

David paused and raised an eyebrow. She rolled her eyes. "Don't even get me going on Mrs. V's antique grenade collection."

"Definitely a pattern."

Victor shouted across the room to one of their classmates. "You must respect the jigsaw! Don't give it attitude, or I'm going to have you scrubbing the bathroom floors with your toothbrush."

* * * * *

Mr. Rightoff stood in the lobby of the school, staring down the empty hallways. He was the master of his kingdom. He had been working at the school since it had been rebuilt, and it never ran as smoothly as it did with him at the wheel. He was determined to make himself ruler supreme of Boxford.

He watched as one kid slowly stuck his head out of a classroom door. "You!"

The kid's eyes focused on the administrator and froze. He knew without a doubt he was caught; there was no chance to run back into the class and hide amongst the mass of teenagers.

"Come here," barked the principal.

The kid let out a sigh as his shoulders slump down. He walked to the principal. The kid kept his eyes on his feet and never met the gaze of the principal, carefully avoiding eye contact. The principal pulled out his tablet and punched the screen a few times. Within moments, the camera snapped a photo of the child and ran it through a student database. Seconds later, the screen was showing a plethora of information about the young student.

"Rob," the principal started, "I see you've missed school once this year and that you're receiving a C- in 'Modern Warfare and You.' You're currently suspected of petty theft and smoking far too much weed."

"Mr. Rightoff, I..."

"Don't lie to me Rob, the computer doesn't lie."

The principal spun the screen around and showed him a photograph from one of the school security cameras. He was outside walking into school and had a goofy look on his face. "It appears that you're high in this photo, Rob."

"I always look like that."

"That's why I think you smoke too much weed."

He spun the screen back around. "And what were you doing now? Cutting class? Trying to leave the school so you can smoke some of your marijuana? Or do you kids still call it Mary Jane? What is it, Rob?"

"I had to go pee."

"You'll have to start peeing in a cup and get tested if you don't shape up fast. I'm going to contact your parents and tell them about your recreational activities."

Rob's defensive posture gave way to fear. If his parents suspected any of this, he'd be grounded for life. They wouldn't let him leave for any reason. "Mr. Rightoff, you can't tell my--"

"Too late."

"What?"

"I already emailed them?"

"When?"

"Now."

"But you--"

"Look at that," he said quickly, "Your mom just said she would meet me during the parent teacher conferences tomorrow. Make sure you're on time, you don't want to disappoint me and your mother."

"I can't believe--"

"You need to hurry to your next class. Rob."

"But the bell--"

Ring. Ring. Ring.

"Don't argue with your elders, Rob. That's what got you into this predicament in the first place."

Period 7

Version 1

The girl screamed as her classmate collapsed to the floor. She watched as his body suddenly went limp, the life flowing from his lips. She leaned in close and threw her arms over his chest, crying how life wasn't fair. She beat her fist into his chest, hoping that a miracle would happen, that her boyfriend would rise from the dead.

She paused as she heard a small rasp from his lips. She slowly sat up to see his face. His eyes were open, blinking very slowly. She leaned in to kiss him when she saw his eyes were still lifeless. She pulled away in horror, until he grabbed her neck and started mumbling, "braaaains."

Version 2

She backed away quickly as her boyfriend's dead body shot up at the waist. She could feel herself slipping in the copious amount of blood left behind by the neck wound. The taste of bile filled her mouth as she fell backwards into the puddle. It was only then she began to scream at the oncoming dead boyfriend. His hands clenched her sweater, and he pulled himself along her body until they were face to face. She could see his lifeless eyes as his teeth met her neck.

Version 3

She skidded backward in the blood covering the cafeteria floor. She dropped to one knee and waited until her dead boyfriend lunged. Grappling onto his shirt, she leaned into a backward somersault. She pushed off with her feet, sending him several feet away.

She could feel the blood dripping down her white blouse, staining the satin fabric and clinging to her ample bosom. She reached back and pulled the pin out of her hair, letting it drop in a wet mess across her back. She brushed the hair out of her face, leaving streaks of blood across her cheek. "Die you fucker."

Her dead boyfriend worked his way to his feet, intensely focused on his one-time girlfriend. She grabbed his outstretched hand, spun him around, and kicked his knee, knocking him to the ground. She grabbed his skull and spun as hard as she could muster. The lifeless body fell to the ground, dead for a second time that day. "I dumped you because I'm a lesbian."

"Seriously? I'm turning into such a lesbian," Cadi muttered, looking at her screen.

"I won't complain," Xander said from the doorway, "well, as long as you let me..."

"Finish that statement and zombies won't be your only problem," she said with a laugh. She gave him a hug.

"No luck?"

"None," she admitted, "I think I might be tapped out. What if I really am out of good ideas? I had a student call me a hack today."

"You're seriously basing your self-worth on the word of a sixteen-year-old?"

"Point made," she said.

She sat down at the computer and closed her laptop screen. "I think I'm going to need to wait until the zombie apocalypse begins tomorrow night."

He raised an eyebrow. "Tomorrow? What makes you so

sure that tomorrow is the day?"

"You know every time you question me, it comes true," she said with a smirk. "As long as I keep saying random stuff and you all argue with me, it happens. It's been my secret ever since we first met."

"And here I thought your secrets were deep, dark, and mysterious," he said, sitting on the edge of her desk.

"How goes your class?" she asked.

"You know, students just sit there and look like they're dead on the inside. I have to keep resisting the urge to pop a cap in their asses. I think they look like zombies either way. Might as well just jump to the end game and get it all done."

"Mine isn't much better. I had a girl today try to tell me all about how Shakespeare used guns and how he had a show down in a Mexican church."

"Romeo and Juliet was on TV again, was it?"

"I swear to God," she said, "I'm not asking much. I just want the little bastards to learn something. Anything really!"

He began to laugh at her. She furrowed her brow and pouted at him. "What?"

"You're starting to sound like a real teacher. Who knows, after the apocalypse maybe you can teach the new world order about how Shakespeare influenced the world."

"Screw that," she said, "I'm going to teach them how Max Brooks was right and they should have been teaching World War Z in freshmen English."

"Maybe you should go back to painting."

She threw up her hands in defeat. "Life hates me right now."

She was about to continue on her rant, but paused as Xander held up his hand. He kept his finger against his lips and looked around the room. Turning around, Xander glanced at the door. He put his hand on the shoulder holster beneath his blazer. He motioned for his wife to stay put as he slowly walked towards the door.

Xander stepped out and quickly scanned up and down the hallway. He paused for a moment, looking for to anything out of sorts. His wife held a concerned expression on her face. "Sorry, I just got the feeling that I was being watched."

"I miss conspiracy you," she said.

Outside the door, down a row of lockers, Kevin had his back pressed against the wall, hidden from the doorway. He held his breath, trying to keep his heartbeat to a dull roar. Crumpling the overdue history paper in his hand, Kevin slid it into the trashcan next to him.

He waited for a moment and slowly leaned his head forward to look down the hallway. He leaned back against the wall again. No, he must have heard them wrong, he thought to himself. Was his history teacher just talking to his wife about the zombie apocalypse? That couldn't possibly be right.

Kevin pushed off from the wall and jogged away from the room. He couldn't believe what he had overheard. Mr. Winters was logical, even humorous under the right circumstances. He was obsessed with...

Kevin's slowed until he was standing still. "He's obsessed with zombies." He thought about all the conversations they had in class and started to piece things together. It was hard to believe his teacher could really be concerned about the zombie apocalypse. That was just one of those things that everybody joked about, right?

Kevin scurried down the hallway, putting distance between him and the crazy teachers. "I'm not sure he's joking."

* * * * *

"That's a mocha latte, anything else for you, sir?"

The gentleman purchased his coffee and slid his credit card back into his wallet and shuffled toward the bar area. He followed the cup as it traveled from the cashier to one of the baristas. The scarf scratched at his neck, catching on his day old stubble. He noted the careful manner in which he poured the milk into the cup, and then scooped on a little extra foam for him.

Just as the young man was about to hand the drink to the elderly man, a young woman grabbed the cup and quickly took a sip. She paused and looked at the barista, then at the elderly man. "Quality check," she said.

"How dare you drink my coffee."

"I couldn't bear the thought of you having to drink this swill," she held the cup close to her chest, away from the man's outstretched arms. "We'll make you another."

The man stared at her in disbelief. "I want to talk to your manager."

Lauren's face lit up at the mention of her title. "That's me. What can I help you with?"

The man scoffed in disgust. "You just took my drink."

She looked at the cup nestled against her bosom. "This drink? I don't think so sir. I've had it the entire time we've been talking. Sorry."

"But you--"

"Possession is nine tenths of the law."

"Where's your--"

"If you want a drink sir, you'll have to go to the cashier."

"Why I never--"

"Maybe you should?"

"What?"

"This conversation is confusing."

"I think you're a bitch."

"A bitch with a coffee," she said taking a sip.

The old man cursed under his breath and stormed out of the store. Lauren smiled and took another giant swig of the warm liquid. She turned to walk into the back room and saw the barista staring at her. "What? You should have made him his drink."

The man glared at her. "You know you're the worst boss ever."

Lauren slammed the coffee down on the counter and jabbed the man in the chest with her finger. "I have the power. Don't make me fire you. I have no problem with that. Do you want a paycheck? I can have you out of here in no time."

"I'm calling the regional manager."

Lauren gasped at the mention of her boss.

"You come in here every morning, twitching like a crack head looking for a fix. Then you spend all day stealing drinks, eating the food, and doing absolutely *no* work. You're the reason our store is the lowest ranking store in the United States. I hope the coffee gods strike you dead."

Her eyes darted toward the roof. "Tempt not, and do not use their names in vain."

"You're a crazy bitch."

Lauren stopped and looked the small man over. Nails dug into her palm as her fists clenched. The edge of her lip quivered as she tried to wrangle in her anger. "I should hurl this coffee at you. But I won't. It tastes too good."

The man slapped her. Before he could give a sly retort,

she was on top of him, grabbing his by his apron and straddling his falling body. Lauren screamed as they hit the ground, continuing to hit his head off the ground. She finally stood up, watching as he checked the scratch marks on his face.

"Don't call me crazy," she said as she reached out to a display case filled with coffee and dumped the contents on him. He winced as the pounds of coffee from the rack pelted him.

She stopped her attack as an elderly woman cleared her throat. "Lauren, I think we need to talk."

Lauren saw the old woman, her reading glasses dangling around her neck. The crossed arms and tapping foot of her district manager spoke volumes. The manager had promoted her a while ago, and Lauren had hoped to make the coffee aficionado proud, but the look of disapproval wounded her.

"Yes ma'am."

The two women walked into the storage area of the store. As they walked through the doorway, the older woman shut the curtain to provide a bit of privacy.

"I'm disappointed in you Lauren," the woman started.

"But he started it."

"I'm sure he did," she said, "but this doesn't have anything to do with that."

"Then what?"

The two women took a moment to take long swigs off their respective Starbucks cups. They both gave a sigh of relief as they swallowed the precious brown liquid.

"I think you know what I mean."

Lauren's eyes darted back and forth attempting to avoid the woman's gaze. "Sampling every bag of coffee in the store?"

The manager took another long swig. "You know that's not it. I do that at every store I inspect."

Lauren quickly took another gulp, trying to hide her anxiety. She could feel the caffeine coursing through her veins, bringing new life to her body. "The customer assault? The closing the store for private taste testings? The--"

"The having the distributor place half his order in your car."

Lauren froze mid sip. She had been caught. The woman was on to her. She was about to cut off her supply. Lauren quickly evaluated the situation. She could run. She could deny the fact. She could kill the woman, hide the body and create an elaborate scheme in which she could take over Starbucks and own all the coffee herself.

"Lauren," the woman said calmly between sips of coffee, "stop contemplating killing me for a corporate take-over."

Dammit, thought Lauren.

"I was once in the same position as you; a young woman, drunk on power and the deliciousness of bold coffee. I'm going to do to you what I wish my district manager had done for me."

"Rehab?"

"Too costly."

"Promotion?"

"Too radical."

Lauren paused at the next suggestion. "Termination?"

The elderly woman nodded her head calmly. "I'm doing it for your own good."

Lauren began to panic. She finished her coffee and thought it could be her last gulp. She was about to go cold turkey. She reached for a bag of ground coffee and held it close to her, taking solace in its fresh blended goodness.

"You don't want to become me," the woman said calmly.

Lauren's eye began to twitch, "You can't do this to me."

"Lauren," the woman said calmly, "I'm doing this for you."

"No," Lauren said, "you can't do this. You can't."

The woman put her hand on Lauren's shoulder. "You need to be free, before," the woman paused to look at her coffee cup, "before you're forced to decaf."

Lauren let out a gut wrenching scream, competing with the brain freezing power of an iced chi latte .

* * * * *

Kevin walked back to class and sat at a table with Jessica and David. He ignored the teacher's comment about his lack of a hall pass. His eyes were staring off in the distance, processing the new found information.

"Are you okay?" asked David. David waved his hand in front of Kevin's. He looked at Jessica, "What's wrong with him?"

"It looks like he caught his parent's having sex."

"Ew."

"See," she said, pointing at David's face. "Kevin, are you okay?"

"Maybe we should tell the teacher," David said.

Jessica snapped her fingers. "That's what it is. Dude is fucked up on his own drugs," she said.

"Drugs?"

"Shhh," Jessica said. "Yeah, he's the local dealer for the school. He supplies everything to everybody. Half the school uses him as a pharmacy."

"Wow," David said. "I wouldn't have thought it."

"Neither does anybody else," she said. "I've never seen him on drugs before. He's one of those crazy dealers who doesn't use their own product."

"Honor amongst thieves kind of thing," David added.

"Stop being smart," she said.

Jessica waited until the teacher's back was to her group. She wound back and slapped Kevin across the face. The teacher spun around. "What was that?"

"I sneezed."

"A sneeze?"

"Yes," Jessica said, "must be my allergies."

"Sounded more like the righteous fury of a scorned teenage female," the teacher said.

"Yeah, my sneezes always sound like righteous whatever you said."

Slowly, Kevin reached up to his face and his eyes began to focus on Jessica. "God damn girl, keep that paw off me."

"What the hell are you on?" Jessica whispered across the table.

"I'm not on anything," he said, rubbing the hand print on his face. "Jesus that hurts."

"Be glad I didn't use my ring hand," she said pulling back her hand. "What's wrong with you?"

"Catch your parents having sex?"

Kevin paused at David's statement. The senior looked confused as David shrugged his shoulders. "Who the hell is he?"

"David," she said, "he's new here. Now step off before I sneeze again."

Kevin looked confused, gaze fixed on an empty space as if he had come back from war. "I just overheard something from some of the teachers that is starting to make some things very clear."

"Cryptic much?"

Kevin frowned at her. "You do know you have some serious mood swing issues."

"I'm a woman," she said. "Deal with it."

He took a deep breath, still rubbing the increasingly red hand print on his face. "I overheard Mrs. and Mr. Winters talking. They said something that was a little bit weird, but it's starting to make some sense about a bunch of our classes."

David leaned in, whispering loudly to the other two. "That they're too easy and we should just skip to college."

"Besides that," Kevin said.

"Then what?"

"Notice how Mrs. Winters is obsessed with zombies? I mean like completely and utterly obsessed."

"My mom has all seventeen of her books at the house. They're pretty good," Jessica said.

"Well that's not enough, Mr. Winters is always talking about zombies in popular culture. You know, movies, comics and all that crap."

"Sounds like they make a perfectly logical couple," David said.

"I don't think they're obsessed with it though. I mean, not like we think."

"I've known Mr. and Mrs. Winters for years," Jessica said, "they're perfectly normal," she paused, remembering how excited Cadence had been when Xander bought a new set of brass knuckles for the woman. "Well, kind of."

Kevin leaned across the table and whispered, "They're convinced that the zombie apocalypse is really going to happen. Not like that stupid 'what would you do if zombies attack', but like seriously worried about it. I overheard them talking, they think it's going to happen here."

"So they're a bit weirder than usual," Jessica said.

"Maybe they're a bit *too* into their comics," David added.

"Guys," he said, "have you noticed that there is a bit more than a zombie obsession at this school?"

"Oh, please explain, crazy conspirator," Jessica said.

"Dude, the library had 'Zombie Preparedness Month,' and then Mr. and Mrs. Winters are always talking about the do's and don'ts of zombies. Don't get me started on your mother, who I'm pretty sure was trying to teach me how to decapitate somebody today in gym class."

"Really?" asked David.

Jessica nodded. "She does that to everybody though."

"Then why was she talking about my 'assailant' trying to eat me?"

"Hmmm, that does seem a bit odd," Jessica said. "Not outlandish for her, but definitely odd."

David shook his head, trying to digest what the two older students were talking about. "I'm not completely convinced there is a zombie apocalypse," he said. "I feel like we need more proof."

"Did you hear anything else?" asked Jessica.

"I freaked out and ran," he said, "but they definitely sounded like it was something that was going to happen soon."

"Like 'Dawn of the Dead', the whole world is going to fall apart type thing?"

He shrugged. "Do you think we should ask them?"

"Since when have adults ever told us the truth?"

Jessica waved at them to stop. "Let me think for a moment. There is something weird here. I'm not sure if it's crazy ass people coming back to life to eat me weird, but there is something weird. I mean, everybody you just listed off has been at my house in the last few weeks for dinner."

"You know them all?"

She nodded. "Even Mrs. V," she said, "they're all friends outside of school. They normally talk about..."

Her jaw dropped.

"She's onto something," Kevin said quickly.

Jessica thought about the last time Mrs. V had come over; in her usual manner she showed up with a pie in one hand and a rifle case in the other. They had dinner and then, as always, they went outside for a glass of wine and target practice. Her mother never participated firing weapons. Her motto was if she couldn't kill it with her bare hands, it didn't deserve to be killed. The others had no problem.

"What is it?" asked David, waiting for Jessica to finish her thought.

"Hold on," Kevin said. The boy tilted his head, mimicking the girl and pointed at her eyes. "She's having a flashback."

Xander and Cadence would always laugh about the ragtag group of individuals. They would comment on how messed up it was, having weekly suppers like normal people. At the table every week, they would toast to missing friends and there was always an empty place at the table where they filled a glass to respect their fallen comrades.

She was the only kid at the table, and most of the time she would zone out with her headset on. She frequently ignored their ramblings, but she couldn't help but notice that everybody at the table had the bulge of guns under their dinner jackets, or a least a thigh holster. They thought she never noticed, but after binge watching all of Law & Order:

SVU, she was very aware they were packing heat.

"Jessica?"

Kevin stopped David. "Wait for it. She's coming back."

"How can you--"

"Holy shit," she said.

"Told you."

"I don't know if they're worried about the zombie apocalypse, but I know everybody that's involved."

"What do you mean?"

"My mother, Mr. and Mrs. Winters, Mrs. V and Mr. Spear," she paused "they're all part of it."

"Really?"

"Then there's my dad, Angelica, and Lauren," she said. "They don't teach here though."

She paused at that thought. There was something about the group of people around that dinner table that worked here. There was some sort of connection that she couldn't figure out, something that would unravel the entire mystery.

"What are you thinking?" asked Kevin.

"I'm missing something," she looked at David. "You're wicked smart with computers. Think you could figure out the connection between the teachers?"

He gulped at the request. "Are you sure you want to find out?"

She nodded. "Kevin might be a psycho drug dealer, but he's not entirely wrong on this."

"I resent that."

"More like youyou resemble that," she said. "So shut it."

"I think it's zombies," he said, "it has to be zombies."

"You realize how ridiculous this sounds," Jessica said.

"Isn't that how it all happens," he said, "all you have to say is--"

"There's no such thing as zombies."

Kevin's palm smacked against his forehead. He reached out and smacked David too. "You just killed us all."

The teacher spun around again eyeing the three of them. "Was that another sneeze? Sounded more like the slap of a limp-wristed pansy."

* * * * *

Mrs. Staller, yes I understand that my manuscript is a few weeks late. You have worked with me for years and know that I'm a diligent writer and I will have something noteworthy to you shortly. I'm currently...

Cadence stopped typing her email and looked up around the empty room. She could feel the hair on the back of her neck stand on end. Slowly, the chill ran down her spine and her fingers twitched. She hadn't felt the sensation since that fateful day at the mall.

"Yes," she declared excitedly, "somebody's good as dead!"

I'm currently about to write a masterpiece that would put Cadence Winters back on top of the zombie genre. I'm going to want a PR blitz like no other. Just hold on for a few more days and you'll be reading the best thing since...well, since my first book.

* * * * *

"You're an idiot," Jessica said. "Class is about to end. Give me your cell and I'll call you soon as we have anything else for you."

"I'm still not sure this is a good idea," David said.

"What's the worst that could happen?"

"Will you stop saying that shit?!" Kevin said, loud enough to make the teacher turn. "You must never pay attention in Mr. Winter's class!"

"You three are going to need to see my after class" said the teacher.

"Jesus," said Kevin. "Yes, Mr. Kringle."

Kevin looked back at Jessica who was shaking her head. She thrust her finger into his chest. "First we get a lecture, then we get eaten alive. I'm going to blame this all on you."

Ring. Ring. Ring.

Period 8

"Tina," the principal said in his most concerned voice. "I'm sure you had nothing to do with that vicious fight that broke out today in the quad."

"Absolutely not, Principal Rightoff."

"I didn't think so."

"Jessica East just attacked me for no reason. I was trying to study, and she just went berserk," she lied. "I think she's jealous of me or something."

"It might have something to do with her overly violent mother."

"I'm sure it does, Principal Rightoff," she said. "I try not to question your judgment, but I'm not entirely sure why you hired a woman who is so dangerous to young developing minds."

"To tell you the truth Mrs. Sacarin," he said, "I'm not sure how she was hired. I received an official email from the super attendant and he gave me a list of 'adjustments' happening to my staff."

"Adjustments?"

"Yes," he admitted, "some stranger characters began to show up in my school. The newest is the ROTC instructor, who is now also the shop teacher. He doesn't have a single credential that would allow him to teach in a high school."

"That's mighty strange, Principal Rightoff," she said.

"Yes it is," he pondered for a moment. "Now come to think of it, none of the new hires are certified to teach. I might have to bring this predicament up at the next school committee meeting."

"I would be more than willing to stand behind you in that decision," she said proudly.

Mr. Rightoff thought about the predicament. It was a conundrum, and he would have to send the Super an email to discuss the situation. He looked down to the young woman sitting in his office, her face slightly bruised and her lip still crusted with dried blood. "Now on to the real reason you're here, Mrs. Sacarin."

"This isn't a creepy old man thing, is it?"

"Uh--"

"I have mace."

"What?"

"And a stun gun."

"No."

"Just warning you, sir."

"About Parent's Night tomorrow."

"Oh thank fucking God," she exhaled.

"What?"

"What? I didn't say anything," she said with a smile.

"I would like you to be the opening speaker. As the class president, you are the very best Boxford High School has to offer. I would like you to give the opening address and then present me to the audience."

"Alright."

"The parents will be gathering in the auditorium. The students will be in the cafeteria and gym, watching the presentation simulcast. I think we'll have the Irish Step Dancing team do a number, and then turn it over to you. You'll have to be dazzling, charming, and show them that we are the best."

"I can do that," Tina said, straightening her back.

"But not too haughty about it. We also need them to take

a little pity on us, since we are looking to raise their taxes for the eighth time this year to make money for the new Astrodome for our football field."

He stopped and looked at the young, beaten woman. She was the perfect mix of obnoxiously smart, and with the black eye, they would admire and pity her. "I think you can do that pretty well too."

She gave him a snarl. "Watch it."

"What?"

"I said, 'Good idea sir.'"

He raised an eyebrow at the busted girl. "From there, the parents will go to the child's homeroom. Each period will last ten minutes. That should be long enough for each teacher to perform a song and dance for the parents. Then they'll move onto the next class on their child's schedule. We should have the entire evening over in a couple of hours."

"It sounds absolutely delightful, Mr. Rightoff," she lied.

"I'm still on the fence about having the swim team put on a synchronization extravaganza. We'll have to see if the mood hits me."

She rolled her eyes. "It's all for my Harvard resume," she mumbled.

* * * * *

Sam strummed along his guitar, playing yet another song from his favorite indie rock band. His music teacher cringed at the horrible sound coming from the instrument. "Okay, enough noodling around on the guitars. We're going to try and perform as a class."

The small room contained five students all holding acoustic guitars. The teacher waited for the brat to stop playing and looked to his most apathetic pupil. "Rob, are you going to join us?"

"Why bother?"

"Because I asked you."

"But what does that mean? What does it matter? Why does anything matter?"

"Oh shut up," said Sam.

Rob, all dressed in black, stood up and pointed at the hipster, his arm shaking as he tried to will the guitarist's head to explode. "Someday, you spoiled brat, I'm going to go apeshit on your ass and beat you to a pulp."

"Try it," Sam retorted. He slipped his guitar pick between the strings, his hand resting on the bridge. "My father's lawyers would be all over you."

"Of course, your father to the rescue. Someday he won't be there to protect you, and then I'm going to beat the life out of your annoyingly tight-jeaned body."

"If the two of you down sit down and shut up," yelled the teacher. "I'm going to use a guitar string to strangle you both."

The three small girls all holding guitars clapped quietly.

"Now, you spoiled rotten hipster wanna be, sit down and shut up."

"Haha," Rob pointed.

"And you," the teacher continued. "You poor excuse for a goth, sit down before I cut your wrists for you."

The three girls all struck a power chord on their guitars.

"Now start playing, or I am going to go all Ozzy Osbourne on your tiny little heads."

* * * * *

David sat down at one of the twenty-five computers neatly organized in rows in the class. Each of the giant black monitors had a child sitting behind it, clicking away at the keyboard. The teacher sat at her desk in front of the class, texting on her cell phone.

David eyed the assignment posted near the keyboard of every computer. They were supposed to be working on creating memos. He scoffed at the work. They were in a computer class and it had been dumbed down to simple typing. Granted, it was a skill that would serve 90% of the class when they became office assistants. However, he had taken the class to hone his computer skills, actual skills, something he couldn't already do with precision.

He grumbled as he began typing away on the computer. Students around him used their pointer fingers to work through the assignment. He stared at the paper intensely as his fingers danced about the keyboard, and within the minute the memo was finished. The clacking of keys had alerted the teacher, who looked up from her cell phone. "What are you doing?"

"I finished," he said meekly, trying not to alert his peers.

The teacher walked over to him in a hobble, dragging her wooden leg with each step. "Let me double check that you did it correctly."

She leaned over his shoulder and he could smell the overabundance of baby powder and lavender. He choked back a cough as she pointed at the screen. "Well this..." she stopped, "and what about..." finally she leaned back, "it's perfect."

"I fixed your typos," David said.

"Thank you, David." He noted the aggravation in her voice.

"Should I do another one?"

"I don't want you getting ahead of the class. Just look

like you're busy in case the principal shows up."

He wanted to argue that he was already ahead of the class. However, he learned in his few short years that it was usually best to blend in. As the teacher walked away, David watched the boy next to him give him an evil glare.

"Stop showing off."

David didn't bother answering. He ignored the kid and went back to his computer. He clicked around, looking for solitaire. He found the network people at the school had locked out all the fun stuff.

"Eff that," he grumbled.

He looked over the giant monitor to see the teacher busy again on her cell phone. He could hear the familiar sound of Angry Birds being whipped at defending pigs.

With a few clicks of his mouse, he opened a terminal program granting him access to the guts of the computer. He ran command after command, his fingers whipping along the keyboard.

The blinking cursor demanded a password before he could enter the gates of technological freedom. He pulled a tablet out from his backpack and plugged it into the computer. With a few taps of his finger on the screen, he watched as a program began to scan passwords. It only took a moment before the terminal on his computer accepted the password: boxford.

"Seriously?" he whispered, "these guys are idiots."

Clicking away at the keyboard again, he pulled up a map of the school. He had access to all the automated functions of the school. With several clicks, he could see through the camera currently located in the hall outside their classroom. "Nifty."

He scanned through various cameras, watching

classrooms, hallways, and oddly enough, a discreetly located camera in the girl's locker room. He wanted to test the limitation of the program and he found the classroom they were sitting in. David now had access to the temperature controls, lights and even the ability to control other computers in the classroom.

"What kind of high school can do this?" he asked.

He clicked on the lights toggle and the lights shut off. With a quick click again they came back on.

The teacher barely pulled her eyes off the phone. "What was that?"

All the kids shrugged, ignoring her, their focus directed to the radiation being emitted from the computer monitors. They were like moths to a pixel-generated flame.

One of the girls in the back of the room stood up and walked over to the teacher. "Do you have any hand moisturizer? My hands are so dry."

"Here you go," the teacher said, barely taking her eyes off her phone.

"Thanks," the girl said as she massaged the scented lotion into her skin. "Where did you get this? It smells awesome."

"They were handing out free samples at the cafeteria earlier."

"I'll have to get some," she said, heading back to her chair. "Thanks Mrs. Brown."

David watched the skinny girl walk back to her chair. He couldn't explain why, but for some reason there was a knot in the pit of his stomach. Something was going on that he couldn't pinpoint. Between Kevin's babbling and Jessica's gut feeling about the teachers, something was unfolding. What he couldn't figure out--how were the teachers and the impending doom connected?

He tapped a few buttons on his tablet, and the school schematic moved from the computer monitor to his portable device. He detached the cord and slid it into his backpack. Opening another screen on his desktop, David punched in command line after command line.

Switching programs, he clicked on the security camera located in the library. He could see Mrs. V moving from computer to computer, checking in books and cleaning up magazines scattered across the lounge area.

He switched back to the other screen and accessed the terminals in the library. The computer closest to her blinked with the message, "Have Information."

She moved away before the blinking cursor caught her eye. He moved to the computer closest to her, and realized she was in a zone and didn't stop long enough to see the computer screens. David swore under his breath. "Slow down, woman."

He finally stopped accessing the computers and flipped to the staff directory to scan her profile. He found her cell phone number, punched in the number on the computer, and sent her a text. "I see you."

He watched as Mrs. V stopped for a moment at the vibration of her phone.

The woman made no attempt to hide dropping the F-Bomb as she stared up at the security camera. She finally looked around to all the computer screens and saw them flashing his message. She threw her hands up and went into her office, closing the blinds.

David punched in a few more keys. He opened a terminal on her personal computer and sent her a message.

Delaware: I think I have more information.

V: Who are you?

Delaware: Not important. There is a conspiracy at the school.

V: It's called school board.

He frowned at the computer. She wasn't wrong, but it was the wrong conspiracy for today. It was rare he found himself stumped. The older woman had the answer; he knew it.

Delaware: You know something.

She didn't respond right away. He stared at the computer, waiting for the reply. He imagined she was concocting a story to tell him, an excuse for what was happening.

Delaware: You're part of it.

Between Kevin overhearing the apocalypse story, and Mrs. V constantly rummaging through news feeds and databases about the school, David knew something was up. He didn't get transferred to this school without doing some research. He knew it had a weird history, and there were things that simply didn't make sense.

V: Yes.

He stood upright. It was the first time she had provided him with any piece of the puzzle. Up to this point, she had relied on him for intel. David had hacked the school computers weeks before moving here. His work led him to several computers sending out some mysterious search quires. It only got stranger when he realized that some of the machines were sending encrypted information.

He didn't like encrypted information.

Delaware: What is your connection to Mrs. and Mr. Winters, Mr. Spear, and Mrs. Li?

He wished there was a camera in her office so he could

see the look on her face. He thought about it for a moment and switched to another program. Within moments, her webcam betrayed her, the concerned look turning grave.

V: Who are you?

Delaware: Not important right now.

V: Only a handful of students capable of this work.

He knew he was overplaying his hand. It was only a matter of time before she figured him out. Now the question was, could he get the information he wanted from her first? He was excited to draw out the conspiracy, but he didn't want to get wrapped up in it. David wrote again.

Delaware: What's the connection?

She let out a long sigh, giving away her defeat. As she clacked away on the keyboard, he held his breath, the anticipating growing with each second.

V: They were my students ten years ago.

He thought about it. She didn't have any reason to really lie about that. But it didn't make sense, how was that the great connecting conspiracy? He felt like he was just handed the answer to the entire puzzle. Maybe he didn't know the right question?

Delaware: It's happening.

He wasn't even sure what he meant by that. But he knew something was going on in the background. He didn't like to think about his gut feelings, they weren't exactly facts, but he couldn't resist. Something was wrong.

V: How do you know?

Delaware: Gut.

V: Do you even know what is going on?

He wanted to argue with Kevin logic from earlier, but he knew it was big.

Delaware: The apocalypse.

He could see her nod at the camera and give him a thumbs up. Mrs. V wasn't as swift as him on the computer, but she wasn't an idiot. He watched as she reached into her refrigerator and pulled out a hand gun. His eyes widened as she pulled back the slide on the weapon to check that the chamber was loaded.

She reached the keyboard.

V: Be very aware. When it happens, you're in danger. Stay away from the school.

He could see her typing on the keyboard in a furious manner. He was ready to switch programs and track what she was typing.

V: David.

Shit. He was found out.

He punched a key on his keyboard and looked up to the speaker in the room.

Ring. Ring. Ring.

"Mrs. Brown, is the bell early?" asked a girl near the back of the room.

"Yeah, whatever," she said playing her game, "have a good day."

After School

"Did you talk back to me, cadet?"

"Uh," the kid stammered, "no."

"No, what?"

"No, thank you?"

Victor leaned into the kid's face and yelled so loud he was spitting on the young military hopeful. "That's no *sir*, cadet."

He looked at his three recruits. They were shameful. During Victor's tenure in ROTC, the sergeant would have slaughtered these teens. The drill sergeant wouldn't have dealt with their lack of commitment, he'd have simply told them to hit the road.

ROTC had changed in ten years.

He could see the camo fatigues weren't fitted properly to the three young boys. Scuff marks covered their boots, and their few pins were placed improperly on their uniform. Victor was happy to be here. The sergeant was about to turn around these bunch of sorry trainees.

"At ease soldiers," he said.

They clapped their heels together and rested their arms at their sides. He had seen the notes from the previous sergeant. His work was shameful. Victor had already sent a letter to his commanding officer demanding that he be removed from military service. He had tried to politely express his displeasure, and had added that a rifle squad shooting may be appropriate for this level of offense.

"Why are you here, cadet," he asked the small kid standing directly in front of him.

"Uhm," he paused, "discipline sir? My parents say I need discipline."

"And you?"

"I want to be a trained killer."

He looked at the last one. "And you?"

"I don't like gym; this is the only alternative."

Victor recalled the first day he had met his drill sergeant. He had been like these kids, expecting it to be an easy grade getting him out of gym. As a confused sophomore he thought it would be cool to get a little buffer and maybe learn some kick ass self defense techniques. Then he had met his savior.

His drill sergeant was the love of his life. Not just a gay kind of love, but certainly that as well. Teenaged Victor worshipped him like a father. The man had taught him to respect himself, respect others, and to be a proud soldier. The broad, sturdy, clean-shaven man had inducted him into the brotherhood of ROTC, and taught him to be a proud citizen who would someday stand up for his country.

Victor looked at the sorry bunch in front of him, he owed it to his drill sergeant to do the same for these kids.

"Today, we're going to start with a demonstration."

They raised their eyes in disbelief. They weren't used to a drill sergeant who got his hands dirty. Their previous instructor had been fairly lame, refusing to participate and treating it like Boy Scouts.

"I've invited Mrs. Li here today to show you some of the things you'll learn in ROTC. I will teach you respect. I will teach you to become a valuable part of society. Most importantly, I will teach you how to kick the crap out of anybody who doesn't respect their country."

Mrs. Li walked in from the doorway. "White man thinks

he can beat me."

Victor flashed her a smile. They began to walk in circles around one another. "Mrs. Li is a world-renowned Chi Master. I'm going to show you some of the finer parts of unarmed combat. You won't get to this right away, but I want you to see how much of a warrior you can become with focus and practice."

"You're going down, pansy cracker."

He smiled at the small Asian. "Going to break you like a fortune cookie."

The cadets all shifted nervously. They took a step back as their drill sergeant squared off with their gym teacher. "Cadets, Mrs. Li is a formidable foe, you might not know it from her small stature..."

He stopped speaking as Min's hand smacked him across the face. He looked at her, his face showing his shock. "Not yet."

"White man too slow," she said.

The cadets chuckled at their instructor's expense. Min took a step back and got into her fighting stance. "Won't hurt you too much."

"I'm going to wreck you," he said through clenched teeth.

She lunged at him, her palms out flat. Before it could connect with his chest, he knocked her hand aside. He attempted to grab her wrist, but she stepped in to slam her other hand into his kidney. Victor sidestepped the blow, pushing her harmlessly wide and the two of them squared off again.

"You're pretty good."

She smiled at him. "You're almost good."

He pulled at his jacket, ripping off buttons, and threw

his fatigues to the side. Standing in his wife beater, he flexed his arms, "Let's try this again."

The cadets watched as their instructor blocked a punch, threw up a knee, ducked out of the way of a kick, and attempted to throw Mrs. Li. They were impressed with how neither combatant managed to land a punch or a kick. The speed at which the fighters moved astonished them.

Finally, Victor's fist connected with the edge of Min's jaw, sending her face sideways. She backed away and checked her lip for blood, coming away with crimson on her fingers. "First blood goes to you."

She pulled off the top of her gi until she was standing in just pants and a sports bra. Min tossed her uniform top aside and flexed her arms. "Now I'm ready."

As they traded blows, the cadets backed up further and further. The fighting got more and more violent, and the speed continued until suddenly Min was standing behind Victor with a blade in her hand pressed against his neck. "I win."

He reached down to his boot. "Hey, that's my knife."

"Finders keepers." Min gasped as she clutched his ass cheek. "Been waiting years for that."

Late After School

Cadence and Xander sat in the car, unsure if they should get out and venture into the small suburban home. The radio spat out advertisements, first for a car dealership, then a furniture store, and finally a wrinkle reducing cream.

"I don't know if I want to go in," said Cadence.

Xander reached over the stick shift and rested his hand on Cadence's leg. His wife had changed from her typical teacher clothing to a black dress. He would have said it was lovely except she accented it with small skull earrings and a skull necklace. It reminded him of the girl he fell in love with a decade before. She was rediscovering her goth roots.

"It's not that bad."

Her eyes locked with his. The man couldn't help but notice how thick she had applied the eyeliner. Her lashes seemed to go on forever, drawing him to her icy blue eyes. If his wife had been wearing a veil he'd think it was a funeral they were attending, not a dinner party.

"You don't understand Xander. It's the end of the world," she pouted, forcing her bottom lip to curl. She slumped in the passenger seat, crossing her arms to complete the fit.

"It'll be okay."

She let out a loud sigh. Even her husband in his pressed white dress shirt and tie couldn't change her mood. She mumbled about pushing him from the vehicle and driving the car off a cliff. She pondered if the car, spinning out of control, lit on fire, and crashing into the ocean would put this behind her. There was a spot in her heart turning black, a sensation she hadn't felt since high school, and she liked it.

"It was one Amazon review," Xander said, doing his best to placate her.

"One review? It was a *one star* review. Do you know what that means? Do you?"

He pushed away from her, squishing himself against the door. He knew he had wedged his foot into his mouth. There was nothing he could say to calm his wife. He decided to go for broke and get it out of her system before they went to the dinner party.

"It's not like--"

"SusanL1778 said, and I quote, 'Cadence Winters has lost her edge. Her zombie books have become repetitive and it's starting to look like she's run out of ideas. Her last book was derivative and had no original plot. I've read romance novels with a more complicated story line. She compared my work to *romance*."

"Maybe she meant it as--"

"I've already done some research. Her average rating is four stars. She reviews mostly young adult action adventure, and occasionally she delves into the horror genre. She has a Facebook, Twitter, and Instagram account where she likes to post photos of her three cats. She also likes to read recipe blogs, mostly focusing on gluten-free meals."

"Wow," Xander said, becoming even more terrified of his wife. Cadi had a knack for being scary when she was in a good mood, but now, she was past the point of breaking. Usually when this happened, she shot things.

"You've certainly done your homework."

"She lives at 72 Acorn Drive and has a rock wall in the front of her yard. She pays her mortgage each month, but has a tendency of paying her electric late. Her driver's license is up for renewal next month."

"Cadence," he said, "you're worrying me." He pulled his hand off her leg. He was thinking it might be time for him to leave the car. The handle of the door was cool in his palm as he thought about popping it up and running.

"She dated a sprinter in college, but he wanted kids and she was too in love with her cats for that. When she was in grade school, she wanted to be a ballerina and received a C- for effort on a school science fair project."

He could run. He could make it to the bushes before she reached her leg holster. If he was lucky, the tight space would mean she'd only be able to graze him.

From the backseat of his compact four door, Lauren leaned through the space between the two seats. "I know you're having a break down. I get it. It happens to me a lot. But we need to go inside. I need to pee. I mean like *really*. And I need coffee. Like really times two."

Cadence turned in her seat, staring at the black woman. The car was dark enough that she could only make out the white of the woman's eyes. Cadence wanted to reach out and slap the barista. But she decided against it. If she let her rage slip out, she wouldn't know how many people would die before she wound up on SusanL's front door step.

"I'm going to pee in your seat," Lauren insisted.

"Let's go," Xander said. He pushed open the door and waited for the other two to follow suit. It took a moment, but Lauren jumped out and hauled ass to the front door. Cadence opened her door and slung her backpack over her shoulder as she walked next to Xander.

"You were in no real danger," his wife said.

Xander gave her arm a squeeze. "Yes, I was."

Cadi smiled at her husband. "Yes, you were."

They walked up to the stairs to the porch as Lauren pounded on the door. The knocks were in rapid succession, she danced back and forth on her feet, performing the universal "pee dance." From somewhere inside, a scream started in another language, barking orders.

"She sounds like she's in a bad mood."

Cadence nodded. "Maybe *her* bestselling novel got a one star review."

"You're not going to let it go, are you?"

"Not until SusanL feels my righteous fury."

"It's going to be a long night," Xander said as the door cracked open.

* * * * *

Jessica sprung over the back of the couch, dashing out of the living room. She slid across the hallway in her socks until she reached the door. The teen pulled at the locks and swung the door open.

"Thank God," she said, "mom is in such a bad mood."

Xander gave Jessica a hug. Cadence repeated the gesture as Lauren pushed through, bolting towards the back of the house. Jessica eyed the black girl as she bounced off a wall, trying to turn the corner toward the bathroom.

"Too much coffee?"

"Is anything new?" Cadence asked.

"What's Min mad about?" Xander asked, kicking his shoes off into the corner of the entry way.

"Dad hasn't gotten home yet. She's been slaving away in the kitchen. She keeps saying, 'If I wanted this treatment I'd go to Asia.' Then she starts speaking Mandarin and yells some more."

"Where's your dad?"

"He's been at work all day. I haven't seen him since yesterday."

Jessica didn't miss the worried glances between the two guests. She thought back to Kevin's conversation earlier. The raised eyebrows and Xander squeezing his wife's hand wasn't lost on her. She wondered if her Dad was doing something other than working for the cable company.

"I'm sure he just had some late installations to take care of."

She nodded at Cadence. "I'm sure that's all it was."

Or perhaps he's out slaying zombies trying to prevent the end of the world? Jessica thought. "You can find mom in the kitchen," she said. "I have to go do some homework."

Before she could head down the hallway to her room, the doorbell sounded. She waited for the usual scream from her mom. Her foster mother always assumed she had her headphones on and required screaming, loud enough to wake the dead. As if on cue, "Open the door!"

Jessica opened the door again. It was the librarian. They had met frequently in the school when Jessica was hiding from her mom in the back of the periodicals.

"Hello, Jessica."

"Hi Mrs. V, I hope you're hungry, mom has been cooking since she got home from school."

From nowhere, Mrs. V pulled out a pair of ivory chopsticks. With a couple of skilled clicks, the woman smiled. "I've been waiting for dumplings for a week now."

The door knob jingled as somebody fumbled with the handle. Jessica grabbed the door and pulled it open. Hank gave her a smile. "Thanks."

"Mom is *so* going to kill you."

"So, nothing's changed."

Angelica pushed past him into the house. "Dumplings!"

* * * * *

"Jessica, why don't you head to your room and get your homework ready for tomorrow," asked Hank in his best dad voice.

"Yeah, have an algebra test I need to pass, or I get to do my senior year one more time." Hank noted the four educators pausing at the statement. His poor daughter forgot that half the adults in the room worked at her school. It couldn't be easy, he thought.

"I was kidding," she said taking, several plates into the kitchen. "You need to lighten up, it's not exactly the apocalypse."

Enough tension you could cut it with a knife. Hank caught the slight grin on her lips as she backed through the kitchen door.

Min smacked Hank in the shoulder. "She knows."

He shook his head. "She doesn't know anything. That's just something teenagers say." He saw the concerned expression on everybody's face. "It is, isn't it?"

"You really are out of touch with what the youngsters are doing these days, aren't you?"

He narrowed his eyes at Mrs. V. She was easily thirty years older than him, but she was probably right. She probably had more of an idea of what was "in" and what the kids found hip these days. Hank smiled, taking solace that being the least hip parent wasn't a bad parent to be.

"So, what do we know?" Victor asked. The room got quiet. The large table was covered in food, dirty plates scattered everywhere across the surface. Even though it appeared a food bomb went off in the dining room, it was quiet. The mood shifted as they all leaned in on the table.

"The daycare is," Angelica tried to think of the right word, "cute."

Hank nodded in agreement. "It's a daycare. There are ankle biters running around."

"Worst thing we saw all day was a teacher picking her nose more than the toddlers. Woman is convinced there was gold up in them there hills."

"Uhm, ew," Lauren said, pushing her plate further away.

"You'll go back tomorrow. If necessary, get access to the daycare. Maybe it's a front for something. I can't believe the intel is bad."

"Speaking of," Cadence chimed in, "are you finally going to tell us where you are getting this intel? It's not coming from the CIA or FBI."

"The dark web has been silent. I can't find any mention of going ons around here.," said Xander.

Mrs. V was impressed. Cadence and Xander had been formidable in their intel gathering abilities while they worked at the agency. She was always surprised at how dangerous they could be, even unarmed. Her team was impressive, even if it was a little less than conventional.

"NSA and Homeland say you're wrong." Angelica spoke up. The fiery redhead had taken a small vacation after her father died. During that time, a string of Russians were found dead. Drug dealers and human traffickers were going missing. Mrs. V had suspected her step daughter was mourning her dad's death the only way she knew how, by killing everything in her line of sight.

"I have somebody on the inside. For now, we do our due diligence. We need to make sure we're covering our bases."

"Is it wrong that I'm hoping they turn into zombies so I

can shoot them?"

They all gasped at Victor's words. "Don't act like you don't have your hand on the trigger half the day. Besides, I said *after* they turn to zombies."

"You may win the title of new disgruntled member of our group," Lauren said. The girl reached down to her purse and pulled out a flask. She screwed off the top and added coffee brandy to her cup. Lauren realized everybody was staring at her. "Shut up, I had a rough day."

"Do you know when this thing is supposed to go down?" Cadence asked.

Mrs. V shrugged. She didn't want to tell them it was a student who was feeding her information. She was pretty sure Cadence, Xander, and Min all had the kid in their classes. She didn't know his credibility, just that he was getting access to something that was giving him far more information than he was letting on.

"Okay, so, something is going to happen. When are we thinking?" Angelica asked. The red-haired woman was holding a steak knife in one hand, spinning it about her fingers in a well-rehearsed act of boredom.

Mrs. V didn't have an exact answer. She thought the homecoming game would have been the perfect time to assault the student body. However, there was the possibility of prom, the cotillion dance, or even the battle of the bands.

"Parent's night?" asked Hank. The big guy held up a sheet of paper with information on it. The note demanded all parents were required to be at the event.

"Let's go over what we know." Mrs. V said, inviting the rest of her team to add to the discussion.

"We know Ms. Shelly worked for a pharmaceutical company. We know that Bryce interned with her when he

126

got back from that stupid game show." Cadence remembered the events as if they had happened yesterday. They were detailed in her novels, telling about the nefarious plot of corporate executives determined to destroy the world.

"We know that Sonya was a super model," Xander said, remembering the ample bosom of the runway model.

Cadence elbowed her husband, knocking him from his trance. Teeth flashed as he smiled at her, trying to brush away thoughts of Sonya walking the runway in nothing more than a lace bra and skimpy underwear.

"Oh God, he's thinking about her runway show again," Victor said, pointing at Xander. "Whose smart idea was it to show him that video?"

They all turned to Hank. The chubby man's face turned red. "I thought it would be relevant."

"The beauty cream is our link. The scientists made it, the model distributed it. I mean, if I were her, I'd want to keep that body." Cadence couldn't argue with her husband's logic. She would smack him when they were alone for staring at that fake redhead.

"We already checked the entire Provasive company. The bottles were stolen and the machine was one of theirs, but they're as benign as a body image destroying company can be. The only thing they're guilty of is making teenage girls throw away their money." Hank realized they were at a dead end. They could keep chasing outbreaks, but eventually they were going to get caught in the middle again and it was going to end badly.

"I can call in a favor," Mrs. V. added, "and have the guys at the agency start pulling every shred of information they have on other beauty companies. Maybe there's a lead."

Lauren slurped down her drink. "Until then, we go to parent's night. We blow up anybody in our way."

"Chocolate crazy is right," Min said.

"So what do we do to be prepared?" Mrs. V unfolded a sheet of paper and whipped out a pen from nowhere. "We're not getting caught with our skirts hiked up this time."

"I want every automatic weapon we have." Xander tossed out a sheet of paper from his pocket. Mrs. V picked up the sheet and saw the three dozen weapons listed. "What? I just happen to keep my inventory on me."

"Everybody needs to be carrying." Cadence nodded.

"Swords," Min added.

Angelica pointed to the Asian and hi-fived the girl. "I'm with Min. Blades. Switchblades. Swords. Hell, if you have a meat cleaver, I want it."

"Blow torches," Hank added.

"Coffee." They paused to look at Lauren. She took another swig from the flask, wiping a drizzle from her lips with the back of her hands. "Remember last time? Yeah, coffee bitches. It saved your asses."

"Grenades. Rocket Launcher. Can anybody get access to one of those portable helium lasers? It'd be nice to not need ammo. Chainsaws always seem to show up. Might as well get that. I'm thinking one of the NASA exoskeletons with modified digging drills."

They all paused to look at Xander.

"It's not like I said a tank," he paused. He slouched down in his chair. "There's no chance we can find a tank by tomorrow, is there? I promise to only use it if there's an apocalypse."

* * * * *

David watched from the street as she crawled out the window of her second story home. She slid her window shut, taking care not to slam it. Jessica carefully walked to the edge of the roof and jumped off, landing in some bushes between the house and the garage. Her head popped up over the brush, turning to and fro, looking for any adults in the vicinity.

Jessica ran down to the end of the driveway. She motioned for him to follow her around the corner, and laughed when she saw his face. He suspected his shifting eyes and all black outfit weren't exactly what she had in mind for going out this evening.

"Where are we going?" he asked hopping onto his bike.

"It's called the Dining Room." She dropped her skateboard onto the ground and kicked off, sailing down the street.

David peddled along to catch up and rode next to her. He only knew the girl for the better part of a day and already she was leading him to a life of crime. He was a straight A student in several advanced classes ahead of his grade, and at this rate, he'd be able to have his pick of colleges. But here he was, in the middle of the night, going to some place called, "The Dining Room." This was not going to help with college applications.

They only rode about two miles away from her house. David and Jessica had to cross through a train yard to a slightly seedier part of town. As they left the train yard, the abandoned buildings became more frequent. He gripped his bike a bit tighter, expecting somebody to jump out from the shadows at any moment.

"Kid," she said, "don't worry, I've got you covered."

"Sure, you can beat up a cheerleader, but how are you

against thugs with guns?"

With her head hanging down, she threw up her arms in defeat. "Thugs with guns are going to steal your bike? You so sure about that?"

Okay, he admitted, it was foolish. "It's ten speeds," he mumbled to himself.

As they walked down an alley, he noticed music starting to fill the air. They turned down a side road between empty buildings. Lights filled the street and dozens of people hung outside a massive metal door. She signaled for him to stash his bike behind a dumpster. Jessica slid her skateboard under the huge green bin.

"A rave?" he asked?

She nodded. "You sound surprised? What can I say, I'm a girl who likes to let loose a little."

"It's not that. We were just in the middle of suburbia, housing developments and all that. Now we're in the middle of a barren warehouse district where people are gathering illegally to listen to house music?"

"Now that you mention it, it does sound a bit out of place."

They both paused as a white Escalade drove up to the door. Two teenagers hopped out of the back of the car, sporting the latest in street designer wear. Their mom leaned over into the passenger side and waved to her kids. "You have fun," she said as her kids walked in the front door.

"Okay, that's a bit more of what I expected," said David.

David pushed his bike behind the dumpster, trying to hide it from sight. He could only imagine which one of these yuppies might want to steal his sweet ride. "Okay. Farewell suburbia, hello ghetto."

They both paused as a woman in tight white leather

pants and stiletto heels made her way to the door. She wore a white halter top and a poofy almost-furry jacket that looked like a living animal. The middle-aged woman made her way toward the door, blowing kisses to the boys hanging around the outside of the door.

"Was that their *mom*?" Jessica hissed.

"The cougar epidemic is out of control," David said, astonished at the forty-year old woman and her ability to walk in such tight clothing.

"Okay," she said, grabbing him by his hoodie, "we need to set some ground rules."

"What?"

"Do not drink from any glass somebody hands you. Do not take any pills somebody gives you. Do not lick, snort, ingest anything somebody offers you."

"Yeah," he said, "cause I do that all the time."

She jabbed him in the chest with her pointer finger. "Most of all, have yourself a good time. People are here to let loose."

David had no idea what she meant. The girl strutted toward the entrance, each step more confident than the last. She bumped fists with two of the guys at the door who opened it wide for her. The moment the door opened, the intensity of music increased. His eyes went wide as the bass thumped loud enough his chest cavity vibrated.

She motioned for him to follow. It was now or never. In his memoir, this is where he'd tell the world he became evil. He'd call her out by name as the reason he turned to a life of crime. With a deep breath, David rounded the door, following her toward the increasingly deafening sound.

The Dining Room was a large, gutted restaurant. The smell of fish still hung in the air, or sweat; it was hard to tell them apart with this crowd. It opened into a large seating area, except all the tables and booths had been torn away, trashed long ago. The floor was nothing more than bare cement, and only parts of the bar on the far wall remained. What had once stocked the finest liquors was nothing more than cheap wholesale booze.

To his right, there was a DJ raised up on a temporary stage. The speakers on either side were larger than the man playing music. Lights above him spun about, casting rays of different colored light onto the crowd in front of him. There couldn't be less than three hundred people crammed into the tight space, crowding the stage.

To his left, there was a dead space where nobody danced. Instead, ravers stood in small groups talking to one another. It wasn't until he saw Kevin the drug pusher hanging out that he realized what was going on. It was like everywhere else David guessed; some came to party, and others, they came to *party*.

Jessica was at the bar. He judged her quietly as she ordered a drink and slammed it down on the counter. Apparently, she wasn't as cut and dry as David had imagined. There was a bit of a sinister undertone to her personality. He pointed at him, and then at Kevin, and waved them both toward the back of the club.

David slid past two girls grinding on one another. He paused to smile at the sight, getting scared when one of the girls winked at him. He moved to the back of the club until he was next to his high school companions.

"Find out anything?" Kevin shouted over the music.

Jessica shook her head. She pulled her headphones down off her head and wrapped them around her neck. "They were talking all polite like nothing is going on. Not one mention of zombies. When I mentioned the apocalypse though, they all froze."

"They know," he said.

David leaned in to listen to the two of them shouting over the music. They were lost. They didn't know how to go about the conversation without involving the adults. Jessica was annoyed, and Kevin went from being concerned to reveling in the conspiracy theory.

"It's happening tomorrow afternoon," the new kid blurted out.

Kevin and Jessica stopped to look at him. Kevin leaned in close to David's face. The smell of aftershave wafted off him, which was ironic because David bet money the kid had yet to start shaving. Kevin grabbed David by the back of the neck and pulled him close. "How do you know that?"

David cursed under his breath. He didn't want to tell them, but by the increasingly tight grip Kevin had on his shoulder, he knew he had backed himself into a corner. Even Jessica was starting to look angsty at the new information.

"I hacked into a whole lot of computers. I have software that looks for the world of weird. I've been stalking this whole zombie thing for a while."

Kevin's teeth clenched tightly and furrowed his brow while letting out a low growl. He grabbed onto David's hoodie and started to lift him from the ground. "You knew about this the whole time? You *knew* there were zombies? You were going to let us be eaten?"

"I wasn't certain. I didn't know anything definite until you filled in the gaps. I mean honestly, who believed zombies were really happening?"

Jessica nodded. "How do you know for sure?"

"Mrs. V."

Jessica's eyes lit up. The whole time she had been sitting at dinner, waiting for them to slip up, David was piecing together parts of the puzzle. She pushed Kevin away and grabbed onto David's collar. He was going to need to explain to his mom how his clothes got so stretched while he was studying for an algebra test in his bedroom.

"You knew my mom was involved and didn't say anything!?"

"I've known you for a day. A day!"

She paused to think about it. "True." Jessica set him down. "So we have confirmation. Zombies tomorrow?"

David nodded. "My software is still running. I don't know details. I still don't know who's doing it."

Jessica brushed off the kid. "You don't need to. We know some adults that know who's going to do it."

Kevin pulled out a bottle from his jacket. He read the label quickly, squinting to see it in the dark, and popped it open. He swallowed the pill while the other two stared. "I have heartburn," he said, shoving the bottle up for them to see.

"So we avoid school tomorrow?" David asked. "Maybe we alert the authorities?"

Kevin didn't know what to say. "What do you think?"

Jessica shook her head. "We can't skip school and let everybody die."

"You want to go?" asked David.

"You're not serious," Kevin asked. "You know zombies eat people alive, right?"

"No shit," she said. "Like I don't watch The Walking Dead."

"We'd just be eaten alive," David added, agreeing whole heartedly with Kevin on this one.

"We can't let them die. And it doesn't sound like the grown ups are exactly nailing this one. Besides, we're the ones who were brought up on zombies. I'd like to think I've learned a few things reading World War Z."

"Doesn't everybody die in that book?"

She shot Kevin a dirty look. "Besides, if we go in there ready, how hard is it to stop zombies? I mean, they're already dead. We just poke a few holes in people's heads."

"Shouldn't we try to stop it from happening at all?" asked David.

Jessica shrugged. "Yeah, I guess that way makes more sense too."

"Okay, I have an idea," she said. She motioned for them to gather closer. They made a three-person huddle, screaming ideas and suggestions at each other. For the next fifteen minutes, they plotted how the three of them would prevent the apocalypse.

* * * * *

The plan was in place. They each had their role to play during the first few periods of the day.

Jessica didn't think it'd be a problem. They were only zombies. With a few well placed locked doors, they could easily escape. If lucky, they could find out what was causing them. She didn't want to admit it to herself, but stopping a zombie apocalypse might finally make her mom proud. And think of the college opportunities after saving the world-- Harvard bound.

She was tired of being serious. She was tired of dealing with the boys. Jessica was tired of school. Simply put, she was kind of tired with the boredom of her life during the daylight hours. She walked toward the DJ, sliding her away along the writhing bodies. Her skin was coated in sweat as she pushed to the middle of the crowd. For now, there was only her friends, and a DJ leading them toward bliss.

Jessica began to dance in the crowd, her body grinding in rhythm with the mass of people. She noticed a woman in all white--the cougar from outside. The woman gyrated her hips with the crowd, sweat pouring down her artificially-tanned body. Jessica couldn't help but smile. Everybody here came for a reason, some to be lost, some to be found. As she danced, she couldn't judge.

Jessica reached into the deep pockets of her baggy pants and pulled out two neon blue glow-sticks. With practiced ease, she broke them and danced. Her hands moved in a hypnotic pattern, her body seeming to flow like liquid, defying the joints and clunky working of human anatomy. The crowd parted for a moment, giving her a bit more of the dance floor as she swung her arms to and fro. She spun around and was surprised to see Kevin standing in front of her.

Kevin reached into his jacket and she expected for him to pull out a pill bottle. He pulled out what look like two small orbs. Her eyes showed disbelief as his body started to move in time with the music. The kid wasn't unfamiliar to the rave scene. She just assumed he was here on the hunt for new clients. It hadn't dawned on her he might also be a raver.

As his hands spun above his head, the two orbs flew outward, attached to his hands by thin colored wire. The orbs spun and lit up, glowing a bright red. As he continued to spin his hands, the orbs danced about his body in a mesmerizing pattern. The crowd pushed back, the dancers watching his performance. She had seen countless poi dancers in the audience before, but Kevin was by far the most elaborate.

The spinning balls changed color in mid-flight. He ducked down, having them spin over his back and then around his legs. It appeared she had misjudged him. Jessica began to dance again, hopping back and forth and letting the music wash over her. They were here for a good time, there was no point in her dwelling on him being a bottom feeder at school.

Kevin pressed up against her as the crowd pushed back in. He was holding the two balls in his hands as his body began to move along with hers, a serpentine dance, gyrating as the sweat rolled along their bodies.

She leaned in close until their lips were nearly touching. She admired his eyes, the DJ's lights illuminating Kevin's face enough to see his baby blue irises. She could feel his breath on her lips, and as their hips pushed against one another she reached up and slid her hands along his wet neck. She licked his lip, enticing him to close the final distance between them.

Kevin tasted like cherry. As his teeth bit down on her lip, Jessica realized she was making out with the resident drug dealer, and she didn't care. She grunted as he grabbed her hips, pulling her closer while he explored her mouth with his tongue. She figured if they were going to save the world tomorrow, might as well enjoy their last night of normalcy.

Past Bedtime

"When did you start renting a storage locker?"

Xander paused, his key still in the lock. His storage locker was one of the largest in the complex. It faced the far end of the facility and had several video cameras pointed on the door. He paid a handsome stipend to the attendant to pay attention to the cameras, but mostly to keep his mouth shut from what the guard might see go in and out of the locker.

Xander turned the key and pulled the padlock from the door. He lifted the gate with his foot, and as it rolled up the track, the lights turned on automatically. Cadence's eyes went wide as her brain began to process what she was seeing.

"Remember when you said, 'No more guns in the house' and I said, 'Sure'? Well, I might have kept buying them."

She stepped inside the twenty by twenty storage space. Lining the walls were racks holding enough automatic weapons to stage a military coup. Crates stored in the middle held grenades, more than she had ever seen before. She knew her husband had a problem, but she hadn't been aware of how bad it had gotten.

"Where did you get these?"

"Well," he said; the tone in his voice told her it was going to be a story she didn't like. "I got involved in a chatroom with a guy who belongs to a drug cartel. When we met, I bought a bunch of weapons, mostly small stuff. Then I decided to see what I could get military grade. You'd be surprised how fast government officials are willing to hand over their goods when you slip them an envelope full of money."

There was even a *rocket launcher*. Cadence just pointed at it, unable to form words. Her husband had his hobbies, mostly origami and the occasional pistol, but this was something new to her.

"Oh that! Well, remember when I said I was going with Angelica to see a man about some intel? Well we did, except intel really meant heavy arms."

"Where did you find the money?"

Xander paused. She wasn't mad he was storing enough artillery to wage war on American soil, Cadence was more concerned about his funds. "Funny story, not haha funny, but more ironic."

Cadence's gaze thinned into a glare. "Xander Winters, I will kill you."

"When I turned twenty-five, I might have inherited a trust fund."

She spun about and grabbed him by the throat. He was glad to see she had been keeping up with her Booty Buster Workout tapes, but the lack of oxygen reaching his brain made him see spots. His wife pushed him back until they bumped into a wall. Her deathlike grip didn't relent.

"You're a trust fund baby?"

He managed a slight nod as his eyes rolled backward in his head.

The seventy-two automatic rifles. The eight crates of high yield explosives. The three foot lockers holding rocket launchers. The giant thing that looked like a robot in the back. None of that mattered. She was pissed that she was married to a trust fund baby.

"How. Much."

She released her grip enough for him to suck in air. "Twelve million or so."

She clenched his throat again. "My life as a struggling artist. My entire marriage, it's been to a member of the bourgeois? I've been living a sham."

"Honey," he spat out.

"I've secretly been living a life of privilege? What would my younger self say? I married a yuppie; a gun toting yuppie on top of it all."

"Can't..."

"I would despise myself. I would point at myself and say I was a poseur, a fake, a harlot. I would hate myself."

"Breathe..."

"I don't know if I can ever look at you the same."

"Ghhrhir..."

She paused. Off to the side there were several mannequin legs, an odd sight unless her husband had a bizarre fetish she wasn't aware of. It took a moment, but she noticed the leg holsters wrapped around the fake woman's legs. She smiled at her husband and pulled her hand back, letting him fall to the floor. He inhaled, trying not to hurl on the storage room floor.

She examined the holster closely. It was the one she had asked for Christmas. She pulled at the Velcro and admired the durability of the cloth, the way it curved to hug a woman's upper thigh. She had been eyeing it for months, but decided to hold off until the holidays.

"You like it?" he said through a scratchy voice.

"Load up the U-Haul," she said, "I need to test this out."

"You're not mad?"

She turned, her eyebrows slanted so far that she looked like a caricature of herself. He knew that face, she typically reserved it for her agent when a book deal fell through. He had married a beautiful woman who could stop traffic with a single look. He would be sleeping on the couch.

She grabbed a rifle off the wall, jammed in a magazine, and pointed it directly at him. "We'll talk about this when we get home."

He choked, nodding. "Yes dear." Zombies, those he could handle; a disgruntled wife, they didn't make weapons large enough to deal with that.

* * * * *

The duffle bag sat on the living room table. It was filled with guns. Next to it sat several green tin boxes, each one filled to the top with different types of ammo.

"I still feel I'm packing a bit light," Angelica said, pushing her red locks behind her ear. She counted the guns-- thirteen total--and at least a few thousand rounds. She didn't like to be unprepared.

"Back in my day," Mrs. V said from the other room.

"Oh no," Angelica replied, "you did not just pull that 'When I was young' bullshit, did you?"

"Listen," Mrs. V said, "my first zombie apocalypse, I had six bullets, an American flag, and a couple grenades. We did pretty damned good on our own. I'm sure you have enough ammo to kill every one of those little bastard students twice. Wait until you see the arsenal Xander is bringing. I think he even has a military exoskeleton with lasers mounted on it or something."

"Have you ever thought, 'Wow, the people I hang out are just a step away from being homicidal maniacs?' Cause I'm starting to think they might be dangerous."

Mrs. V. tossed her favorite bayonet onto the table. "If

they weren't scary, we wouldn't be friends. And this coming from the woman who asked permission to kill her ex-boyfriend because he was getting married."

"That's different."

"You broke up with him, Angie."

"How can I be with a man who doesn't like cats?"

Mrs. V paused. "Really? That's the reason?"

Angelica shrugged. "A girl has to draw the line somewhere."

Mrs. V walked around the dining room table, put her hands on Angelica's shoulders, and turned her. She pushed back the hair on the young woman's head, smiling at the girl. "You know," Mrs. V said, "your dad would be proud of you."

"I hated him when you got married."

"I know."

"I hated you even more."

"I know," Mrs. V said, giving the stepdaughter a hug. "Your mom was an amazing woman, and your dad is a hero. It's hard to measure up to that."

Angelica turned her head, faking something caught in her eye. She pushed away the tears. Angie didn't cry. She refused to let it happen, instead letting out a long sigh. "You know, you're not half bad Renee."

Angelica turned back to the woman, her mascara running down her face. She missed her parents, her dad was her entire world, but she had to admit, she had a pretty amazing stand-in-parent. "You make a pretty good mom."

Mrs. V hugged her tight. They embraced. It was the first time Mrs. V had seen Angelica let down her guard. It was a moment. She was happy she had finally won the girl's trust. It had taken time, but finally Angie didn't think of her as a commanding officer, but a step-mom.

"Have we hugged long enough?" Angelica gave a slight laugh.

"Yeah," Mrs. V said, "hugging with this much ammo nearby is making my trigger finger itchy."

"We're not going to tell anybody that just happened, are we?"

Mrs. V shook her head. "I'll shoot you if you do."

"Ditto."

Angelica started to walk out of the room, and turned back to the elderly woman. Mrs. V had been a librarian once upon a time, now she was a data expert and fierce fighting machine. Angelica wouldn't admit it out loud, but she looked up to the woman. Turning out like Renee wouldn't be half bad.

"Thanks mom."

Mrs. V shot up, her eyes going wide. She hadn't expected that.

"Whoa," Angelica said, "let's just say that never happened, Renee."

"That's commanding officer to you."

"Yes ma'am."

Mrs. V smiled. It was on the eve of the apocalypse they had begun their relationship. It'd be a funny story to tell the grandkids when Angelica stopped beating up her boyfriends and threatening to castrate them. Someday, someday she would find a boy who would treat her right and take her to the shooting range for date nights.

Mrs. V head back to the library. Her old house, a Victorian she bought when she had first started dating Beau. He had moved in, and between operations fighting the zombie scourge, he had helped her restore it to its former

143

glory. He had tried to convince her to move to a beautiful loft in the city, but she had stayed firm. This was where she wanted to spend the rest of her life.

Mrs. V walked up to the large door leading into the library, and pressed her hand on the scanner beside it. A small slit opened in the door and a red beam scanned her eyes. Of course, there had to be some upgrades when Beau moved in. The garage constantly scanned for explosive devices and tracking technology. The living room had a full surveillance system, and even the basement had escape tunnels with reinforced steel doors. It was the perfect home, she thought.

As the library door's hydraulics hissed, opening the eight inch thick steel door, she slid inside. Only she and Beau were permitted into this room. During their courtship, they would help prevent government take downs in foreign countries, even thwarting terrorist organizations. However, it was during an excursion in which they were captured and tortured for information on nuclear technology that Beau won her heart.

Once the killed everyone holding them captive, they fled through a dictator's house. They had been split up, and agreed on a rendezvous point. She later found out he had taken a different avenue to leave the man's house, one leading him right through the library. Beau had gifted her an original Gutenberg Bible for their first year anniversary. Even with the spattering of blood from the dictator on the cover, it was the most thoughtful gift anybody had ever given her.

She proposed. A man who would risk their lives to acquire literature was her soul mate. It helped that he had excellent marksmanship. Later that month, when they were saving the Pope from a religious extremist group, the holiest of men married them. It had been the perfect ceremony, Latin verses read aloud while they dodged bullets and nearly lost their lives. It was the honeymoon she had always wanted.

Now he was gone. Angelica was the legacy he had left behind, and Mrs. V would do anything to protect her step-daughter. As she moved through the eight foot tall rows of books, Mrs. V passed the Bible in a glass display case. Just above it on the wall was a picture of her husband trying to stitch together a bullet hole in his shoulder. It was the Beau she liked to remember, the tough man with a heart of gold.

The two story library would make any librarian jealous. The second floor had books from floor to ceiling. There was an antiquity collection she found during a raid in Egypt, and a plethora of first editions. When she died, some library would be very lucky to receive Mrs. V's collected works. Until then, she housed them in her temperature-controlled library, savoring the sweet scent of musty books.

She took a seat at the only table in the room. As she adjusted the seat, a monitor rose out of the table and came to life. She pushed her pointed finger down on the pad. A small pin prick and a drop of blood later, the computer greeted her.

Mrs. V opened the terminal on her screen she used to contact David. She wanted to see if there was any more information she could squeeze out of the student before they arrived at school tomorrow.

V: Are you there?

She waited for several minutes. The cursor blinked, nothing happened. She was preparing to log out of the terminal when a message appeared.

D: Nice to see you Mrs. V.

V: Same to you David. Have you learned anything more about the attack?

D: I learned you know far more about the impending apocalypse than I suspected.

V: A woman has her secrets.

D: So it seems. What are looking at?

V: Viral outbreak. Zombies. They're real.

D: I know. We know about your cohorts.

V: We?

D: I'm not the only student at the school who knows what is going on.

V: Don't go to school tomorrow.

D: Why not call off school?

V: We need to find the person responsible for the outbreaks. We can't keep chasing corpses, somehow the source revolves around the high school.

D: We'll be ready.

Mrs. V. was annoyed. Of course, another student who wouldn't listen to her advice. Even David, one of the smartest kids at school, was going to be a typical teen and go against anything she could throw at him. She did admire his bravado, she just hoped it wouldn't get him killed.

V: Put your team on alert. They see anything out of the normal, report back.

D: Same to you.

V: Be careful David.

D: I have to go, the rave is over.

Rave, she thought? The smartest kid in school was at an illegal concert. That sounded more like Min's daughter than the computer genius. She paused as the thought went across her mind. Pieces started falling together. David had an inside source.

V: Keep Jessica safe.

...

D: Will do.

Mrs. V. was tempted to say a prayer for them. She closed the computer on her desk and walked to the picture of Beau above the Bible. She didn't pray, instead she made a promise. "Tomorrow, I end this. This is my final class, Beau."

* * * * *

Cadence's head shot up as she loaded a crate of grenades into the U-Haul. She ignored the hair standing on her neck, but the shiver working its way up her spine gave her cause for alarm.

"Everything all right?" asked Xander.

"I don't know. I keep getting these weird feelings, like somebody just doomed us."

"Doomed us?"

"You know," she said, "like they said, 'Nobody dies on my watch,' or 'What could possibly go wrong' or even the horrible, 'Let me use the title of the movie in my final solution speech.'"

"How bad is it?"

Cadence shook her head. "We are so screwed."

THURSDAY

Breakfast

The cafeteria was one of the largest rooms in the school. At any given moment, it could house nearly one thousand hungry students. The long rows of tables held small circular stools, each a large contraption capable of moving to the side during dances or public events. Most often, the space housed younger students dropped off early from their busses. Seniors waited until the last possible minute to roll out of bed, throw on dirty clothes, and pile in the door like shambling zombies.

In the far corner of the room, Kevin noticed Jessica and David talking amongst themselves. He walked through the door, giving a slight nod to the new shop teacher. The man gave him a slight bow back, but otherwise paid him no heed.

Kevin kept his head down, working his way around the tables. Dozens of students were eating their cereal or eggs. He barely recognized the kids in the cafeteria, as he got older he stopped noticing the younger kids. Few of them were clients and even fewer of them sparked his interest socially. If they were paying, he wasn't paying attention.

As Kevin approached his co-conspirators, they both looked up; their faces showed their displeasure. Kevin sat down at the table and gestured for a kid following him to sit down with them.

"What's *he* doing here?"

Jessica and David stared at Rob. They tried not to judge him, but the copious amounts of eyeliner and the fake raven black hair made him an easy target for ridicule. Kevin leaned in close, bending over the table so they were able to whisper.

"Look, I've known Rob since grade school. We've recently had some differences," he looked back at his one-time friend, "but I think you'll be able to see why I brought him."

"Differences?" the goth hissed.

"Don't start, Rob."

"You mean, how we used to hang out in middle school until you started peddling your Ritalin to the kids in math?"

Kevin rolled his eyes. "Says the poseur."

Jessica gave a slight laugh.

Rob gave her a scalding look. "Kevin's willing to sell drugs to every chump at this school. *I* ask him for a hookup, and he says no."

"Dude," Kevin said, "you don't do drugs. You're like the most straight laced person I know."

Rob grabbed Kevin, pulling him in close. "Shh! I have an image to maintain."

"That's the real reason we stopped hanging out. You got pissed when I wouldn't turn all goth with you. Seriously, do people still dress like this? Isn't this so 90's?"

"Guys!" David interjected. "Kevin, why did you bring him?"

"While Rob has some serious issues with his wardrobe, I couldn't think of anybody who knew more about zombies."

"Figures," Jessica said, "the Lord of Darkness is the expert in all things undead."

Rob stared at her through black bangs hanging down over one eye. She couldn't help but think he looked like a bad high school cliché. She half expected him to wear a cape and claim to be a child of the night. Jessica wondered if he spent his evenings under the moon, trying to call forth demons to purge the Earth.

"We don't have much time till the bell. What do you know?" asked David.

Rob shrugged. "Not much, you know."

"You apathetic eyeliner-wearing ass." Jessica grabbed at him from across the table. "Tell us what you know, and I won't resort to dropping you like a dumb ass cheerleader."

Rob raised his middle finger at her, showing off the chipped black nail polish. She returned the gesture with both hands.

"Why do you want to know about zombies?" he asked.

"School project."

"Personal reasons."

"Pop culture demands it."

He eyed them. He didn't buy it. Kevin hadn't talked to him in years, and out of the blue Rob gets a text message last night to meet Kevin in the cafeteria. It wasn't enough that he got a strange text message, but the new kid and Jessica weren't exactly Kevin's typical friends. Neither of them seemed to be wired on speed or in desperate need of a fix. Something wasn't adding up.

"Tell me, or I walk."

Kevin and Jessica turned to David. The kid hung his head down. "Okay look, the zombie apocalypse is about to happen and we're pretty sure it's going to happen here. We need to know what we're up against."

"Really? You serious?" Rob tried to hide his excitement. He had contemplated more than once going berserk on the kids at the school, but with the difficulty of acquiring a real gun, he felt his bb gun just wouldn't make the statement he wanted.

"We're serious," Jessica said. "So either help us or go away."

They were serious. Rob started to laugh. Either they were taking some serious drugs, or they knew something. He didn't care, he was elated that there was a chance the entire school was going to be eaten alive. "You want me to help you stop the apocalypse?"

Kevin jabbed his former friend in the stomach. "Stop being an ass and help us."

Rob didn't stop laughing. He stood up and flipped them all off again. "I hope it happens. I hope the zombie apocalypse happens and kills you all. I cannot wait to see you feasting on each other. I'll be laughing my ass off."

"Seriously?" Jessica asked in disbelief.

"You thought I was going to help you? You're all a bunch of assholes. And Kevin, you're the biggest one of all. I hope the other two eat you alive."

Rob turned around and began to walk off. All three stared, unable to comprehend the level of jerk from their classmate. The goth kid held up both hands, extending his middle fingers as he walked out of the cafeteria.

"Not how I expected that to go," Kevin said.

"Exactly what I expected," Jessica said. "Kevin, you're an idiot."

David slapped several sheets of paper onto the table. He didn't wait for Kevin to make a retort to Jessica. "Okay, we have maps here. I've labeled each map with our class schedule, so we can stay near one another. If something goes down, we meet here in the quad."

Kevin was impressed with the kid. "What do you want us to do with these?"

"We have till the end of the day to build a cache of weapons. Find them, secure them, mark them on the map. When this all goes down, there's a very good chance we'll need to defend ourselves."

"Dude," Kevin interjected, "you know zombies just drag their feet around. It's not like they can catch up to us."

David brushed off the boy's comment. "You'll be the first to die. Me on the other hand, I already know some places where we can build up a good stock of weapons. Remember, if you see anything suspicious, you text right away. If somebody looks sick, text. If they look like they might die, text."

"If they look like they just came back from the dead and are trying to eat somebody," Jessica said, "text."

"Got it," Kevin added.

"All right, we need to get to class. Everybody knows the plan? We're on alert for this. We're going to be heroes," David added.

"Not too bad, little man," Jessica added.

They started to get up when Kevin leaned in to Jessica. He was close enough he could whisper into her ear. "About last night--"

"It never happened," she said.

He gave a defeated nod. "Of course, nothing happened."

As they each grabbed a map, rolled it up, stashed it in their pockets and began to walk away, a boy at a table not far from them looked up. Pulling back his hood, he watched the trio walk away with a light bounce to their step. He found it hard to believe he just listened to the three of them talk about zombies invading the school. He knew Kevin was an idiot, but this was his time to use the information to his knowledge.

"Kevin," Sam spat out, "today is the day you're going down."

Period 1

Sam grabbed the chair, snarling at Kevin who attempted to swipe it out from under the boy. Sam gave a haughty chuckle as he sat down in the anchor's seat. He snaked a microphone up through his shirt and clipped it on the collar.

"So it seems your girlfriend isn't such a fan of you."

Kevin tried to brush off the snot nosed kid. "Even a rejection is more than you get from the ladies."

"And you know all about rejection, don't you?" Sam said, trying to hide the smile spreading across his face.

"All right guys," said the teacher to the room full of students running the television studio. He was a slender Asian man with a wispy mustache and long fu man chu. He held his hands in his pockets, trying to hide his overabundance of energy.

"We have the show this morning. Then immediately afterward, we're going to pre-tape the show that will air during parent's night. We need to be on our toes, okay? We need to speed right through this, *okay*?"

The kid manning camera two saluted the teacher. Sam rolled his eyes at the kid's dedication to the morning television show. He was a freshman and didn't have an original thought in his head, instead he took orders from the producer who did all the thinking from him. *Techs*, Sam thought, *they're so beneath me*.

"I know that look," Tina said, leaning over the anchor desk. She had her hair pulled back into a ponytail and her makeup, done so well it was difficult to see the bruise where she had been clocked. "He's condescending somebody in his head."

"Shut up," Sam said coming back to reality.

"I'll be in the control room if anybody needs me. Let Mr. Rightoff know he has to stay behind to tape the second show. Tina, can you do that? Okay?"

"Uhh, yeah, I can do that."

"Okay!" the teacher cheered as he walked to the back of the studio and into the small control room that worked all the sound and lighting equipment for the studio.

"Tina," Sam rested his head on his hands while leaning on the anchor desk. "Did you know that Kevin here has a thing for Jessica?"

"What?" Tina didn't hide her anger at the statement. The adopted wench had made a fool of her, and she didn't like one of her anchors crushing on the crazed Amazonian.

Kevin rolled his eyes at the two. "It's none of business, either of you."

"It is when she decks me in the face. I can't *believe* you. You could have any girl at the school, but of course you go for my sworn mortal enemy."

"Tina, you're overreacting."

Tina held up her hand, walking toward her station on the set. She hopped up on her chair at the small round table, turning away, purposely avoiding eye contact with Kevin.

Kevin socked his co-anchor in the arm. "Why the hell did you have to go and do that?"

"How's it feel to be the center of attention, Kevin?"

Sam took pleasure in his co-anchor's misery. He fought the need to begin laughing--no, not laughing, *heckling*--as his co-anchor tried to find a way to get himself out of a fight with his beloved, beautiful cheerleader friend. Yes, his plan for destroying Kevin was slowly taking route. There was the next matter to attend to.

The lights flared on, the massive canisters of illumination overhead quickly heating up the room. The cameraman moved into position and held up his hand, signaling the show was about to start. The producer ran out, screaming for everybody to be quiet as the camera man counted down.

Kevin began shuffling the papers on the desk and flashed that brilliant smile. The cameras came to life and his back straightened. "Welcome Boxford High, to another wonderful morning. We have a great show for you today. First and foremost, we need to remind you, parents are expected to be at Parent's Night tonight. If it takes guilt, then so be it. We look forward to seeing them."

The camera shifted to Sam. "There was an incident in school yesterday resulting in the arrest of three students. Students claim there was a shortage of tacos in the cafeteria, increasing tensions. When the last taco was taken, a brawl began, resulting in bruised eyes and a fractured arm. The culprit of this travesty? Mr. Simons, a recently hired and now fired English teacher. He is currently awaiting arraignment."

"Wow, that's quiet the feisty fiesta Sam," Kevin remarked.

"Yes it is, now we send you over to Kimberly for the weather."

Sam grunted as Kevin punched him in the arm. "So help me God, if you bring up Jessica one more time, I'll end you."

"Says the zombie hunter."

Kevin froze at the statement.

"So there *is* something you're hiding. I wonder what it could be Kevin? How would you feel if the entire school heard about your crazed theories? Would Mr. Cool become a tool?"

"Shut your face, before I cut my knuckles on your teeth."

The camera switched back to them. "That's great to hear Kimberly," Kevin said. "I'm glad to hear we'll have nothing but sunshine and open skies for Parent's Night. Now, we'll send it over to Tina to give you the morning announcements."

"Before we do that Kevin," Sam interjected, "how about we talk about a real pressing issue facing the school."

Kevin's eyebrows went up as he skimmed the script; this wasn't part of the morning show. He knew it couldn't be good. They never went off script. There was a punishable by death clause given by the teacher if they ever went off their scripts.

"Let's see our very own Kevin having his heart torn from his chest." Sam smiled at Kevin, who still wasn't processing what was happening. The small monitor hanging from the ceiling showing the broadcast switched to a short video of him whispering into Jessica's ear. They could faintly hear the words he whispered to her and her rejection. The screen turned back to the anchors.

"If you see our dear Kevin in the hallways, please take a moment to give him your condolences. It must be hard to have your heart ripped out by such a pretty girl."

A technical difficulties logo flashed across the screen as Kevin tackled Sam, hurling him to the ground. Sam laughed as he tumbled to the floor, the microphone cables ripping out from under the desk. Kevin tried to grasp onto Sam's neck, squeezing, hoping his head would pop off from his body.

"The look on your face," Sam laughed as Kevin smacked him across the face.

Tina started snapping her fingers at the cameraman. The camera spun around focusing on her. She gave her patented seductress smile at the camera as the technical difficulties graphic vanished. "Well, that was certainly an amusing start to the morning, but how about we get back to business."

As she read the morning announcements; a change to a class meeting location, a switch in busses after school, and introducing the teacher replacing Mr. Simons; her back arched. Her breasts became more and more prominent as the shot continued, threatening to rip off the buttons of her blouse.

Mr. Rightoff stepped into the frame and paused for a moment as he found himself lost in the dark cavern of Tina's cleavage. He shook his head, taking off his glasses and rubbing the bridge of his nose. He smiled at the camera. "Another exciting show Tina," he said as Sam tossed Kevin against a wall of the set.

"Never a dull day down here, Mr. Rightoff."

"First thing I need to announce is the new cellphone policy. It has become problematic for teachers to deal with students cheating on tests." Mr. Rightoff paused as he caught Tina checking her texts. "Because of this, starting today, we will be jamming all cell phone signals. This means you're more than welcome to use your phones, for whatever good they'll do you now."

Tina smacked her phone against the table. She could see the zero bars on her screen and a clenching sensation grappled at her chest. She started to feel faint, her breathing raspy and shallow. She thought at any moment she might pass out, or worse yet, have to resort to actually talking to her friends.

"As you can see, it's a pandemic that we have decided to

remedy." Mr. Rightoff smiled at the girl, his eyebrows constantly arching in a way that made him look maniacal.

"Tonight is going to be a big deal," he continued. "Parents will be able to talk to teachers and see what classes are being offered at our amazing school. Most importantly, it'll be a chance for us to convince them we desperately need that seven million dollar AstroTurf football field so we can once and for all let Wessford know that we're the superior school."

"I'm sure we can do that," Tina said, batting her eyelashes.

"We'll let's turn it back to...," the cheerleader paused as Kevin wrapped a cord around Sam's throat. "How about we end it here. Good morning Boxford, you have a great day at school."

The camera cut off, and Mr. Rightoff jumped off his chair and grabbed Kevin, pulling him off Sam. Sam uncoiled the microphone cord from around his neck, sucking in air. Mr. Rightoff tossed Kevin to the side, holding out his hand, and helped the strangled child to his feet.

"Sam, how about we go to my office? I want to make sure you're okay." Mr. Rightoff unwrapped the cord and gave a scolding look toward the other boy.

"Glad you came right away," Sam hissed.

"I didn't want to offend your manhood," Mr. Rightoff spat out. "Now let's go talk about that sizable donation your father is going to be making to our chemistry labs."

* * * * *

Rob sighed deeply as he caught a reflection of himself in a mirror across the classroom. While he didn't loathe taking Introduction to International Cooking and Foreign Cuisine, he did hate the frilly apron he was required to wear. He had won the fight against needing to wear the chef's hat. In a class where he was the only boy, he fought every rule to maintain some semblance of masculinity amongst his female cohorts.

While he watched the timer on the oven tick down, he began to ponder his interaction with Kevin this morning. Was he seriously concerned zombies were going to attack the school? Were they concerned about a virus outbreak? Could they be overreacting to the flu? He couldn't fathom they were serious about *real* zombies, dead people coming back from the dead. While he was certainly okay with the idea, the likelihood that his prayers would be answered were slim to none.

He paused.

Rob slowly reached out as the girls around him gabbed and complimented each other on their mildly attractive chocolate soufflés, and wrapped his hand around the hilt of a cleaver. He eyed the teachers, squawking about some trendy vampire show on television last night. He quickly slid the blade into his backpack. He wasn't sure Kevin was sane, but he didn't want to find out the hard way. If zombies were going to attack, he would find a way to be their king and reign supreme.

"Like oh my God, our soufflé looks magnificent." Rob eyed the girl, imagining what they would look like as zombies. Rob hated his classmates. The thought of missing flesh and mindless moaning made him smile.

"I know Biffy, isn't it awesome?" He could sound excited, but he couldn't lie with his cold dead eyes.

As they took out their chocolatey decadent dessert, the class gathered around to see just how perfect it was. If he couldn't take over the world and cause suffering, he could manage as a pastry chef.

"Wow Nycoale, you smell so good," said a girl to her neighbor.

"Like Chloeee, I know right? It's this new beauty cream I'm using. I got free samples at the job fair. You want some?"

"Totally."

Rob turned to see the girl squeezing dabs of the cream on several girls' outstretched hands. Each of the girls sniffed the cream and began applying it to their t-zone: the space of their forehead down their noses in a well-rehearsed motion. He didn't know why, but in the pit of his stomach, got a sinking feeling. Perhaps Kevin and his newfound friends weren't totally wrong about the apocalypse descending upon Boxford high.

* * * * *

Min smacked her student on the butt. "Stand up straight." She continued down the line, forcing students to arch their backs while they balanced stacks of books on their heads. Each student held a stack in each hand, held out, while standing on one bent leg. They were stronger than she had anticipated. When she started this exercise, she hadn't lasted a full minute, and they were nearing four. Perhaps they were beginning to take her class seriously. Maybe she wouldn't fail them after all.

Scratch that, she'd fail them just because she could.

The seconds continued to tick down and Min watched as muscles ached, causing the books to shake. She had threatened the first person to drop the books would have to run laps around the gym. They were terrified of running laps. They were terrified of her. The scent of fear in the air made Min smile, she finally understood why teachers got into the profession--the rush of crushing children's dreams.

"I. Can't. Do. It." A young boy grit through his teeth. His legs were shaking and his arms were beginning to droop under the increasing weight of the books. As the texts came crashing down, Min had to fight the urge to point at the child and mock his inability to sack-up.

"You know the punishment," she barked.

The kid didn't argue. The large sword strapped to Min's back proved to be the most effective classroom management tool she had come across. She couldn't understand how some teachers were incapable of keeping their classes under control; all it took was a three and a half foot T'ai Chi blade.

Min clapped her hands twice, signaling for students to rest. As she continued to walk the line of students arranged shoulder to shoulder, she stopped at the sickly sweet scent emanating from one of the girls. She scrunched up her nose at the smell of youth and joy, and shook her head as she walked in front of the small army of gym students. "Today, we continue sparring."

"Uhm Mom," Jessica called out from the end of the line. "I mean Mrs. Kim," she corrected herself. "Would it be possible to spend some time practicing with the compound bows? I could use an archery refresher course."

Min couldn't argue with that. During her last survival preparedness drill at the house, her daughter had barely been able to hit the bullseye. She couldn't argue that it was essential for them to have silent fighting tactics, it would serve them well during the zombie invasion.

"I agree, Jessica," the woman said. She had a feeling her daughter was up to something, that parental intuition she had read about in the self-help books going into overdrive.

She couldn't place her finger on it, but there was something her daughter wasn't telling her. Maybe it was a boy? Min hoped it was a boy. Preferably one of the hot ones. Anything but the small geeky boy she had befriended; Hank was all the geek their family could handle. Once they defeated the wave of zombies, Jessica was going to be grounded until she spilled her secrets.

Min handed the key to the supply closet to her daughter. "Bring out the archery cart, I will set up the targets."

Min didn't miss the head nod between Jessica and David. The two of them were conspiring about something, but Min couldn't figure out what the two had in common. It wasn't like her daughter to befriend weak children with thick framed glasses. She hoped it was just a phase.

The gym was the length of two basketball courts side by side. A partition down the middle divided the huge room so several teachers could use the space at once. The bleachers were retracted into a giant wall of wooden benches on each side of the court. Min approached a small stand near the massive rock wall that stood at the end of the gym. She pressed a button, and panels in the floor opened. Ten archery targets raised out of the floor across the court. She held back a laugh as the boy running laps ran into one of the targets, falling to the ground in a mess of jellied muscles.

Jessica approached her mother, dragging behind her a giant cabinet on wheels. The girl opened the cabinet and looked back to her mom. "We have a slight problem."

"What?"

Jessica stood to the side, showing her the rack inside. There should have been a dozen bows hanging from hooks inside. Instead, there were only ten of them. On closer inspection, she realized all the razor tipped arrows were missing. All that was left were the training arrows. "We can't train with these." Min said. "They're for novices."

Jessica rolled her eyes. "They'll do for now mom. You can order more of your bull killer arrows later."

"True," Min said.

A few minutes later, each of the students was drawing back the fifty-pound strings of their bows. The familiar twang of flying arrows filled the gymnasium. Min was impressed nearly all of the first shots landed near the middle of their targets. She walked down the line, eyeing each student, admiring their stances.

"Nice posture. Keep legs apart."

"Lower your elbow."

"Don't pull on your release."

As she reached David, she thought her daughter must be crazy. "You too weak to pull back the string?"

He scowled at the teacher. "Some of us don't plan on fighting for our lives."

"What if you're stranded on an island? What then? How will you hunt?"

"I'll order take out."

She took the bow from the boy. He let go without a fight. Min wondered for a moment how much trouble she would be in if she loosed an arrow at the child, not to kill him, but to give him a bit more ambition to fight back. She pulled back the string until it touched her cheek. Without looking at the target, she let the arrow go.

With a thwoom, it was off. The arrow wasn't remotely close to the target. Instead the purple bolt flew near the bleachers, to where the young man was still doing laps. The arrow struck him through the shirt just under his armpit, yanking him against the bleachers. He looked down at the arrow thrusted through the fabric of his gym shirt, and fainted.

"The weak deserve no less." She thrust the bow back into his chest. "It's them or us, cracker. Do not become a liability."

"Who is this *them* you speak of?" he asked.

Min narrowed her eyes. She was beginning to think the little pasty white brat knew something. Perhaps he was in cahoots with his daughter. For a moment, she feared her daughter was bumping uglies with the small albino boy. Min shook her head. Her daughter knew better than to date a boy who couldn't beat her in a fight. It was a household rule.

"Hope you never meet them." Min said as she walked away. She sniffed the air again, very aware of the disgusting smell radiating from several of the girls. She would have to hose them off in the locker room, perhaps spray them down with a power washer. Their scent offended her. This could not be tolerated.

* * * * *

Xander handed his wife her leather briefcase. The two teachers hovered inside the doorway to her classroom. As she took it from him, she leaned in, giving him a kiss. She pulled back quickly, touching her lip, surprised by how his scruff tickled her lip.

"If we survive this," she said, "you're going to shave off that goatee."

He rubbed his hand along the stubble of his face. "You sure? It was starting to grow on me."

"Not a chance in hell."

"Speaking of," he said, switching the subject to more nefarious subjects. "Do you think we're doing the right thing?"

"I told you multiple times, there was no way we were going to get all those weapons in here. We'll have to wait till lunch to bring them into the auto shop."

"Not about that," he said, "but I still think you're wrong. I mean about not alerting the authorities? The kids? Hell, even their parents?"

"What could any of them do?"

The concern was written across his face. It showed in the way he furrowed his brow, or how he blinked slowly as he reflected on the decisions they were making. It was one of her favorite things about her husband. He was more than capable of making things explode, but deep down underneath the conspiracy theorist, he was a big softie.

"I don't think we give the kids enough credit," he turned to walk to his classroom. "There's a good chance they'd be better at this than us."

"They're kids, how good could they be?"

Period 2

David tried not to gag as he worked to solve for X. It seemed there was some new craze amongst the students and their desperate need to keep germs at bay. He watched as one of the girls in front of him applied copious amounts of moisturizer to her skin.

"It smells so good," whispered her neighbor.

David eyed the paper in front of him. It was difficult to concentrate on the math problem. He was working on quadratic functions, his personal favorite, but he was consumed with the idea of something bad happening. He reached into his backpack and pulled out his cell phone. Jessica was sitting in class with Mr. Winters; his class was on the far end of the school.

There were no texts. He examined his phone more closely and noticed there was no signal. The wifi was gone. The cell signal was nonexistent. He stopped to ponder if his parents had finally noticed the cell phone bill. He may have downloaded a few too many apps since he got his iPhone. He scrolled through the settings and saw there were no available networks.

The girl next to him was banging her phone on the desk. There were at least a dozen students staring blankly at their cells. Then David recalled Mr. Rightoff's announcement. Of all the days to eliminate cell phones, it had to be the day zombies were expected to strike.

His teacher walked by in the aisle between the desks. He hemmed and hawed over the work the students were doing. The teacher was a great mathematician, but the man had no idea how to teach. He wrote problems on the board and let the kids freak out as they raced to figure out the answers. David thought zombies might be the least of their worries, the American Education system was doing doing more damage than any flesh eater.

In the back row, one of the tiny Asian girls raised her hand. Isabella stretched her limb out, waving it about in an effort to be seen. "Mr. Moho, would it be possible to see the nurse?"

David's eyes lit up. It was happening. It was the first sign of the apocalypse. It only took one student getting sick before the outbreak occurred. He stopped for a moment, pondering if he would be able to kill the girl if it meant saving the world. It wasn't like he knew her, matter of fact she was kind of annoying and it was only his third day there. He nodded to himself, convinced that if it came time, he could strangle the girl for the better good.

"Go ahead, make sure you get a pass when you come back."

"Uhm," David stood up, "she doesn't look too good. Maybe I should escort her to the nurse."

Mr. Mentel stopped and eyed the most talented student. The teacher had been leery when he was told he was getting a new kid in his class, but so far, the kid had proven he was at the top of his game. The teacher just waved at the student. "Go ahead, don't cause trouble."

The Asian girl scoffed at David as she walked by. In the hallway he kept giving the girl sideways glances. "Are you sure you're okay? Not feeling ill? Don't want to eat people do you?"

"God, you're weird. Why the hell are you following me?"

Isabella didn't look at him when she talked. She was too busy rolling up the sleeves on her designer button-down shirt. David couldn't help by admire her pleated skirt. It didn't escape him that she was almost wearing the stereotypical Asian school girl uniform. "I wanted to make sure you were okay."

They passed by Mrs. Winters room. As they passed by the door, the woman looked up from her desk to meet David's eyes. He tried to convey the whole incident to the woman with a single glance. He wanted to let her know that it was beginning and the madness was going to break out. He was convinced all he conveyed was that he had crazy eyes and perhaps that he was constipated.

"I was just going to the bathroom."

"Why didn't you say that?"

She reached into the purse hanging from her arm. She pulled out a small white object and held it up. "Going to the nurse gives me more time to spark up."

"You're going to get high?"

She rolled her eyes and pushed into the women's bathroom. He stopped at the door, a forcefield being projected from the small black "woman" sign not he door prevented him from entering.

He contemplated pushing inside the door and stopping her, but he found himself unable to violate the sanctity of the bathroom. At his last school, all the bathrooms were gender neutral and they lived in an academic utopia. Here, he found himself vexed by a simple piece of plastic.

David sighed and continued walking down the hall. He turned the corner and headed towards the giant red and white plus sign. If he wasn't going to barge into the bathroom, he could at least go check in on the nurse. He had to assume her office would be where he'd find patient zero. If he was lucky, it would be as simple as locking the door and keeping the crazy contained inside.

* * * * *

Isabella took a deep drag off the joint, letting the smoke fill her lungs. She could feel the scratching at her throat, tempting her to cough. The girl held it as long as she could and let out a long sigh. Her eyes were already watering, the tears flowing down her cheeks as her muscles calmed.

She froze as she heard the door open and another student take the stall next to hers. She waited for the familiar sounds of the girl scuffling and sitting down on the toilet. Isabella silently cursed as the girl next to her stood still in the adjacent stall. She was going to save the rest of her joint for after school, but she didn't dare get caught with it on her. Tossing it into the toilet, she pushed the handle, flushing down her alternative medication.

Isabella walked to the sink to wash her hands. Looking in the mirror, she saw the girl's feet in the stall were facing the wrong way. She started to wonder if maybe one of the boys was drunk and stumbled into the bathroom. It wouldn't be the first time. After pep rallies, most of the boys in the school were drunk.

She started washing her hands, making sure to use plenty of soap, hoping to hide the smell of pot on her hands. There was a girl standing behind her in the reflection. She jumped and started swearing. "What the fuck is wrong with you?"

The girl didn't move.

"You're such a freak."

As she reached for the paper towel dispenser, the girl

lunged, grabbing her hand. She tried to pull away, but the girl was fast and grappled at her hand, making sure she couldn't get away. She was going to scream, but the girl pushed her down on the floor, knocking the wind from her lungs.

Isabella had always worried about being raped at this school, but never worried about being beaten up by some ugo in the bathroom. Just as she thought she might get away, the girl leaned in close and started biting at her arm. She barely managed a squeal as the girl broke skin and chewed away at her flesh.

* * * * *

David's eyes rolled back in his head as he took a whiff of the Nurse's office. He had expected it to smell sterile, perhaps like alcohol swabs. But no, it was just more of that nasty lotion the girls were wearing. He hoped Mr. Rightoff would ban it, or at least swear never to let the company who provided the samples back into the school.

The Nurse was a hefty woman sitting behind a desk in a white nurse's outfit that hugged her in all the wrong places. He nodded to her and she gave him a smile back. "How can I help you?"

"I was sent down by Mr. Moho to check on a student," he lied.

"Don't get too close, it seems there's an extra potent case of testitis going around today."

David couldn't help but smile. He had assumed the office would be filled with sick kids, but he didn't expect her to be very aware of why they were secretly coming to her office. He walked by several hospital beds where students were lying down with ice packs on their heads. It didn't seem any stranger than usual.

He was hoping one of them would be frothing at the mouth. David was starting to get excited about the possibility of having to slay one of the undead. He thought if he could add that to his college resume, he'd be a shoe in for any university of his picking.

As he passed a table filled with supplies, he noted the copious amounts of gauze and bandages. He waited until the nurse had her back turned and stuffed his pockets with several rolls of each, thinking if it was going to happen, he best be prepared for more than just weapons. He made a final grab for a bottle of Tylenol and shoved it in his pants, trying to hide the obvious bulges in his jeans.

"It doesn't look like she's here now," he lied, "I'm just going to head back to class."

"Careful, you don't want to turn into one of these germ ridden zombies." He froze at the choice of words. Was the Nurse in on it? Could she be the medic for this group of adult commandos? He let out a slight chuckle. He couldn't imagine the school nurse being part of their cohorts. What good could possibly come from having a school nurse on the team?

* * * * *

Rob ducked inside the long snaking corridor leading to the darkroom. The teacher was beginning another lecture about the use of light to create depth in photography. The woman used the phrase so many times he was starting to think she was crazy. Usually he was amused when she lost it, she would grab at her curls and begin to pull. Today, however, he just wanted to be alone.

The winding hallway prevented light from reaching the

darkroom. At the final stage of the journey, he pushed open a large wooden door, entering the space. The room had a faint red glow, dark enough to make it difficult to see, but just enough light it wasn't pitch black. His eyes took several moments to adjust to the dimness.

Once the door shut behind him, the room turned eerily quiet. The sound of the teacher's gabbing vanished, all was left was the hum of the ventilation system. The room was fairly large. Around the perimeter, photo enlargers were placed in little cubicles, and in the middle was a giant sink with water slowly feeding into several trays filled with photographs. It was the one time he got to be alone during the school day. The general quiet in the darkroom was inviting. Covered in only black clothing, he seemed to vanish from the world.

He laid out light sensitive paper and placed his negatives on the machine. Clicking a shutter release, the light poured out, bombarding the white paper. For a moment, he was blind, then the light vanished. He repeated it over the course of several sheets of paper.

Just as he was about to drop the negatives into the liquid that would forever freeze the picture into the fibers of the paper, a light turned on. The darkroom was flooded with bright white light. He dropped his papers and swore out loud, threatening to annihilate whoever turned on the light and ruined his photographs.

The door started to open and froze at his swearing. Whoever was about to enter knew they had done something wrong. They backed away from the door slowly until it latched shut. He watched as the feet moved away from the door. When they were gone, he let out a sigh and got down on his hands and knees, looking for the paper that had fallen underneath one of the cubicle stations.

"I'm going to kill them," he muttered under his breath.

Rob reached underneath the station and felt around for the paper he had dropped. He paused as he felt a wire binding. He pulled out the notebook and blew off the years of dust collected on top. It wasn't a standard student notebook, but a notebook teachers used to record grades.

"Random."

He opened the first page to see a teacher's name he had never heard of before. He flipped through the book and found scribbles along lined sheets of paper in the back of the planner. He started to read her rantings until he came across one that made him freeze. The woman was writing to God, asking for an escape, talking about things outside the door, threatening to break in.

"Zombies."

He paused as she talked about their assault to get into the room and devour her alive. He threw the book across the room, pages fluttering as it landed on the ground. His breathing quickened. "They weren't lying."

He tried to rationalize it. They were somehow messing with him. He opened the door, and got down on his hands and knees. The light from the small hallway illuminated the scratches along the bottom of the door. He could see them clearly, sets of five along the base. The world was beginning to get dark. He was feared he might faint. He froze at the stillness in the room. The teacher had stopped talking. Nobody in the main classroom was speaking.

Rob looked up, and in the open doorway was the familiar face of the teacher. As she stepped closer, he could see her white blouse was soaked a dark red. Where her lips should have shined a bright fuchsia, there were no lips. He screamed loudly, slamming the door shut just as she reached down for him.

He spun the lock and scooted back from the door, his breathing labored. He pressed his back against the far wall and felt the teacher's notebook under his hand. He was doomed, just like the teacher who had written in the notebook. Death, it was coming for him. He would either be eaten alive, or die of starvation.

Just as he was ready to admit defeat he leaned his head back. In the dim red light, he focused on the sound of the air vents. *The air vents,* he thought. He wanted to laugh. He wanted to curse out his schoolmates and call the teacher who died in the darkroom an idiot.

As he stood up, grabbing onto the sink, and stepped up toward the vent. The grate opened easily and fell to the ground in a loud bang. He almost laughed at the freakishly loud noise. "I'll just escape through the vents. Can't believe nobody thought of this before. Bunch of idiots."

* * * * *

"We are not merely the keeper of photographs," a kid announced to the class, "we are the archivist of memories. We are the creators of design, the recordist of dreams, we are the spirit of Boxford High School."

The kid paused for a moment, waiting for the applause to begin. A single female in the front hair clapped loud enough it sounded if the entire class joined in. She dragged her chair closer to the speaker, notepad in hand, documenting his every word.

Kevin leaned back in the metal computer chair, the back of his head banging against the wall. It had been nearly a week since the yearbook editor had given a speech. If history was any indication, it was three days overdue. Each time a deadline approached, he would whip out the thesaurus and give another speech filled with rhetoric, and when the yearbook staff would begin to fall asleep, he'd preach louder. Eventually his speech would turn to cackling--laughing at his own joke or devising an evil plot, nobody was sure of which.

His right hand henchman sat in the front row, spurring him onward. Kevin picked up his phone and noticed class had only been going on for four minutes. It was going to be a long day. He eyed the flagpole in the corner of the class, the American flag hanging from a spear like pole, and jotted a note down on his map. As he glanced at his phone again, he realized there was no signal.

"Shit," he mumbled to himself.

"Please Jose Verequez," the girl in the front of the class called out, "what can we do to make the yearbook gods happy?"

They were *serious*. Kevin had been placed in this class against his will. He needed another credit to graduate, and for some reason they thought it would be good for him to be placed in geek central. He was pretty sure he was the only person in class without braces. Probably the only one who had ever been on a date.

The teacher shopping for boots on Amazon wasn't lost on him. When Jose began his tyrannical rule, he made it known that he was a force to be reckoned with. By himself, he would just be a power hungry dweeb, but it was his crony Alexis that made it so much worse. Kevin had no doubt that they would go home tonight, synchronize their dvd players, and belt out show tune lyrics together.

"Perhaps zombies aren't the worst thing that can

happen," he said to himself.

The rest of his classmates, while nobody in his social circle, were somewhat normal. They worked on the pages that would go in the yearbook, taking photographs and interviewing the outgoing seniors. They could be mistaken for human. Even despite their non-stop work, Jose would sleep in the classroom, threatening to delete people's work if it wasn't up to his standards.

The editor smiled, the light shining off his braces. Kevin hadn't noticed before, but the kid was wearing a letterman jacket. The sacred varsity "B" was pinned on his left breast, a symbol highlighting a talent in sports, not journalism. He wondered if being a geek was now recognized as a professional sport?

Jose turned around, standing on a chair, motioning to the row of past editor photos hanging on the wall. "Someday, we will look back, and I, I mean we, we will be immortalized."

On the back of the editor's jacket, a giant YB was sewn into the fabric. It shouldn't surprise him. The kid probably went home and broke out his sewing kit and attached it himself. Either that or he threatened to break out into a lecture about the significance of yearbook to the embroiderer.

Kevin watched as the teacher's head hit the desk, thoroughly disenchanted by her student. Last week, the woman had mentioned she needed to step out to take a phone call and Jose had nearly lost it. His "We are yearbook," speech begun as it did normally. Usually it ended with him holding his hands up, listening to the chanting in his own head. This time however, he pointed at the teacher and called her a fake and one of the "unworthy." Her eyes rolled back in her head loud enough to be heard as she took her phone call, speaking to the other party through Jose's speech.

Before the end of class, Kevin heard Alexis, minion of Jose, ask the teacher, "Are you really dedicated to the cause?"

Kevin started to count the days until graduation. He could stomach the class, he could survive, he just wasn't sure if Jose would. Kevin contemplated the sedatives stashed in his right inside pocket; he had enough to put the kid in a coma. He considered sprinkling some into the kid's seltzer water. "It'd be worth losing out on the money."

Alexis screamed. Her voice echoed off the brick walls of the classroom raising the head of every student. She managed to drown out Jose, who was holding his hands out, trying his best to appear like Jesus on the cross. Jose turned just in time to see a growling teacher lunge at him.

"Holy shit!" screamed another student.

Kevin stood, jaw slack. It was happening. He should have known the apocalypse would start in yearbook.

The teacher grabbed one of the sports writers and bit down on his neck, the screams growing louder. Instead of running for the doors, the students pushed their backs against the wall, frozen at the gruesome sight unfolding in front of them. The student fell to the ground, gasping for air as the teacher lunged for one of the freshmen.

Kevin hadn't been ready. He knew it was going to happen, but the muscles in his arms froze. He forced himself to move, to grab the map, to inch toward the door to safety.

"Jose," Alexis yelled, "run!"

"We're journalists, we must document!"

A door on each side of the room would get them out of

the room and into the hallway. Kevin only had to make it to one of them. He could hold it shut, contain the zombie teacher. He gasped as the first victim started to jerk, flipping over onto his stomach. This was how the zombies won, they could reproduce faster than the living.

"Shit," he mumbled out loud.

"Don't forget to use your flash!" Jose said, grabbing a yearbook off a shelf. He hurled it with the precision of a true yearbook geek. The book caught the teacher in the back of the head. Just as she turned, Alexis snapped a photo of the blood-soaked instructor.

Jose started to cry out as the teacher descended upon him, her jaws snapping, trying to feast on his face. Jose grabbed another yearbook off a shelf and swung it hard, smacking the woman in the face. The undead teacher growled, perhaps still annoyed with his earlier speech. She clutched one of his arms, teeth sinking into his wrist.

Jose flashed a smile, just in time for Alexis to snap another photo. The woman was on him, chewing away at his arm. Jose cried out as she devoured his arm, working closer to his neck. He reached out with a bloody fist, "Have my senior quote read, 'Death in the name of yearbook: achievement unlocked.'"

Kevin's hand touched the handle to the door leading to the hallway. His fingers were mere inches from granting him freedom when the teacher's face turned upward, facing him. Kevin grabbed the flag pole and lunged forward, the metal tip of the pole sinking into he woman's rib cage.

The woman pushed forward, using her body weight to squish her way down the wooden pole. Kevin backed up until his feet reached the wall. She was only mere feet away from her bloody hands touching his face. He closed his eyes and turned his head, accepting his inevitable fate.

"Not on my watch!" Alexis jumped off a desk, camera strap wrapped around her hand. She let out a war cry, screaming at the top of her lungs. She let the camera slip out of her hand and swung it by the strap, bring the metal body in an arc over her head. As her feet touched down, the heavy camera smashed into the teacher's skull, embedding itself into the woman's cranium.

Kevin peeked enough to see the teacher fall to the ground. The girl had taken blood and smudged it on her cheeks in war paint. For a moment he was more scared of the underclassman than he was of the several zombies climbing to their feet. Where they had started as one, now a half dozen filled the room, moving toward the few remaining living.

"Run!" she screamed.

Kevin grabbed onto the door handle and swung it open. As he turned to wave her out, he noticed the bite mark just below the wrist of her leather jacket. His savior was about to become one of them. Kevin shut the door as she took another swing with the camera, clubbing the sports writer across the head.

He watched through the glass. Her feet slipped out from under her as she prepared to swing again. She landed on her backside. Jose's corpse was crawling, reaching out for her. His teeth bit into her leg, ending her high school career.

"I did it for yearbook!"

Kevin sighed. Maybe the zombie apocalypse wasn't such a bad thing. "Really, is anybody going to miss them?" So maybe they wouldn't have a yearbook, but how many of those portraits would be labeled with the words, "Presumed dead." At least for the moment, the apocalypse was contained in the yearbook classroom.

"Shit."

Through the classroom, a student early to their next class walked through the door on the opposite side of the room. Poor Maria started bellowing at the sight of so much blood plastering the floor and walls of the classroom.

"We're so screwed," Kevin said.

Ring. Ring. Ring.

Period 3

Kevin pushed students out of the way as he ran down the hall. He tried yelling, tried telling them there were people with guns. The majority of the students shuffling in the hallways listened to music on their phones, ignoring the outside world. The few students who did hear him, paid him no attention. It was exactly what he expected. The apathy of his generation would be their undoing.

For a moment his heart leapt. Tina emerged from the stairwell leading downstairs toward one of the quads. She made eye contact with him, her face registering the panic he radiated. "What the hell is wrong with you?"

He turned around and saw there was nobody following him. At the far end of the building, he had just stabbed a teacher through the chest with the American flag. Here, people were shuffling to algebra like it was nobody's business.

"I just saw Jose get eaten alive."

She rolled her eyes. "Did you take some pills?"

"Tina," he said, "I'm not making it up. There's something going on. There are zombies. The dead are coming back to life."

"You mean like on that TV show?"

"Tina, this is not a show!"

Her eyes rolled backward again, conveying her annoyance. They were friendly, but really, Tina didn't like dealing with him. His reputation as being a pill pusher was a real harsher on her popularity. She couldn't have the other cheerleaders thinking she got her pep from a pill, they'd dethrone her faster than the time Melissa got fat.

"Follow me," Kevin dragged her by the arm. She scoffed at him as she plodded along, following him through the double doors into the library.

"Okay, long story short. There are a group of teachers here who fight zombies. They've known the apocalypse was going to happen. Jessica--"

"Ugh," she said, "I should have known it was because of her."

"Will you just shut up, Tina?"

Her jaw dropped. She hadn't been talked to like that in roughly twenty-four hours. The last person who did caused the bruised lip she still sported, the same person Kevin was apparently in love with. Now she had to deal with her co-anchor spouting on about his obsession with the jungle princess.

She shook him off, taking a step back. "Okay, first, don't touch me. Second, you're crazier than usual. What is wrong with you, freak?"

"I just watched the yearbook editor get eaten alive by the teacher."

"Are you sure she wasn't making out with him? I've heard rumors. I mean, ew and everything, but if they're in love, it's beautiful."

The kids cleared out from the hallway, moving into their classrooms. Kevin pushed by Tina. He pressed his face to the glass, waiting to see if there were any more students in the hallway. A freshmen with a backpack on wheels headed toward the library, ignorant to the world around him. The underclassmen was about to reach for the door when he was hurled against the glass. Blood splattered across the glass as the freshmen grunted, sputtering blood up as a young girl attacked him.

"Oh sweet mother of God!" Tina screamed.

"Believe me now?"

"Stop it!"

"Sure, let me ask him if she'll stop eating him."

Five more shuffling students started feasting on their classmate. Tina continued to back away from the door, pointing, trying to scream, but the sound caught in her throat.

"They want in," Kevin said as the zombies started clawing at the handle to the door.

"Kill them!" Tina said.

"Will you be useful? Or does barking stupid orders come naturally to a cheerleader?"

She was about to karate chop him across the back of his neck, but she was pushed aside by a woman in a flowing skirt. Kevin jumped to the side, rolling along the floor as the woman held up a gun in each hand.

As the doors busted open, the world slowed. Kevin pushed backward, trying to stay out of reach of the incoming zombies. He heard the first pop, then a second, and it continued. For every shot fired, a zombie hit the floor, a single bloody dot in the center of the forehead.

"No dead in my library!" bellowed the librarian.

The head of each zombie exploded, sending red-soaked brain matter across the glass doors. The librarian had her feet shoulder width apart, a gun in each extended hand. For every bullet she fired, a zombie hit the ground. Before he could yell, before he could react, she was tucking her firearms into shoulder holsters. Her skirt flowed; its pattern reminding him of something from the sixties, possibly a former hippy. However her firearm expertise was anything but peaceful.

Mrs. V launched herself at a bookcase just to the side of the door. Bracing herself against the six-foot-tall wooden structure, she pushed, grunting as the furniture gave way. It fell, mostly blocking the door. Her hands were speedy as she pulled at curtains in the rest of the windows looking into the space. Within moments, there was no way to see inside the library. She was trapped with the two teen survivors.

"You've practiced this before," Tina said while she wiped blood off her face.

"Once or twice."

"And you just happen to keep guns on you?"

"Have you seen what fourth period study is like in here? Every day I'm tempted to pistol whip the bastards."

Kevin was frightened of the dead students on the ground. He knew it was happening, he knew they were going to strike, but he hadn't been prepared for this. He wondered if he'd be capable of killing one of them before they ate him alive.

"We need to alert the school," Kevin said.

Mrs. V whipped out her cell phone and let out a sigh. She held up the small rectangle, waving it around in the air. "Damn thing never gets a signal when I need it." Mrs. V tossed the phone onto the floor and pulled out a phone with a large antenna. She flipped it open and punched in her security code. The satellite phone showed no signal as well.

"Mr. Rightoff," Kevin said. "He made it so cell phones don't work."

"That moron is going to get us killed," complained Mrs. V.

"What is going on? What was wrong with them? Why do you have guns? How did you both know?" Tina began to sob. "Does someone have a wet nap?"

The librarian inspected her kills, making sure none of the bodies were moving. She ignored the overreacting girl; it was almost as if the cheerleader had never seen the living dead before. Mrs. V. held up her hands. With two fast claps, the lights in the library turned off, leaving the room is almost absolute darkness.

"To my office," she said.

"Are you seriously ignoring the fact she just killed a bunch of students? She killed Emilee. I mean, her back handspring needed work, but that's no reason to kill her."

"Does she always talk this much?" the librarian asked.

"You have no idea," Kevin replied.

Kevin took Tina's hand and dragged her through the library and into the woman's office. The librarian was rummaging through her mini-fridge when she pulled out another gun and several boxes of ammo. She pulled out her weapons and started feeding ammo into the magazines. She put them back into their holsters and placed the newest weapon in her waistband. She paused as the two students stared at her.

"Ever shoot one?"

"No," Kevin said.

She drew back the slide and chambered a round. "You have fourteen bullets. See red and they're dead," she said flipping off the safety. "Got it?"

Kevin took the weapon from her, unsure if he was capable of pulling the trigger. He pushed the button, turning on the safety, and slid it into his waist band like he had seen in numerous gangster movies. It didn't matter that he wasn't sure he could use it, let alone shoot a peer between the eyes, having the weapon made him feel safer.

"How did this start?"

Kevin shrugged. He didn't know what answer she wanted. Did she want when they found out about the zombie apocalypse? Or did she want when his classmates decided to wake up from the dead?

"Yearbook. The teacher ate somebody. It spread until everybody was dead."

"Not dead," she said, "just hadn't risen yet. They're undead now."

"Zombies."

She eyed the boy. "What do you know about zombies?"

"Whoa. Whoa! Can we take a moment here?" Tina got between the two. She put her hands on Kevin, pushing him back across the room. "I can understand her shooting some students. I can understand you being a bit crazy. But zombies? You mean they're going to start *eating brains*?"

"Zombies eat more than brains."

Tina glared at the librarian. "Your expertise on the matter is appreciated."

Kevin ignored the hysterical girl. "We knew it was coming. We knew you were in on it."

"David," Mrs. V cursed under breath.

Kevin nodded. "Me, David, and Jessica are in on it. We were preparing to stop the apocalypse."

"Where are they now?"

He shook his head. "Hopefully some place safer than this."

* * * * *

"What did you say you were making?" Victor asked.

Jessica smiled at the man, saw dust collecting on her goggles. "Oh, we're making stakes for," she paused, trying to think up a reason to be making a dozen pointed sticks.

"Our vampire cos play," David interjected. "We like it to be authentic. I'm the heroic vampire hunter."

Victor didn't believe a word out of their mouths. Min's daughter wasn't stupid, she was frighteningly swift. It was worse that she was developing her adopted mother's temper, a lethal combination. There was no chance that the daughter of Min Kim would be caught dead helping a cos player. David on the other hand, Victor could easily believe he was the president and dungeon master of the local Dungeons and Dragon's club.

"How about you tell me what you're really doing?"

Before she could dig in her heels and perpetuate David's ridiculous lie, screams erupted from the hallway. David and Jessica jumped back as Victor lifted the back of his shirt and pulled out a gun. They stayed close to the man, out of the way of his gun, but close enough if he needed to save them.

"What was that?" David asked.

"Nothing," Victor said, inspecting the area just beyond the shop doors. He was about to put the safety in the on position, but spotted streaks of blood on the ground.

"Liar," Jessica said, her voice mustering every bit of her mom's sass possible.

"Zombies. They're here. They're going to kill us all," Victor said.

"Knew it," she said.

Victor paused. He had suspected Jessica knew more than she was letting on. "I'll explain it all later. For now, we're on the offense. You see something that looks like a zombie, kill it."

"What if it's just another student?" asked David.

"I suppose we should save them."

"Suppose?" David repeated.

"Can't tell me you haven't thought about it."

Jessica nodded. "Well yeah, but that's a whole different problem. We knew it was happening."

"How?" asked Victor.

Jessica looked at David. The kid pushed his thick black framed glasses up the bridge of his nose and shrugged his shoulders. The pieces were starting to connect. "You're her informant."

"Yeah," David admitted, "kind of guilty."

"I'll want answers once we're safe."

David spun about in the wood shop, the room void of any undead. "We could stay here? The doors are thick. There are no zombies, and we're alive. It sounds like a great plan. Don't you agree? I think so."

"No cell phones," Victor said. "We need to get to the main office so we can make an announcement. The faster we get there, the faster we alert the others. The faster they find out, the faster we bring in enough weapons to squash this outbreak."

"This?" Jessica asked. "You mean like the current apocalypse, or do you mean like *this* apocalypse?"

"It's not my first time to this rodeo."

"Oh, so you're like a zombie expert?"

"It's on my resume."

David watched the two of them banter. "Is witty repartee part of the job description? Or do we start running?"

Victor ignored the young geek, instead making note Jessica was far too much like her mother. "Our first directive is to secure the school. This cannot get out."

"Get me to the main office," David said.

Victor and Jessica eyed the smallest person in the room. David pushed his glasses back up his nose. "I can lock down the school."

Victor reached down into his boot, pulled out a six inch knife, and handed it to Jessica. "We're going to see just how much you're like your mom."

"Jesus," she said.

"What about me?" David asked.

Victor jumped into the hallway, turning one direction then the other. Once it was clear, he motioned with his head for them to follow. "Unless you can make a headshot at fifty feet, we've got this."

"Dammit," David said, trying to stay just behind Victor, out of his way, but close enough he could scream for help. "I am so dead."

* * * * *

Lauren swore under her breath as she tried to balance the tray filled with coffees in one hand while locking the car door with the other. She swung her hips, smacking into the door and knocking it shut. The former barista picked up the other tray off her roof--eight drinks in total--and headed toward the school.

"If it's the apocalypse, I want coffee." She eyed the eight venti cups with extra espresso shots. She was almost a bit guilty. "Maybe I should have asked if they wanted anything.

"If I ration it, I'll survive. I need one coffee per period. I can do that. I can make it. I did a double shot before they made me leave. I can't believe they won't give me my discount anymore. I went from store manager to *plebeian*. I feel so normal. My life is over."

Once this was over, perhaps she would heed the advice

of her district manager and consider joining rehab. It couldn't be so bad, could it? Perhaps she could take up smoking and drink less. Maybe there was a drug she could take. Lauren wondered what sleep would be like; she heard it was delightful.

She reached the dozen doors entering into the school. She pressed the handicap button with her knee. One of the doors eased open slowly. Lauren scooted inside the door and stole a sip of coffee from one of the cups.

The school was quiet, almost too quiet. She expected there to be a dozen students in the lobby, either coming in late or leaving early. She turned to where the secretaries normally sat. Instead of the two older women with giant curly hair, an empty window greeted her. Lauren set down her drinks on the counter and checked the sign out log for the school. Nobody.

"That's weird."

She picked up one of the cups, ready to bask in the delicious dark nectar, when a scream sounded over the PA system. "Zombies!!!"

She jolted, gripping the cup tightly, sending its contents onto the floor. Before she could cry over the loss, gates slammed down around the doors. She watched as one-by-one the windows were covered in metal, blocking anybody from coming in or going out.

"Okay," she said, "this seems more normal."

She took another cup and drank deeply, consuming the whole thing in one gulp. "Where to run and hide first?"

Ring. Ring. Ring.

Period 4

"What do you mean the building is locked down?"

David pointed at the metal bars on the windows of the computer lab. "I hacked into the school's security system. Why we have retractable bullet proof plating on the windows, I'll never understand. But they're there."

Victor banged his head against the wall. "Dear God," he turned back to the kid. "You've trapped us in here with them?"

Jessica shook her head. "Better they're trapped in here than roaming outside."

Victor shook his head. "That's not the point. Our weapons are out there!"

"Can you open it?" Jessica asked.

David shook his head. "The encryption is too complex. Why does this have military grade encryption? I didn't see how complex the security is in lock down. Maybe if I had my laptop, I could open it up."

"Where's that?" she asked.

"At home."

Victor tried not to growl too loudly. He pointed through the metal slats covering the window. In the parking lot, triple parked, was a small U-haul. Inside was enough fire power to take down the government of a third world nation. The truck was close enough he could make out the license plate, but beyond the security gates, it was light-years away.

"So what now?" asked Jessica.

"We kill our way out."

* * * * *

Angelica had her back pressed against the concrete wall just outside the daycare. She slowly peered over her shoulder into the glass door overlooking a large play area. There were telltale signs of children; the blocks, the toys, and even the tray filled with small sippy cups. Everything was there, except for the actual children.

She slowly opened the door and slid inside and clicked off the safety on her gun. Sounds eminated from the back of the play area through a swinging door.

"Do you hear that?" she whispered.

"Is that kids laughing?"

"Yeah," she said, "this place smells like an evil genius' lair."

"Of course it does," Hank said over the intercom. "The sound of children laughing always makes me think of evil."

"I knew you'd understand."

She looked down at the juice cups and could see a spill on the tray. She reached out to touch it and realized that it had long since been dried. She scanned the room for any other signs of life. There was a layer of dust on the counters. "Nastiest daycare ever," she mumbled.

"Your glasses aren't picking up any heat," Hank noted. "This place is either entirely empty, or there's nothing in there with body heat."

Angelica moved along the wall until she reached the swinging door. She knelt down and carefully pushed it open. She expected to see a kitchen or perhaps an office, but there was only a small landing with stairs that lead into the basement.

"What's her rule?" asked Hank.

Angelica rolled her eyes. "It's fine."

"No it's not," he said. "You never follow a sound down stairs."

"Who's the veteran?"

"Cadence is. She knows more about these zombies than any of us ever will. Angie, do not go down those stairs."

Angelica took her first step down the rickety stairs. "She's a writer. She reads stupid zombie novels. We've been in the field hunting these things for years. I think I know what I'm doing."

"If you keep setting yourself up like that, something dumb is going to happen, and you'll be sorry."

"Don't worry about me."

She eased herself one step at a time, taking stock of the stairwell and looking for any movement. Angelica finished climbing down the stairs and pressed her back to the wall, looking under the stairs for any wayward hands.

She looked around the basement. It was a solitary room with only one door leading out. The basement looked relatively normal, shelves with food on them and unopened boxes filled with supplies.

"Are you dead yet?"

"Shut up," she whispered.

She touched the side of her sunglasses and the lenses turned a lighter color. She knew Hank was seeing what she was seeing now. He'd be analyzing every bit of data they picked up. "There's nothing here."

"Pan the room again," he said, zooming in on the various boxes and items lying on a fold out table.

"Go over to the table."

She walked backward toward the table, keeping the solitary door in her line of sight. "Everything looks five by five," she shrugged.

"Is that a chemistry set?"

Angelica looked down to the box. "My First Chemistry set," she read aloud. "Yeah, it looks absolutely sinister."

She looked at the box a bit closer; there was a spattering of blood on the side. When she flipped it over, she could see a small hand print. "Okay," she admitted, "it just got sinister."

"Is that a child's hand print?"

"Only thing worse than zombies are zombie babies."

He snickered. "I have the urge to tell dead baby jokes now."

"Juvenile."

The lights dimmed and flickered. "I'm reading a spike in the power grid. Whatever is going on in there is taking up a lot of juice."

Angelica began averting her eyes from the door, examining the floor as she walked. She could live with zombies, she had no problem blowing away people. There was something oddly disturbing about the idea of a flesh eating baby corpse chasing her down.

"God I hate kids," she mumbled. "Dead or alive."

She reached the door and realized that it wasn't a typical door one would be seen in a commercial building. She ran her hand along the surface. Without feeling the weight, she knew it was closer in size to a door found in a bank vault. There was something definitely off about this place. She checked around the frame looking for any traps and began to pull at the door.

It was only a crack, but she could see that it lead into a much larger room. Angie wedged her fingers into the gap and waited. She leaned back, using her weight to pull at the door, causing it to creek open. The thunderous noise of electricity inside the room grew louder. As it reached a crescendo, the door swung open.

"Holy shit," Hank said over her headset.

The room was at least three stories tall and filled with all manner of electrical equipment. "What the hell is this?" she mumbled.

Hank could see on the monitor that Angelica was on a metal platform circling the room. In several places, metal stairs led down to the next level. In the middle of the room was a giant metal contraption, the thing hogging all the electricity.

"Can...this...sure..."

"I can't hear you anymore. There's interference. I'm going to try and boost the signal from my end."

She was on her own. She knew the familiar silence. There was the typical quiet on a phone, but when the line went dead, even the white noise faded. She was alone.

Angie tried to look over the railing but she could only make out shadows on the ground below. She scurried alongside the wall as she made her way to the stairs. She could see she wasn't actually alone. They had blended into the shadows of the room, but the light of the device was beginning to show just how many soldiers were housed in the massive space.

"Fucking daycare," she said.

She looked around the room and realized she was trapped. The only way out was the way she entered. The only obvious answer for her was to cause as much damage as possible and pray she didn't get shot in the process.

She felt along her waist for her spare ammo magazines and down to her hips for her two spare weapons. She took a deep breath. "This is what you do best, Angie," she told herself.

She began charging down the stairs in fast sprint. Before she could reach the top of the stairs, she heard gunfire beginning all around her. It was too dark in places to see all of the enemies. Angie slapped the side of her glasses and the lenses coated themselves green; she could see the soldiers lining the walls. The night vision worked great, except for the occasional flash of blinding light coming from the device in the middle of the room.

Angelica raised her gun and took a shot. The bullet pierced the forehead of a soldier. She tucked and rolled along the scaffolding. As she sprung to her feet she held her gun out, and took a shot. Another head shot.

She continued running around the scaffolding, trying to take shots before she reached each of the soldiers on her level. In her zeal, she missed one tucked away in a small alcove. She could feel him clothesline her before she saw him on her glasses. She felt the wind leave her body. Try as she might, she couldn't inhale.

The scaffolding smacked against her back as she landed. Before she could force herself to inhale, the cold dark spot of his boot flashed toward her face. Angie dropped the gun and reached out with both hands, grabbing the soldier's foot and twisting hard until she felt the pop of his hip.

She raised her foot up and slammed her heel into his groin, knocking him backward into the alcove. More of them began swarming in her direction. Grabbing the gun, she fired three shots and watched as all three men fell were they stood.

"Damn," she coughed, "I'm good."

She stood up and dropped the magazine out of her gun. She inserted another, and assessed her situation. Cracking her neck, she started counting out the enemy. Her mind was beginning to lose its rational self and go into attack mode.

Without thinking, Angelica ran, and at the last possible moment she leapt off the platform, swinging over the banister. She grabbed onto the pole, slingshotting herself onto the platform below. Her feet slammed hard into one of the men, knocking him backward. She fire twice into his chest as she took him to the ground. Kneeling over his body, she fired at the feet of a soldiers above her.

Her vision was beginning to tunnel; she was going to that happy place where she transformed into the perfect soldier. She stood and fired once to each side of her, taking down oncoming soldiers. Stepping back up onto the banister, she pushed off, flying backward away from the scaffolding.

As if it was in slow motion, she threw her gun away. Reached to her thighs, Angelica pulled out two more hand guns and began shooting towards the scaffolding she had lunged from. With each shot, a body fell to the ground. At the last minute, she pivoted her body in the air and tucked into a roll, skidding to a stop.

"92% hit rate," she muttered. "I'm slipping."

"Yes," came a voice, "yes you are."

Angelica's eyes widened upon hearing the smooth silky voice. She stood up slowly and paused for a moment, letting the situation sink in. Guns at the ready, she spun around and fired each weapon. She watched as the bullets whizzed into the voice's owner.

"Not getting any smarter either," said the woman's voice.

"You're dead."

"How astute," said the woman.

"We watched you die," Angelica said firmly.

"Wouldn't be the first time," the woman said, taking small steps forward.

Angelica tapped the side of her glasses and the night vision vanished, letting the electricity snapping from the large device illuminate the room. She could only compare it to a mad scientist's laboratory. The moment the glasses reverted, she could see the woman staring at her.

"Sonya," Angie hissed.

"Angelica," Sonya said calmly. "I didn't want to miss an opportunity to school you again."

"If I remember correctly," Angelica spat back, "I've schooled you each time."

"Well consider this payback," Sonya said.

The woman stampeded toward Angelica. Out of habit, Angie pulled the triggers, knowing they would be empty. She threw one gun to the side, and used the butt of the other to slam Sonya's oncoming fist.

Angie couldn't block the oncoming blow to her face. The taste copper filled her mouth as her lip exploded in a bloody mess. Angelica spat out the blood. She was pissed, but she never started a fight she couldn't finish. Sonya coming back from the dead, was ruining her track record. There was a smug sense of satisfaction knowing, she would get another chance to finish the job. Maybe she'd get lucky and the woman would beg for mercy, Angelica would take delight in that.

"Holy shit," came a voice in her ear, "Is that Sonya?"

"Yes it is," she answered. She stepped up to the undead woman, and with both of hands forming a fist, she slugged Sonya across the face. Blood oozed from the woman's lip, a cut nearly identical to her own. Angelica let out a sigh as she saw the blood absorb into the woman's skin, the cut knitting itself back together.

"Why won't you die?" Angelica asked. "You're going to make me work at it, aren't you?"

"Seems more likely you'll die first."

"Fat chance," Angie said, reaching down to the pockets on either leg. Looking up through her disheveled bangs, she sneered at the zombie. "Just means I'm going to work a little harder to watch you--"

"Can we stop with the dialogue already? You hate me, I hate you. We're going to talk a big game and then fight to the death. Let's get on with it."

"She has a point," Hank said in her earpiece.

Angelica pulled two small sticks out of her pockets. With a flick of her wrist, they extended into three-foot long batons. Sonya's smile grew once she saw the choice of weapon. Angie wasn't sure if pain even mattered to the former model's undead corpse, but she was going to find out how much the bitch could take. There was nothing like working up a sweat while beating the crap out of somebody. With a swipe across Sonya's face, the fight started.

Angie dropped to her knees and slammed the baton behind Sonya's knee. As the bitch fell, Angie stood, her fist slamming the underside of the toppling woman.

She watched as Sonya flew backward onto the ground. Walking over to the woman, she saw Sonya was still smiling. The undead chick was beginning to laugh softly at the Angelica. "You just don't get it."

Sonya rolled backward onto her feet. The undead model turned evil villain charged Angelica. Ignoring the woman's batons, Sonya wrapped her arms around the Angelica's torso and brought her to the ground. As they landed, Sonya clapped Angelica's ears, making a loud ringing sound in her ear.

Angelica's eyes rolled back in her head as she bit back a scream. She tried to focus on the broken baton. She stretched to grab the stick while Sonya continued laughing. Angelica shoved the baton through the woman's jaw and out the back of her brain.

"Tickle?" Angelica asked, despite not being able to hear her own voice.

Sonya finally screamed. Angelica had suspected that she was just another type of zombie, a unique zombie they hadn't encountered before. It only made sense that like all the others, a head shot would inflict the most pain.

She pulled the baton out and went to slam it again but Sonya's hand stopped her. Angelica looked in horror as the hole she had made was already mending itself. Sonya's screams were beginning to turn into maniacal laughter.

"I am going to enjoy this," the zombie growled.

Before the Sonya could pull the baton from her mouth, her head snapped to the side. The zombie queen paused for a moment, and then jerked several more times.

"You're welcome," came Hank's voice.

She looked up to the scaffolding to see Hank standing there with an assault rifle. She was thankful for the support, but pissed that she wouldn't be able to kill...

"Guess again," came Sonya's voice.

Angelica was starting to get pissed. "Die already!"

"What the hell," came the voice in her ear.

"Hank, the machine," she pointed to the giant lightning maker behind her. "Black out."

She tapped the side of her glasses as Hank fired into the large machine. Sparks flew in every direction, and little explosions made the motor powering the device quit. She waited until the lights vanished, and then she opened her eyes. She could see Sonya looking around in the dark. Angelica smiled. "My turn, bitch."

Angelica threw Sonya toward the ground. Sonya was confused, scurrying around in the dark. The zombie took pitiful swings at Angelica, but nothing came close to connecting.

"Thought you had it won, huh?"

As Sonya turned away and started to run, Angelica jumped on her back. She grabbed onto the woman's head and turned it hard, until it made a familiar *snap*. As they went down to the ground, Angelica pulled out her bayonet. Before Sonya could begin to repair herself Angelica sliced into the woman's neck and began sawing away.

"That's just nasty," came Hank's voice.

"No," she replied, "it's satisfaction."

She continued to saw away at the woman's neck until she felt the head detach from the body. She pushed the head away from the body and stood up. Looking down at the corpse gave Angelica deep satisfaction, but not nearly the level she wanted. She wanted to make sure that the woman never came back. Again.

"Do you have something that burns?"

Hank came down the last set of steps. He walked over to his companion and the body lying on the ground. Hank grimaced at the slick of blood covering Angelica as her chest heaved, the knife still tightly gripped in her hand. "I have an incendiary grenade."

"Good start," she said, taking it from his hand.

Angelica pulled the pin and slammed the small canister into the body's neck. She grabbed Hank and ran away. With a loud bang and a bright light, they watched as the body burned away. The sparks soared through the air, burning brightly for a few seconds and then dimmed. All that was left was a mound of ash and the woman's head.

Hank looked at the head. "Think she can grow a body?"

"We're going to find out," Angelica said, picking it up. "It's coming with us."

"Seriously, just nasty."

She grabbed the head by the hair and picked it up. Looking at the face, Angie didn't see any signs of life. "So far it seems to be dead."

"What the hell is she?"

"I killed her once before. I'm pretty sure she's a zombie."

"Not like one we've seen before."

"With all the science crap that we've seen, I'm wondering if this is what they've been trying to do. Not the flesh eaters, but something like her. She could heal any wound and she doesn't look a day older than before."

"Makes sense," he said. "Bryce did put the solution into a youth cream once. It would go with the terribly ironic theme."

Hank motioned with his hands toward the shadows, pointing and then holding up a single finger. Angelica reached down into her boot and pulled out a small handgun. She signed for Hank to cover one side of the shadow, and she would take the other.

They walked quietly in the dark. The sound of the machine in distress behind them made their footfalls impossible to hear. Angelica squinted to try and see the room. Suddenly the emergency lights flashed, drowning the room in red.

"There, much better," said Hank.

They both stopped in their tracks as they looked a woman staggering toward with ropes hanging from her wrists. Their jaws were both slacked as the woman coughed, and dusted off her clothes. The woman gave them the same astonished look.

"About damned time! Are you bitches going to get me out of here or what?"

*****

In rapid succession, Mr. Rightoff tapped his pencil against the desk. Sam resisted the urge to lunge across the desk, grab the pencil, and stab the man in the neck. Sam disliked the principal. A lot. The man was an idiot. How he rose through the ranks to be in charge of Sam's education was a mystery.

Sam was about to speak up, but his father cleared his throat. "Mr. Rightoff, I'm glad we could have this meeting."

Sam was fully aware the only reason Mr. Rightoff was having this meeting was so the principal could get into his dad's pockets. Sam was hoping somebody would show up with one of those giant checks, the amount line holding more zeroes than was reasonable. His dad used it to his advantage, dangling the possibility in front of the principal, making the man dance for the money.

"Can I offer you coffee? Some tea perhaps? What about a scone? I can have the secretary whip some up."

Sam's dad held up his hand to silence the man. His father's expensive watch sparkled in the fluorescent light of Rightoff's office. Mr. Sinning was a powerful man, and he had no problem exuding that position over those around him. Sam knew someday he would take over for his father. The pharmaceutical world would bow before him.

"I'm here to discuss our arrangement."

"Oh, well you'll be glad to know, the female population has been very pleased with your product. I couldn't go through the hallways without seeing girls applying your beauty cream."

Mr. Sinning nodded, pleased with the statement.

"And have you noticed any," Mr. Sinning sat back in his chair and thought about the next words, "changes in your student body?"

"They smell better."

Sam wasn't exactly sure what his dad attempted to get from the man. Sam wasn't entirely sure why he was at this meeting at all. Typically his dad kept his business entirely separate from the family. He claimed he didn't like to bring work home, but Sam knew it was because he was always knee deep in some top secret project.

"Any other changes?"

Mr. Rightoff didn't know what to say. The man was perplexed as to what Sam's father was asking. "You'll have to be more specific, Mr. Sinning."

"Any insatiable hunger? Any sickness? Any," he paused again, the dramatic silence emphasizing his words, "deaths?"

Sam's eyes went wide at the statement. What could his father be working on that might cause death? He was cryptic most of the time, but even this was more obtuse than usual.

"No," Mr. Rightoff pondered the questions, "no change in appetite reported by the lunch ladies, and to my knowledge, nobody has been sick or died. I would think the school nurse would report as such."

"I expect an update if anything changes."

Mr. Sinning stood up, brushing off the front of his suit.

Mr. Rightoff was quick to his feet, holding out his hand. "Now about that football field?"

Mr. Sinning made no move to shake the principal's hand. He sneered at the man's gesture, amused the principal believed this to be a partnership. "You will get your money when my experiment runs its course."

Mr. Rightoff gave a slight stomp of his foot, as if he was going to break out in a temper tantrum. "You had better hold up your end of the bargain."

The phone in the business man's suit began to ring. He held up his finger, halting Mr. Rightoff's tantrum. Mr. Sinning pulled out the device and examined the number.

"Your phone won't work in here. We have signal dampeners on."

"Cute," the man said, flipping open his phone. He lifted it to his ear and listened to a frantic voice on the other side of the call. "Fanny, you should be happy, your experiment is going fantastic. No. No. No, nobody has returned from the," he paused at eyed the principal, "brink."

Sam watched his father's face become more intense. His nose scrunched up as his glasses fell down his face. It was a look that always spelled disaster in their mansion. His father's face went slack at the fast spaced speaking on the other end.

"What do you mean *she* got away?"

Some more fast talking.

"She'll be coming for me. Fanny, you had better fix this. I don't care what you have to do. Make it right."

The phone snapped shut. He started walking out of the door. "Sam, we need to leave now."

"But what about the..."

"Your check will be mailed to you." The man eyed his

son again. "Sam, now."

"That's funny," Mr. Rightoff said, looking at his computer screen. "It seems somebody has activated the school lock down protocols."

Sam thought back to the conversation this morning. The panicked look on his father's face, and the stupid expression in Mr. Rightoff's eyes seemed like the perfect start to the apocalypse. Maybe Kevin hadn't been wrong?

* * * * *

Cadence reached for the holster hidden at the top of her stockings, just below her skirt. A football player threw her backward before she managed to grab the gun. The large student's face was a wreck, his ear and cheek missing, a large chunk of his face only hanging by a few threads of skin.

Cadence flipped over and jumped to her feet. She knew zombies were going to attack today, and yet she still felt it necessary to wear heels. She would have to rethink her wardrobe when she got home. Right now, the stiletto spikes were making it difficult for her to find traction on the floor.

"Fucking fast zombies," she cursed as she grabbed a pencil off her desk. The boy grabbed onto her shoulder and pulled her backward, closer to his snapping teeth.

She reached back, slamming the pencil into the kid's skull. The pencil splintered as it impaled itself on the bone. She slammed her head backward, knocking the zombie in the forehead. The football player stumbled, falling to a knee. She spun around and slammed the heel of her foot into his head.

"Jesus Christ," she yelled as the heel of her shoe broke off in his forehead.

The football player crumpled to the ground. Cadence kicked off her shoes and pulled out the gun. She plopped down in her desk chair. Pulling out a small notebook from her briefcase, she started scribbling notes.

"They're faster. They're angrier. Piercing the brain seems to work still." She wrote furiously, trying to document every moment of the zombie invasion. She froze in mid-sentence; two more football players in full uniform jogged into her classroom.

"Ugh, should probably have shut that."

With her left hand, she lifted the gun, flipped the safety off, and took two shots. Both of the zombies stumbled, jostled by the bullet slamming into their helmets. She dropped her head down, annoyed at their refusal to die.

"Seriously, bullet proof helmets? What the *hell* is wrong with this school?"

She looked down her desk. A stuffed penguin, a zombie bobblehead, a pad of paper, and a few highlighters were the only objects within reach. She was beginning to think she had been too excited for the apocalypse, that she missed a few opportunities to prepare. This would be the perfect time to have a grenade handy, but no, instead she asked for a zombie bobblehead for her birthday. Stupid present.

She lunged over her desk as the zombies rambled in. She tried to put distance between her and the two lumbering giants. Cadence made it to the other side of the desks, and started pushing the desks with attached chairs in the way. The zombies bumped into them, confused at what kept them from reaching their meal.

"Get away from her you bastards."

Lauren was panting, her chest rising and falling quickly. Her eyes were dilated, the black of her pupils expanded until there was nothing left of the iris. She was already covered in blood, and the baseball bat hanging at her side was coated in dripping innards of deceased students.

"Oh thank God," Cadence said as the two zombies found themselves more interested in the black woman.

The two football players tripped their way toward the woman holding coffee cups. Lauren set the coffee down on a stack of Romeo & Juliet books. Lauren cracked her neck and started jumping around. Her movements sped up, starting to create a blur as she fake jabbed her invisible opponent.

The first football player stumbled away from the mess of desks and reached out, his gnarly hands threatening to snag her arm. Lauren kicked, her foot connected with his knee, knocking him to the ground. She kicked as hard as she could with the toe of her shoe, nailing the burly student under the chin. He flew backward, slamming into the ground. His companion walked over him, stepping on his chest as he approached his meal.

Her blood pulsed through her body. Her heartbeat thudded in her ears. Lauren was one with the coffee. The world around her seemed to move in slow motion as she gave over to her addiction. The football player didn't bat an eyelash as she struck his sternum with the heel of her palm. The bone crushed, impaling itself into his innards. She latched onto his wrist, and with a fast strike his bone snapped, leaving one arm dangling at his side. She repeated the maneuver, debilitating the star quarterback.

Cadence couldn't look away from the frightening girl. Lauren acted so fast it was hard to keep up with her movements. She jumped up in the air, bring both fists down on the student's helmet, driving his head down into several vertebrae. The kid slumped to the floor, his brain impaled by his own spine.

"Holy shit, Lauren."

The black woman didn't register there was another living person in the room. She was focused on her sole mission, destroy the dead. She straddled the fallen zombie, pinning his arms to his side. She untaped his helmet and peeled it off his sweaty head. The boy had a sparse growth of three-day stubble, barely old enough to need to shave. Lauren held his helmet in both hands and brought it down, striking the snapping jaw. She repeated the gesture until there was nothing but a crater where it's face had been.

"Lauren, honey, can you hear me?"

Lauren stood, the bloody helmet still in her hands. The former barista eyed her friend and gave a slight growl. It took several blinks before she regained her humanity. Cadence watched the woman's posture relax.

"What the hell is wrong with you?"

"I was in a happy place. A bright place. There was endless coffee. It was like Heaven. It smelled better. It was glorious. I want to be there. I was to go back, Cadi."

"Whoa," Cadence said, approaching the girl. "I think you might need to sit down for a moment."

"I can't. Can't stop moving. If I stop, I die. You taught me that. We need to kill. Kill or be killed. We need to leave Cadi. We need to hurry."

"Oh shit," Cadence said as two more zombies appeared in her doorway. "Will somebody shut that damned door already!"

Cadence grabbed Lauren by the waist and the two backed up, stepping over the fallen football players. She recognized the two students, they were in her second period class today. One was practically a zombie already, never willing to bring her head up off the desk. The other was her star English student. Cadence had a momentary pang of guilt that the girl would never be able to go work for the New York Times.

"Keep backing up, my gun is on the desk."

The girls were freshly dead. Their movements were jerky, as if their joints were fused together, making it difficult to walk. Their skin still had some color, not yet reaching the pasty pale gray that would eventually overcome them. One of the girl's arms was covered in shredded flesh, a defensive wound from a zombie. The other had missing cloth on her shoulder where a zombie had bitten down, dooming them both.

Without warning, both the girls dropped to the floor. Their heads rolled along the ground until they bumped into the football player's bodies. Standing behind them, Min, holding a katana, her gui covered in blood. She was huffing and puffing, her face showing the murderous joy she normally kept hidden during school hours.

"Come with me if you want to live."

Cadence grabbed the gun on her desk and contemplated firing a warning shot at the small Asian woman. "We are never inviting you over for movie night again."

"What's wrong with her?" Min asked, gesturing at Lauren.

Lauren's eyes were still nearly all black. She stared off into the distance, unaware that either Cadence or Min were in the room. Cadence waved her hand in front of the girl. Min slapped the black woman across the face with the back of her hand, leaving a bloody handprint on the girl.

"What? Where was I? How'd I get here? I need coffee."

"Whoa," Cadence and Min said in unison.

Min slid her katana into the sheath on her hip. "So, zombies?" The small Asian held up her hand as Cadence's face started to light up. "No, we're not taking photos for your book."

"Boo," Cadence said.

"What's the plan?"

Cadence thought back to last night. They had talked about weapons. They had reviewed tactics for killing zombies. They had discussed the CW's TV fall lineup. There had even been a lively debate about how coffee flavored ice-cream was America's third favorite ice-cream. Her face showed her displeasure. "We never made one."

"I told you, leave coffee ice-cream alone," Lauren said.

Cadence checked her gun, making sure there was a round in the chamber. "At least we can get to the guns."

Lauren shook her head. "The doors locked. Windows are barricaded. We're trapped."

Cadence climbed behind her desk and lifted the blinds. Behind the white shades, blocking the window, just beyond the glass, metal gates covered their escape. Cadence smacked her head against the glass several times. "I have nine bullets and two thousand students to kill."

"So we stand behind Min and let her do all the work, like usual?" asked Lauren.

"Best plan I've heard so far," Cadence said.

"Where to?" asked Min.

Cadence smacked her head against the window one more time. "You know the drill."

Min's shoulder's slumped as she turned around to head out the door. "God damn auditorium."

* * * * *

"Seriously?" Xander head had been down, correcting a paper comparing the accuracies of Schindler's List to the realities of the Holocaust. He was knee deep in the disgruntled grading of papers stolen from the internet, copied from one another, and one that attempted to draw comparison's from the Smurfs.

He had begun to write witty comments at the top. "A, B, C, D, you received none of these" and "You and Flourine have something in common." As he laughed at his last comment, he listened to the Advanced Placement class shuffle in to their seats.

"Give me just a moment and I'll be ready to hand back your papers."

The room was quiet, far quieter than it had ever been. Most of the time, they argued if Yale or Harvard was the better ranked school. Now, there was nothing, not even the sound of the wheezing student who sat in the front row.

"If I lift my head and you're all zombies, I'm going to be pissed."

He laid his red pen on the desk and shuffled the papers into a neat stack. He reached into the small safe under his desk, making sure to avert his eyes from the students in his class. His fingers touched the biometric plate and it opened with a slight hiss. He reached in and grabbed his favorite gun, taking two extra magazines of ammo and sliding them into his pocket. He sat up at his desk and examined his class.

"Are we going to get started?" the kid in the front asked. "If I don't ace this AP exam, I'm never getting into Harvard."

He was shocked to see the wheezing kid was alive. "You're not snorting?"

"Oh, I'm on medication now. But can we get started? While the rest of these chumps are satisfied with a pathetic

Yale education, I need to..."

Xander's eyes went wide as a student sitting in the next row lunged at the kid, clamping his jaw down into soft neck flesh. The rest of the room was filled with gray skinned zombies. They were recently dead, still following the patterns they had when alive.

Xander wonder if this was how it had happened the first time. This had been the Teacher's classroom once upon a time. Is this where he fended off his first zombies before getting himself killed? Xander hoped he made it further through this made-for-tv movie than Teacher did.

"You're tardy for class," he bellowed as he pulled out the gun.

He fired the first shot. The bullet pierced the head of one zombie, causing the skull to explode before it passed into the forehead of the next kid in the row. He was thankful he kept high velocity rounds in the safe for everyday student behavior issues. They were going to come in handy until he could reach the big weapons.

He pulled the trigger several more times, sending zombies sprawled across the first couple rows of desks. The bodies of dead students barricaded the rest of the dead from reaching him. He jumped over his desk and stood in the doorway, watching as the poor wheezing student had the skin peeled away from his bones. "That's what you get for supporting Harvard," Xander said as he pulled the door shut.

The hallways were empty. He could only assume that most of the students who turned into the living dead were sitting at their desks, waiting for their classes to begin. There were streaks of blood trailing down the hallways, bloody handprints along the lockers. He had to assume the entire student body was victim to the undead.

Xander tried to think of where the others would be. Cadence's classroom was in the east wing, almost an entire school separating them. He was near the art department; he couldn't imagine that many of the art teachers would be good at surviving the apocalypse.

The familiar growls of a zombie pack grew closer. Behind him, there were no escape; the hallway split into a collection of art rooms. He leaned against the lockers and tried the closest door, ducking inside the painting studio. He pulled the shade down on the window, a necessity when the teacher brought in nude models for the children to draw.

* * * * *

"Tina, stop them."

The window shattered. Bloody hands reached through the windows from the hallway into the library. The moaning was loud enough that the survivors had to shout to be heard. Tina didn't know what to do. She swatted at the hands with a field hockey stick abandoned by an undead student.

"They're going to crawl through," she squealed as she smacked one.

"What are you doing, giving them love taps?" barked Kevin. He pushed a book case in front of another window. "Stab them in the head."

She turned back to the three zombies fighting to get through the window. One of the teen boys pulled himself forward enough that his hand fondled her breast. Her face was a splattered with things far worse than blood. Rage built until she screamed.

Tina swung backward and let loose. The stick smashed the side of the zombie's head. He pulled himself the rest of the way through the window, falling onto the library floor. He reached again, this time gettingt awfully close to her skirt.

"Jesus, you're a dead pervert."

The zombie stumbled and reached out to her legs. She backed up and took another swing with the stick. As it connected with the zombie's head, the equipment exploded in a fury of splinters. The zombie staggered but started to pick itself up, moving to its knees.

"Stop playing with it." Kevin yelled.

She pulled back for another swing. The zombie tripped over loose shoelaces and fell, catching itself by grabbing onto her chest. She could feel the heat from his breath on her neck and she swore she could see the teen boy smile. She spun the stick around in her hand and drove it downward, the splintered tip wedging itself into the side of the zombie's head.

"Stop groping me you pervert!"

Tina yanked out the stick and jammed the point into the skull of another zombie in the window. As the body went lifeless, she saw her chemistry partner clawing her way through the window. Tina screamed and stabbed the girl's skull several times with a ferocity she didn't know she could muster.

"Wow, what did she ever do to you?" Kevin asked as he started to push a bookcase in front of the window.

"She turned in our lab report late."

"And him?" Kevin pointed to the boy on the ground bleeding onto the carpet.

"He touched my tits."

Kevin nodded. "Mental note, don't touch your chest."

Tina ripped the stick from the girl's face with a sucking

sound. "Damn straight you won't."

As Kevin pushed the bookcase in front of the window, Mrs. V showed up carrying her gun. "The windows are all blocked. We should be safe for the moment. We have to find the others."

"Or we can wait here. We can sit right here until the cops show up. Then we'll be alive when they rescue us," reasoned Tina.

Mrs. V shook her head. "We are the cavalry. There won't be any cops. If my bosses find out there's an infection, they'll drop a bomb and eradicate Boxford."

"Effective," Kevin said.

She nodded. "We have to assume the others are alive."

"You sure about that?" Tina snapped. "They could be smears on the wall right now."

Mrs. V eyed the teenager girl. "Aren't you just a ray of sunshine?"

"You have no idea," Kevin groaned.

"The chances of Xander and Victor being dead are slim. Cadence has been preparing for this and Min," Mrs. V thought about the young Asian and her tenacity in these situations, "there's a good chance Min has already slaughtered a few hundred of these things."

The sound of scraping nails on the wooden bookcase broke the quiet. They all froze, turning in unison, hoping the bookcase would hold. The students looked to Mrs. V for words of encouragement.

"We are so fucked."

Ring. Ring. Ring.

Period 5

Her bare arms revealed wiry muscle, evidence of her training for the better part of two decades. She was outnumbered, five-to-one, but far from outmatched. She fought with the fury of a warrior, but despite her punches, kicks, dodging and slicing, they would eventually overwhelm her. They would continue to attack until she was exhausted. The dead had no limits.

At the center of her being, there was a raging inferno of disgust. Min hated the dead. She hated the living. There weren't many people Min didn't hate. That burning pit in her stomach cut her off from her most dangerous weapon. Her grandfather had warned her. He said her anger was the only thing holding her back from becoming the perfect warrior.

Min chopped off the head of the closest zombie. She glanced up at Cadence and Lauren; they were sitting on a table in the teacher's lounger, eating doughnuts and watching her work.

"Do you think in my book I should give her two swords?"

"Totally," Lauren replied, "two swords are more badass than one."

Cadence jotted down the idea in her notebook.

"I hope you both die," Min hissed.

Cadence slid the pencil behind her ear and held up her gun. "I'm almost out of bullets. Sorry." She shrugged apologetically.

Lauren turned her coffee cup upside down. "Out of

killing juice, boo."

"I hate you both."

Min was soaked in blood. It was like every zombie encounter. Somehow she always wound up soaked through, covered in things that she didn't dare ponder. She ducked the swipe of hands from one zombie and thrust forward, sending another back out the door.

She had a moment of clarity as she wondered if Hank was safe. She worried less about her pasty husband. His diet had been paying off. He could outrun the slow zombies. Jessica however, her adopted daughter was somewhere in the building. She wasn't helpless, but it was her first time taking on zombies. Fear was not an emotion the young girl was accustomed to.

Her rage subsided and Min touched the well of power coursing through her body. It ran deep and in these rare moments; she drew the energy upward, wrapping it around the muscles of her body.

"Oh shit," Lauren said.

Cadence nodded. "She found her Chi."

The teacher's lounge filled with a cool breeze, raising the hair on everybody's necks. Min thrust her palm forward, striking chest of a young teenage boy. His upper body collapsed, impaling itself into a void. With a fast snap of her leg, the head of another zombie exploded into a shower of skull fragments. With a final pivot, her sword traveled from groin through the torso and straight up the head of a senior girl.

Min ignored the hair on her companions, blown backward and coated in zombie guts. She slid the sword into her belt. "We need to find Jessica."

"Where would she be?"

Min shrugged.

"Everybody pose."

They both turned to Lauren who was holding her phone out on a long stick. The black girl made a peace sign and snapped the photo. She snapped several more, pouting lips, smiling, squeezing her arms together to show off her cleavage.

"You did not bring a selfie stick to the apocalypse?" asked Cadence.

"You're mad you didn't think of it."

Cadence grumbled at the truth.

They all froze after a thump from the ceiling. They turned their attention upward, looking at the metal ducts working their way through the ceiling. Min growled, recalling having to spend a night in the metal labyrinth.

"What do you think it is?" Lauren asked.

"Do you think it's alive?" Min followed.

Cadence shrugged. Min watched as the metal shook. She reached to the sword on her hip as one of the vents came crashing down in the middle of the room. A body rolled out of the piping, landing on the table just behind Cadence.

"It's a zombie!" cried Lauren.

The boy shook his head, staring at the three blood covered women. He started to back away, worried they were going to kill him.

"Damn," Min cursed, "he's alive."

"You're not like them?"

Cadence hung her dead. "Seriously, Rob, did we not go over this in class?"

"Mrs. Winters?"

"Have you seen Jessica?" Min climbed over the table, leaving trails of blood on the smooth surface. She grabbed

220

onto the chain collar around the boy's neck and pulled him close. "Have you seen her?"

He shook his head quickly. "There's a classroom down the hall with survivors. Maybe ten students? They've barricaded the hallway."

Lauren gave a slight shrug. "Oh that's good. We won't have to save them then."

"Lauren," Cadence said with her teacher voice. "We're not leaving them behind."

Min slid off the table and wiggled her body, loosening her muscles. "I'm not responsible if I kill a living student."

"I said the same thing during my job interview," Cadence said with a smile.

* * * * *

"What are the chances they're not all zombies?" Jessica asked.

Victor turned to his youngest recruit. The girl may have been Min's daughter, but she still had some amount of compassion left. He had to assume that Min was covered in blood screaming a battle cry as she decimated rooms full of zombies. If they waited long enough, she would probably kill all of them.

He shook his head. "I can't imagine they would be prepared for this."

"Night of the Living Dead," said David.

"The Walking Dead," replied Jessica.

"Z-Nation."

"iZombie."

"What?" asked Victor.

"There are more shows about zombies than there are reality TV shows. How do you think we figured it out? Stab them in the head and you're golden."

"But are we dealing with runners or slow zombies?"

Jessica pointed to her young companion. "See, he knows what's going on."

"Doesn't this school have a zombie LARP group? I mean, they already looked like zombies. I bet they're just roaming around excited that they have friends now."

David nodded quickly. "See."

Victor hung his head. "What happened to going outside and playing?"

"No TV," Jessica said.

"Or Wi-Fi," David said.

Victor ignored the smart-ass comments and turned his attention to figuring how they were going to get out alive. There weren't that many zombies, even with the entire staff and student body, only two-thousand kids stood between them and freedom. Between him, Min, and Xander, they could probably handle that in small bursts.

He froze as he watched three figures bolt past the door. The blur of army green was a sight for sore eyes. He had written off his cadets as cannon fodder. They were weak, and wouldn't stand a chance. Victor wondered if the sergeant had thought that about him when he first joined. He had to take a chance on them.

"Were those people still alive?" asked David.

"Yeah, they're my cadets."

"We're not going to go save them are we?" he asked.

Victor nodded. "They're my cadets. I can't turn my back on a brother."

Jessica let out a long sigh. He could tell she wasn't amused by his ramblings. Civilians never understood the sacred bond between servicemen.

"You stay here, I'm going to go get them."

"Okay," David said with a smile.

"Yeah, no." Jessica picked up stake and stepped behind the militant man. "If I let you go out there alone, you'll die. That's how it happens in the movies. Mom would be so pissed with me."

"This isn't a movie," Victor snapped.

"Save your ass, or deal with my mother."

"Point taken." Victor dropped down below the window as a group of zombies ran by the door, in hot pursuit of the cadets.

"That answers that question," David said.

"They're usually slow," Victor said, "these must be track students."

The kids dwelled on that as Victor peaked through the window. The moment it was clear he opened the door. A straggler shambled by the door just in time see him crouched in the doorway. He lunged at the zombie, grabbing its head and spinning it quickly, sending it falling to the floor.

"Run."

They followed behind the swarm of zombies chasing the cadets. As they rounded the corner of the hallway, working their way down the science wing of the building, the zombie horde began to thicken as rambling zombies saw a stir of activity.

Victor looked over his shoulder to see Jessica slide underneath the grasp of two zombies. She grabbed David's hand and tugged at the kid, dragging him along with her. The first time the zombies had attacked, Min pulled the exact same move. Genetics or not, he knew she was the daughter of the crazy Asian.

"We have incoming," yelled one of the cadets.

Victor watched as a rope lying across the hallway was pulled tight. It raised to ankle height. The cadets weren't running, they were luring the zombies into a trap. Victor's heart swelled with pride as the three kids jumped over the rope and skidded to a stop.

The running zombies' feet snagged on the rope, toppling to the ground in a pile of cold bodies. Before they had time to jump back to their feet, a group of girl's wearing skirts and wielding field hockey sticks jumped out of several classroom doors. With a bellowing cry, they started beating the bodies of the zombies.

"The heads," Victor yelled, "bash in their heads!"

One of the girls fell to the ground as a zombie grabbed onto her leg, chomping away at her thigh. Another girl screamed, bashing in the zombie's head. Victor pulled out his gun, but there was no way he could take a shot without hitting one of the kids.

One of the girls wound back her stick and swung hard enough the lower half of a zombie's jaw flew down the hallway, nearing hitting Victor in the chest. He was impressed. They were fighting back. In his day, everybody just died without a fight; he was proud to say millennials weren't as bad as their reputation.

"Behind you," Victor shouted as he jumped over the rope and through a group of swinging teenage girls.

The cadet turned just in time to see a zombie lunge from a supply closet, his pants around his ankles. The cadet tried to push at the kid, but his hand moved too close to its mouth and the zombie clamped onto the bone. The young military student kicked at the zombie's torso just as a female staggered out of the closet, her blouse open and a smile stretched across what was left of her face.

"Ew," the field hockey girls said in unison, taking a moment to soak in the nasty that occurred.

Another one of the cadets stumbled over his companion and fell to the ground. The female was on him, clawing her way up his torso as he tried to kick at her face. She scratched his face, her teeth sinking into a gap between his shirt and pants.

Just as the female zombie pulled back, preparing to invade his torso, a black blur kicked the girl in the torso, sending the undead slutty girl into the air. Victor recognized the ebony Flash. Lauren lunged at the male zombie on the cadet. Her hands snatched its head, and with several smacks against the ground it stopped moving.

"Lauren," Victor barked.

The girl's eyes were glazed over. Her humanity was questionable as she crept low to the ground. From down the adjoining corridor a familiar voice yelled. "She got into the dark roast!"

Lauren caught an oncoming field hockey stick with her bare hand, stopping the assault mid swing. She grabbed the squealing girl by the neck and lifted her off the floor with might only granted to coffee addicts.

"Lauren stop!" cried Cadence.

Min held up her hands feigning protest, whispering just loud enough to be heard. "Oh no. Not that. No. Bad Lauren."

Victor couldn't make heads or tails of the scene in front of him. There was so much blood he had a difficult time figuring out who was alive and who was undead. A girl on the ground reached up, biting the leg of the girl dangling from Lauren's grip. Only several feet away, a dead cadet sat up, his eyes starting to haze over as he adjusted to his recently deceasedness.

Cadence clutched onto Victor's shoulder as she gasped for breath. "What's going on?"

"You know, some quality education time."

"Smartass." replied Cadence.

"Gay man!" Min said with a smile. "You not dead yet?"

"We need to run." Victor said as the undead began to outnumber the living. He backed away, signaling for Jessica and David to stand back. Several loud bangs erupted in the hallway as Cadence blew apart the skulls of two zombies behind her best friend's daughter.

"Mom?" Jessica said with relief.

The small Asian punched Victor in the arm. "You let her come?"

"Stubborn pain in my ass, she takes after her mother."

"Oh my god," shrieked Rob from down the hall, "she's eating her!"

Lauren didn't look down to the chomping zombie. She rested her foot on the girl's neck, pinning her to the ground while she threw her captive across the hall. The former barista stomped on the girl's neck. "What did you think they were going to do? A musical number?"

"Zombies are real?"

David used his backpack like a club, sending a zombie behind Rob to the ground. "You're not exactly helping here."

"They're," Rob sputtered, "They're real."

"So are they!" Everybody paused, weapons held high, halting their zombie slaying. The football team was shambling down the hallway, each of them wearing their gear.

"Seriously? Helmets?" Cadence wiped the blood from

her face, growing annoyed with how poorly it was turning out.

"They shall meet my righteous fury."

Cadence smacked her forehead. "Min, your righteous fury isn't going to help."

A glass door shattered as zombies pushed their way into the hall. She grabbed Min by the collar and pulled the small Asian away from the impending zombie hoard. They were divided. It would be moments before they were overrun with the undead.

"Victor, you know where to meet us?"

"Same place as usual?"

"Keep the kids safe, or Min is going to wreck you."

Victor grabbed onto David and Jessica, pulling them back from the carnage. They backed away from the undead picking themselves up off the ground. With a salute, he started to turn.

"Oh hells no, you are not leaving me."

Victor watched as Lauren waved her hands. "I am not letting you protect her. There can only be one!"

Jessica raised her eyebrow. "Huh?"

"It's a black girl thing."

Lauren marched toward the group of zombies blocking her way. She jumped down to her stomach, sliding along the puddles of blood, knocking a dead cheerleader out of the way. She passed between the legs of a zombie who was far too slow to catch her. She jumped to her feet and started running toward them.

"It's me or you." The barista smeared blood under her eyes like war paint.

"It better be you!" Min screamed.

"Jesus," Victor sighed. "Let's get out of here."

Period 6

JUMPING up onto the model's platform in the middle of the classroom, Xander rested comfortably above the three zombies reaching for him. The top of the table reached the undead teacher's chest, preventing her from being able to reach him. With a swift kick to the face, she flung backward, landing in a pile of easels.

"Okay," he tried to reason with himself, "this isn't so bad."

The female zombie couldn't reach him, her hands harmless waving in the air. Even the young boy, covered in dark blue paint, had difficulty reaching up onto the pedestal. Xander bent over, resting his hands on his legs, trying to catch his breath.

"I'm getting too old for this shit."

The art studio was one of the largest rooms in the school. Easels surrounded the middle table, where students would practice drawing models. Beyond that, drafting tables filled the room. Along the outer wall, collections of paints and random doodads the students used in their artwork littered the space. He scanned the room for weapons of use.

"Is it too much to ask for a Roman spear? Maybe a sword from the Xia dynasty? Hell, I'll stab them with paintbrushes if I have to."

He hadn't set foot in the classroom since joining the staff. It dawned on him a decade ago, this is the room his wife spent countless hours honing her craft. He imagined her slaving over a painting, pouring her heart and soul into whatever project. Her first passion would always be art, the writing came later. At some point, he'd have to ask her why she stopped using the brush and relied on the laptop.

Fingers touched one of his boots as the boy managed to gain a better angle on the table. Xander stepped on the kid's hand, holding him in place and kicked hard with his steel toe boot. On the third kick, the zombie slouched down onto the ground and stopped moving.

He hopped down off the table, letting the female zombie come at him. Grabbing her by the throat, Xander held her at bay, her jaw snapping as it tried to reach its food source. The freshman's shirt was torn at the sleeve, a large bite removed from her bicep. Just like every time before, the switch in his head that saw them as human flipped. All that remained were soulless monsters trying to eat him.

"It's been fun," he spun the girl around, his arm wrapped around her neck. With a spin of the jaw, a snap filled the empty room and the body slumped to the ground. Eyeing the two dead bodies, he had to hold back a chuckle. Something about the dead coming to life, teachers slaying their students, and the impending apocalypse really summed up the education system in America.

Behind him, a crash broke his moment of amusement. He turned to see the teacher caught in several easels, dragging herself to a cabinet on the far side of the room. The undead only had one desire. They ignored personal safety, even from impending death...or redeath.   The woman dragged herself, her legs stuck in the wooden drawing apparatus.

"Is there somebody else in here?"

The teacher's legs snagged on a desk, her clawing hands unable to drag her any further. He found himself thankful at the stupidity of zombies. If they had half a brain, they'd be dangerous.

He laughed. "Half a brain," he snorted to himself.

Littered along the tabletops, a plethora of paintbrushes were left still wet with paint. He grabbed the closer one, spinning it around, ready to impale the first thing that lunged at him. With the toe of his boot, he slid open the cabinet to see a shivering student curled up, hiding amongst the ceramic supplies.

"So, are you going to come out or are you going to stay squirreled away?"

The kid's eyes were closed so tightly his face had turned a bright red. Xander waited for the kid to budge, but nothing seemed to make him move.

With a boot planted on the teacher's neck he stomp hard several times, crushing its neck. Plopping himself down in a chair he waited for the kid to move. "Okay look, hiding is great and everything, but the building tends to burn down when there's a zombie invasion. So you'll need to come out."

The kid opened one eye, going between him and the dead teacher. Xander didn't recognize the kid. He waited patiently, checking his gun, counting the twelve remaining rounds. Once he was done he slid the weapon back into his shoulder holster.

"Okay, I'm going to go save the world. Good luck."

"Wait," the kid said, "aren't you supposed to keep the kids safe?"

"If you haven't noticed, there's a zombie apocalypse."

"So?"

"Not exactly covered in my teaching contract."

"But--"

"Move your butt or I'm going to let one of the flesh munchers eat you."

"How dare--"

"Come with me if you want to live."

"Oh," said the kid, "in that case..."

Xander hung his head down. Zombies were massacring the entire school and the kids still thought it was a bad movie. He needed to reach Cadence so he could start in on his, "Youth in America," speech. She'd agree, she'd probably promote him leaving the little snots to die. For now, this kid was the only backup he had.

"Name is Xander," he held out his hand, helping the kid out.

"Sam."

"Well, Sam, let's go save the world."

"Couldn't we just go to Starbucks and get a frappucino?"

* * * * *

It wasn't going according to plan. Not even a little. The best laid plans couldn't account for human stupidity or zombie ferocity. Cadence hoped the others had made it down the hall. She had a moment of relief when she thought of Victor and Min's daughter working in concert. That was a terrifying double team.

"They're real."

"Yeah," Cadence said for the millionth time.

"I mean, like they're really zombies."

"So we're back to stating the obvious?" Asked Cadence.

"They can't be real. This isn't a movie."

In the utility closet, the sound of metal sliding out of a sheath didn't escape her. "Min, put away the sword."

"But--"

"No," Cadence scolded. "You can't kill him."

"Even--"

"Even though he's annoying."

"And--"

"And he's probably better off dead than whatever horrible death awaits him before we get out of here."

"Fine," the sword sheathed.

"They're--"

Smack. The boy stopped stuttering. "You hit me."

"He's smart," Min said, giving him a dirty look.

"You're teachers, you can't hit me."

Min wound back for another strike. Cadence grabbed her hand, stopping the impending beat down. "We probably shouldn't kill the children."

"Probably?"

Cadence shrugged. "I might change my mind."

Cadence reached into her pocket and revealed a small notebook. She jotted down notes of what had happened. She wanted to make sure she captured the massacre in the hallway. The teens might know all about zombies, but they still died like civilians.

"Are you taking notes? Really?"

She covered her writing so Rob couldn't see what she was writing. She made an extra note about the young man. "Find way to kill whiney brat."

The woman started pushing further back into the utility closet. Metal racks reached the ceiling, holding hundreds of textbooks. The 1963 written on the spine of a history book started to make some sense. "I'm starting to understand why future generations are doomed."

Pushing through a stack of books labeled, "Miracle of the Typewriter," she found a dead end. Electrical boxes had dozens of wires sprouting out of the top, running into the fake ceiling tiles. The familiar blue Ethernet cords made her think they may be somewhere near one of the computer labs used by foreign languages.

"Why did I never listen to Angela's cybersecurity lectures."

"Googley eyes with Xander."

"Shut up," she yelled back at Min. "Like you could do any better."

"I'm more than a pretty face."

"How can you two banter while the apocalypse is happening?"

"He made full sentence."

The Asian was nothing if not insufferable. "This isn't our first time at the undead rodeo."

Rob pushed further into the back of the closet as thumping started at the wooden door. Cadence resisted the urge to squeal when he clutched her hand between his. The kid's black fingernail polish had chipped off, but she was certain he was wearing her brand, "Are you wearing fingernail polish?"

"What of it?"

"Le Petite Morte?"

His eyes lit up at the mention of the brand. "How would you know that?"

"I own stock. Former goth elite here."

His eyes sparkled as he admired her. She wondered if he'd recognize her now as the queen of the zombies, the bringer of undead death, and the former spokesmodel for Le Petite Morte.

"What happened to you?" He asked with a bit of disgust in his voice.

"What do you mean?"

"You must have been so cool."

Min let out a laugh.

"Did you just say that in past tense?"

"I'll never sell out."

She shook free from his grasp while Min's laughter filled the small space. If she had a gun, she'd shoot them both. No, that'd be too quick, maybe she'd clock them with the butt of the gun.

"O.M.G. Cool. You? Oh, my!" Min braced herself against the book stack, doubling over while laughing. "I may die right now."

"She do this a lot?" Asked Rob.

"You have no idea." Rob gave her a sidewise glance. She pushed the boy's face forward. "Don't look at me, I have the urge to pistol whip you."

"Coooooool!"

"I hope we die. Seriously, I'm going to open the door and end this." Cadence banged the back of her head against the electrical box. Yes, she thought, she would kill them all. "I hope Victor is having more fun."

* * * * *

Mrs. V held her hand up to her mouth, making the shushing sound. They had managed to make their way from the library to one of the less used stairwells with only one zombie encounter. The librarian pushed on the metal bar on the door, slowly opening it as she peaked inside.

"It's clear," she whispered.

Waving Tina and Kevin inside the door, she eyed down the hallway to see several undead students rounding the corner. She closed the door, certain they'd forget about seeing her by the time they reached the door. A chuckle slipped out as she realized teen zombies had the same attention span as they did when they were alive.

"What now?" Asked Kevin.

Mrs. V knew the others would be heading to the auditorium. They had made that their ultimate rendezvous point, figuring it'd be easiest to confront the big bad early and just be done with it. "The others are heading to the auditorium."

"Why?"

Mrs. V was about to answer when she realized there wasn't a good explanation. Were they relying on the need for a bad guy to grand stand, confess their plans on the stage with state-of-the-art lighting, or were they just doing what had always been done? She was going to be pissed if they had to burn down another school.

"It's where you go in these situations, I guess."

"You guess?" Tina had a flare for drama. Mrs. V wasn't too far away from pinching the girl's nerve, paralyzing her, and dragging her out of the school.

"Tina, stop being a drama queen," Kevin eyed the librarian, waiting for directions.

"We're going to make a pit stop first. I looked at the blueprints for the electronic security. I believe the doors to the loading dock near the cafeteria weren't part of the system. I can get you two out from there."

"We're going with you--"

"Like hell we are!" Tina snapped.

"I'm not leaving David and Jessica behind."

"*Her*," Tina's face turned bright red. She shoved her pointer finger into the boy's chest. "You are not putting my life in danger because you have a crush."

He swatted away her hand. "I'm not leaving until

everybody is safe."

"Fine. Die, wake up, die again. See if I care if you get twice-dead."

Mrs. V hung her head. The older librarian didn't realize how spoiled she had been the first time the outbreak happened. The others were younger by far, but at least the most drama they had was Olivia trying to steal Dione's chai latte. She appreciated that she inherited a daughter old enough to be done with puberty, and have tactical training.

"You're getting out. I can't have you slow me down."

Tina's hair whipped around as her anger turned to the librarian. "You saying I'm slow? I'll have you know--"

Mrs. V grabbed the girl and spun her around. She planted her hand firmly over the girl's mouth, stopping her from finishing her rant. On the landing, halfway down the stairs, a zombie she recognized from the debate team bounced off the walls. She didn't think they'd be able to make it down without getting within biting distance.

Bang.

Mrs. V stopped holding Tina and covered her ears. The echo of gunfire filled the small space, ringing in her ears. The second shot fired, chipping the cement on the wall near the landing. The third struck the zombie in the neck, obliterating its spine.

The librarian grabbed the boy's hands, jerking his finger off the trigger. With lightning fast reflexes, her other hand grabbed the kid by the neck, pinning him to the wall.

"No," she yelled, "bad teen. Bad!"

Kevin struggled against the woman's vice-like grip. The boy managed to point down the stair to the zombie struggling to gain its footing. Mrs. V didn't break eye contact as she pointed the gun, eased the trigger down. The skull of the zombie exploded, painting the wall.

"OH MY GOD YOU SHOT HIM!"

"Stop yelling," Mrs. V said, trying to adjust her own volume.

"I CAN'T STOP YELLING."

Mrs. V hung her head down. As the boy's face started to turn a shade of blueberry blue, she let go. The kid sucked in air, gasping like it was his first breath. She checked the magazine and realized they only had a few more shots before running out of ammo.

"We need to move," she said.

"WE SHOULD MOVE."

Mrs. V checked the magazine again. There might not be enough ammo to stop the zombie apocalypse, but there was more than enough to stop an annoying cheerleader. She wondered if the others were as annoyed with the new generation of zombie slayers.

"Let's move."

"WE SHOULD GET MOVING."

"Kill me," Mrs. V mumbled.

* * * * *

"Should we stop them?" Asked David.

"Do you really want to get in the middle of two black girls about to throw down?"

"You make it sound like the Real Housewives of Boxford."

Victor didn't try to hide his grin. "I know."

"I told you for the last time, I am not going to kill myself so you can live." Jessica had Lauren pinned against the wall. The small janitor's office held a few desks with computers, a large table, and palettes of cleaning supplies. At the offhand suggestion of Jessica drinking bleach for their safety, her temper finally got the best of her.

"I will not drink bleach. I will not hurl myself into a hoard of dead. I will not," she held up several rolls of duct tape. "Okay, brownie points for thinking of making a noose out of duct tape."

"Thanks."

Jessica slapped the woman. "No."

David leaned closer to Victor. "I'm going to stop them."

"You really don't understand women, do you?"

David eyed the man. "And you do?"

"What's that mean?"

"Woman advice from the resident homosexual?"

Victor raised his eyebrows. He admitted--he wasn't going to try and hide it--but how could the kid know after only working there for a few days? It wasn't as if he showed up wearing his pride speedo and feather boa.

"I Googled you."

"Huh?" Victor still didn't understand.

"Image search."

Victor's eyes went wide. "About that..."

David raised his hand, blocking the shop teacher. "I was an innocent teenager until I hit that search button. I'll never get it back."

"Says the hacker."

"My eyes," David feigned weeping.

Lauren smacked Jessica's pointing finger. "Zombie apocalypse happens, there are rules. We all know in horror movies, the first person to die is black."

"Technically the zombies died first," Jessica chimed in.

Lauren shrugged off the logic. "There can only be one survivor. Dione thought she could upstage me. She blew up in a thousand little pieces. Think I won't--"

"She died to protect everybody."

Lauren's eyebrow arched freakishly high. "That's exactly what I want you to think."

Jessica turned to Victor and David, sitting on the table. "Okay, I'm done with her. I can only handle so much crazy. Quota filled. Next, onto survival."

"We need to make it to the auditorium," Victor said.

"Why? Doesn't that seem like a vulnerable spot to meet up?"

Victor nodded. "You don't argue with Cadence when it comes to zombie stuff. This is the third major outbreak here. If history is any indicator, when we get to the auditorium, the villain who caused all of this will be there waiting."

"You know this isn't a movie, right?" Asked David.

"Have you tried arguing with Cadi before?" asked Victor.

"So what then?"

Victor put his hand on David's shoulder. "We listen to some villain dialogue, there's some maniacal laughter, then we fight until we kill the bastard."

"I'm living in a bad TV series," said Jessica, hanging her head in shame.

They all jumped as a loud thump came from the door. A custodian smacked his hand against the door again, trying to break the glass to get at its next meal. Victor was surprised at how grotesque the man appeared, his face had been a zombie buffet.

"They ate him," David said, his voice equal parts curiosity and disgust.

Another set of hands pounded the window as several teenage zombies gathered around the man. Their weak attempts at breaking the glass weren't their biggest concern. Victor noted that the collective weight of the undead was going to bust the lock open.

"We need to run." He slid off the table and started pushing. "Give me a hand."

The massive piece of furniture slid along the floor until it rested against the entrance. Victor watched the door latch give way as a growing mob of zombies tried to reach their next meal. The table started to slide back, giving the doors a chance to open.

"There's a door," Lauren pointed to the back of the office.

Victor shoved David and Jessica toward the back, making sure they made it before the zombies flooded the small space. He started to turn around when he tripped over something on the floor.

"Shit," he said as an undead janitor crawled from between the crates. He kicked with his foot, freeing himself from the bulky man.

"Help him!" David screamed.

"You know *you* could help him," Jessica said.

"Look," he said, "I'm the brains, you're the brute. Now get bruting."

Before she could step in to help her mother's friend, Lauren slammed a broken mop handle into the custodian's eye socket. The woman stood up, another layer of blood covering the front of her.

"You owe me," she said, helping Victor to his feet.

"Sure."

"Will you kill--"

"I'm not killing Jessica."

Lauren threw up her hands as she stormed off toward

the door. Peaking inside the room, she held the door open. Victor was surprised she didn't try leaving Jessica to fend for herself with the growing number of zombies storming the custodian's office.

"They should mellow out now that they can't see us." Victor inspected the wooden door, checking to make sure it was more durable than the last one.

"I'm not chancing it."

He watched as David toppled a shelf filled with bags of dry cement. When the dust settled, there was no way to get through the door.

"Where are we?" Asked Jessica.

Victor sniffed the air. The smell of stale cigarettes and marijuana lingered. Between the stench and the proximity to the custodian's office, he instantly knew where they were.

"We're in the boiler room."

"I thought the school was solar powered," said Jessica.

"I'm sure that's a lie we tell your hippy crunchy parents."

* * * * *

"That's just a lie we tell your hippy crunchy parents," said Mrs. V.

"So you're telling me that my organic free range, chicken with no GMO's and humanely killed is just *regular chicken*?" Tina couldn't hide her disgust.

"I'm not sure it's even chicken."

The teenage girl started to gag.

"So what's the game plan, do you think we can get to the other side?"

The cafeteria separated them from the kitchen that would lead them to the loading docks. Between them and the bastion of lunch lady land were at least two-dozen zombies scattered around tables.

"If we move fast, I think we can make it," said Tina.

Kevin nodded, grabbing the door.

"No," she said, "wait for it..."

"What?" asked Kevin.

Ring. Ring. Ring.

"Run!" she screamed.

Period 7

It is unclear if the subject's violent tendencies are due to the serum or being a complete bitch. I suspect from her frequent eye rolling she is either suffering from dehydration with the inability to produce tears, or she is just that annoying.

While she remains restrained, she does not appear to be slowing with linguistic skills. While her vocabulary remains somewhat limited, relying on the words, "kill," "you," and "slut," she does seem to maintain cognitive function and higher order executive skills. In the near future, we will begin testing her motor skills.

I look forward to watching the undead cheerleader attempt the Arabian Double Front.

* * * * *

"What is she doing?" cried Kevin.

"She's making a break for it," said Mrs. V pulling her handgun from her waistband.

"Run," she barked.

Through the doors, forty circular tables held eight seats each. The cafeteria held little else, an attempt by those in charge to keep the masses placated on taco Tuesday. A small salad bar was the last line of defense before two large entrances would take them into the food prep area.

Kevin burst through the door into the cafeteria. A girl from study hall had her arms stretched out, ready to grab. A duck and a pivot brought him out of reach. Only a few dozen zombies occupied the area, spread out; he could do this.

"Tina" he yelled, "wait up!"

The gymnast ignored his pleas. Launching herself into the air, she slid across a table and somersaulted off the end. She ducked and weaved, keeping as much distance as possible between her and the undead.

Kevin realized he was going to be blocked in. Following Tina's lead, he jumped up onto a table and started jumping from one to the next. A hall monitor reached for him, blocking his next leap. With a kick to the face, the zombie fell backward.

"This isn't so bad," Kevin said.

A gun fired. Behind him, he watched a zombie only inches from having its jaw around his ankle fall to the ground. The librarian spun the gun in her hand and gave him a slight wink.

"Don't get cocky," she said.

"Help!"

Tina was pinned on the top of a table with four zombies closing in. She batted away hands grabbing at her clothes, but it was obvious they were only seconds from dragging her to the cafeteria floor.

Mrs. V fired twice as Kevin charged toward the table. One of the zombies fell to the ground. Kevin lunged, tackling another of the undead to the ground. He held the kid by the neck, keeping the snapping jaw away from his face. Teeth clacked loudly as the underclassman tried to chew his next meal.

Tina's foot stepped on the side of the zombie's face, giving Kevin a chance to get away. He grabbed onto the girl and dragged her toward the back of the cafeteria. "They're closing in."

"Keep running!" Mrs. V yelled as she fired into the face

of the closest zombie, forcing the back of its head to explode.

Trying to avoid the puddles of blood and less identifiable body parts, Kevin pushed on. As he stepped in a puddle he slid along the floor, skidding into the serving area where students picked up their lunches before eating. He grabbed the overhead metal door on one of the bays and pulled down hard. As it slammed against the floor, he twisted the locks on either side, securing it.

"She's not going to make it."

Tina pointed into the massacre happening. Mrs. V was a sight to behold. She kicked at the leg of a zombie, knocking it to the ground before she fired, nailing it in the forehead. Smacking the next closest zombie in the forehead with the butt of her gun, she fired.

The librarian leaned backward, narrowly escaping two more undead. Reaching into the belt, she pulled the gun she confiscated from Kevin. Down on her knees, she fired up, each gun catching a zombie under the jaw, killing them in their tracks.

"Holy shit," Kevin mumbled.

"She doesn't have enough ammo," Tina said pointing to several more zombies coming at her.

"Run," Kevin yelled.

Tina grabbed a wooden mop resting against the wall and snapped off the end. "Be prepared to slam the door shut."

"What are you doing?"

"Being amazing."

And she was.

The mop handle slammed into a kid from science and knocked the legs out from a girl in gym. The five feet of wood whirled about in the air, knocking zombie after zombie to the ground. Tina single-handedly created a path from the doorway to the librarian.

"You should be hiding."

"Somebody had to save your ass."

"They're blocking us in."

Kevin watched in horror as zombies circled about their upcoming meals. He grabbed the mop bucket to find it full of soapy water. "Get on the table!" he yelled. Lifting the bucket, he hurled it toward the crowd of undead.

Tina and Mrs. V leapt onto a stools as the water washed across the floor. Zombies reached for their prey, falling to ground as they slipped. Tina jumped to the next table and then the next.

"You're almost there," Kevin encouraged.

"Your motivational rhetoric isn't helping!" Tina yelled back.

Arms grabbed him around the waist before he could move. The pale gray limbs squeezed, and the familiar snapping teeth were close enough he could feel the breath of the zombie on his neck. He leaned forward, using the awkward angle to keep the zombie from reaching his neck.

"Help!"

"Tina get the door," Mrs. V said, "I've got Kevin."

He stomped on the zombie's foot, hoping it'd loosen its grip. Grabbing onto one of its fingers, he pulled back until he heard the bone snap, but nothing made it stop. The zombie grabbed tighter, changing its angle so it could chomp on his neck.

Tina ran past as Mrs. V barreled into the zombie, knocking it and him to the ground. Kevin scrambled to get away, but the zombie caught onto his leg. He dared a glance; it's was mouth only inches from his ankle.

He closed his eyes tight and prepared to forfeit his

humanity. The seconds dragged on, but he didn't feel the bite. He listened as something thumped repeatedly against the floor, until finally the hands on his leg loosened.

Turning he saw why the zombie hadn't bitten him. Caught between the senior's bloodthirsty jaws was Mrs. V's arm. He barely registered it as she bludgeoned the zombie several more times with the butt of her gun.

"Inside," she commanded.

He crawled inside the serving area, still in shock. He didn't know what it meant, she had been bitten. Did the librarian have a cure? Of course she had a cure, she wouldn't have let herself get bitten unless she had a way out of this mess.

"Incoming!" Tina yelled.

She yanked the metal barrier down as Mrs. V rolled inside the serving area. With a couple spins of the lock, they were safe, at least for the moment.

* * * * *

Hank smacked the steering wheel, cursing under his breath. Each time the traffic seemed to let up, the lights in front of him flared an angry red and he was forced to slam his brakes. At the rate they were going, they'd never make it to the school before class ended for the day.

"I'm going to get out and walk," he concluded.

Angelica rolled her eyes. It had become her signature move, a single action that summarized both her frustration and her annoyance. "I know Min has you on that diet and all, but unless you think you can jog the whole way..."

He let go of the handle, trying to let the rage subside. "Why is there rush hour traffic before three?"

"It's the burbs, there's always traffic. So let me get this

right. You married Min? You adopted an orphan? And Angie, are the stepdaughter of a gun toting librarian?" asked Olivia.

Hank had a moment to decide. He could end the cheerleader's incessant questions by driving off the overpass and crashing the van below. There would be a good chance they'd all die. He hesitated when he contemplated surviving, waking from a coma to find Olivia at his bedside, stealing his Jell-O.

He really wanted Jell-O.

"Yes, we got married. Yes, we adopted a teenager. Jessica is her name."

"Whoa," Olivia said. "It took a cracker to tame the Rice Queen!"

Angelica turned in her seat, her eyebrow twitching. Hank recognized the tick; at any moment the red-haired vixen would shoot whatever was annoying her. Driving off the ledge started to look more and more appealing.

"We saved your ass," Angelica started, "would it be possible for you to shut up?"

"Yeah, let's talk about that."

Olivia leaned forward, violating Hank's personal space. "So you know it's been *five years* right? Five years they had me trapped in that lab. Did you guys even come looking for me? Did you?"

"Well, after the funeral--"

She grabbed Hank's shoulder. "What do you mean funeral?"

"You were dead, that's what you do for dead people."

Her hand rested on Hank's head, turning it slowly to meet her icy stare. "You're telling me you didn't even look for me?"

"You exploded," Hank said in an uneasy manner.

"Did you find a body? Did you Hank?"

Angelica chimed in. "To be honest, we were busy."

"Doing what!?" Olivia screamed.

"Mourning Dione."

The cheerleader flung herself back into her seat, crossing her arms and pouting with just the right amount of lip; sad, but pretty sad. Hank tried to hide his amusement at the overly dramatic girl.

"So where are the others? I cannot wait to see the look on Cadence's face. O.M.G. Can you imagine how pissed Min is going to be?"

"They're at the high school," Angelica said holding up her phone, punching a few keys. "They haven't checked in for a while now."

"Maybe they're teaching," Hank suggested.

Angelica scoffed at the suggestion. "They play Words With Friends more than they actually teach. How they keep their jobs I'll never figure out."

"Government conspiracy--"

"Wait, you mean they're at *Boxford*?" Olivia wedged herself between them again.

"Yeah."

"This isn't good."

"Why?" Hank asked.

"The owner of that lab you found me in, his kid goes there. He's like a bigwig in the PTO or something."

"What the hell is with that school?" Angelica tossed her phone on the dash, annoyed with the lack of communication. "He wouldn't infect the entire school with his kid there, would he?"

"True. It's not like he's a monster who kept the star

250

cheerleader of the New England Patriots locked up in a dungeon for five years while performing experiments on her. No, he really strikes me as an upstanding kind of fellow. I'm sure in his spare time he feeds the poor and--"

"I get it," Hank had to smirk. The cheerleader had a knack for rubbing everybody the wrong way, yet they talked about her in high regard.

"Last I heard he was reading to the blind and visiting his Nana at the senior center."

"I'm going to smack you."

Olivia let out a low growl. "I'm going to be pissed if I don't get to kill him."

Angelica gave Hank a punch in the shoulder. "You heard the girl, should probably drive faster."

"Though, if you want to stop all the zombie outbreaks, it'd probably be best to go to their corporate headquarters and destroy their servers. I'm not trying to tell the super secret agent how to do her job, but I'd blow up the entire building."

Hank saw the look from Angelica. The cheerleader was right. They might stop this outbreak, but for the first time, they had a lead. They had the living specimen to guide them to their end game.

"Min will understand."

He agreed with Angelica. "Let's go blow up a building, then we save the others."

"It should give us just enough time to make a last minute entrance and save them while the auditorium burns to the ground." Hank didn't miss the eagerness written on Olivia's face. The cheerleader wouldn't miss her chance for a glorious return to the limelight.

"The auditorium?" asked Angelica.

"Yes," Olivia hissed. "You two will be my backup dancers if I decide to do the musical number."

"She serious?" asked Angelica.

Hank spun the wheel and eased the van through traffic until he reached the exit. They weren't far from the school, but for now, they had a conspiracy to end before they stopped a zombie outbreak. "You'll make a cute backup dancer."

"I'd rather be dealing with the undead," she confessed.

* * * * *

"I don't think it's too much to ask for a small donation for--"

Mr. Lazarus held up his hand, stopping the principal before he was able to continue his solicitation. "My company built this school from the ground up. It has state-of-the-art computer labs. It has the best science labs in the state. We even installed that stupid rock wall."

"I'm still not sure how that acquisition made it to your desk."

"Regardless, Mr. Rightoff," the business man continued, "I will not be giving you the money for new AstroTurf fields and a stadium dome."

"But--"

"Enough."

Lazarus had no problem splurging for the sake of this legacy experiment. They weren't very far from unlocking the fountain of youth and ruling the world, first in cosmetics, and then in every market. First they would sell to the elite, and then the masses would demand eternal youth.

Two thousand lab rats were currently being exposed to their beauty cream. The free samples had been a success and at any moment, the school would begin showing results. Of the two thousand students, he hoped they'd find a handful like Sonya and that irritating cheerleader.

"I should be on my way. Do let me know if anything out of the ordinary starts to occur."

Mr. Rightoff, the dumbest man alive, oversaw his lab rats. The man's only purpose was to continue the farce that Boxford High School was nothing more than an educational institute. If the businessman had his way, the children would have been torn from their homes and turned into test subjects. His top advisors suggested their current predicament was more practical than facing the authorities for kidnapping.

A phone rang, breaking the awkward silence between the men. "Excuse me while I take this."

"But, the cell phone jammers are on."

"It's cute that you think I'd lower myself to consumer technology."

Lazarus turned, giving the principal his back as he reached into his interior breast pocket and pulled out a phone. With a tap of the screen he held it to his ear. "Lazarus."

"Sir, the daycare facility has gone dark."

He suspected they were playing it fast and loose acquiring more research facilities. They had always done better at letting loose the serum in public settings and studying the data.

"Who?"

"It's her again."

"Dammit." He loathed the young woman who had made her mission to destroy his life's work. He'd been gleeful when he found out the head of their operation died in the King David Lake Mall outbreak. He had hoped that would end the covert government conspiracy to destroy him. But no, she had regrouped, recruited, and had becomen a constant thorn in his side.

"No worries, we are continuing our primary experiment."

"Sir," the voice hesitated, "we lost the specimen."

"You what?" The rage made his heart thump louder in his chest.

"Hey," Mr. Rightoff interrupted. "There's something weird going on? None of the students are in their classes."

The principal let out a loud gasp. Lazarus looked over his shoulder; Mr. Rightoff gawked at the computer monitors behind his desk. "That girl, Melanie, she's eating the cheerleader's co-captain."

"Send Sonya to find the cheerleader," Lazarus said into the phone.

"About that," the voice quivered, "she's missing. The video shows her being killed. Like really killed."

"Did you find a body?"

"Sir, we can't--"

"No body, no death."

"Yes, sir."

"The experiment is under way. Call me when you have better news."

He ended the call, slid his phone to his pocket and turned to watch the ghastly face of the principal. Mr. Rightoff sputtered nonsense as he examined the cameras throughout the school, giving firsthand accounts of the massacre.

"We need to call the cops."

"You will do no such thing."

Mr. Rightoff's face turned from mortified to perplexed. "Mr. Lazarus, how can you be so calm? Students are dying."

Lazarus waved the man over to the plush leather chair in the front of the desk. The principal's state of shock prevented him from arguing. Lazarus reached out and grabbed the principal's tie, loosening the knot slowly, letting it slide off the man's neck. After unsnapping the top two buttons, he gestured for the man to take a seat.

"I think we should--"

The cheap tie cinched around the principal's neck. Lazarus didn't like getting his hands dirty, but he wouldn't let the man derail his work. Strangling the man wasn't the worst of it, the sensation of cheap fabric against his skin offended him.

He squeezed tighter as the principal started to fight. "It'll be okay," the businessman whispered, "I'll keep an eye on the kiddos."

The educator struggled for a moment, clawing at the tie, before his body went limp. Lazarus released the awful bit of plastic infused fabric, quickly reached into his pocket, and pulled out a small bottle of his company's moisturizer, cleansing his hand of the cheaply manufactured garment.

"Now, let's see what's happening with Boxford's final class."

Rightoff jerked, his body appearing to convulse. Lazarus reached for the gun inside his jacket and turned to the front of the man. With the gun leveled, he waited.

The principal's eyes opened, bloodshot and void of human intelligence. Lazarus smiled at his creation. The undead man got to his feet, trying to groan as he relearned how to walk. The businessman put away his gun, pleased with how quickly the transformation happened.

Lazarus stepped behind the computer to see the carnage erupting on the screen. Pockets of youth were putting up a fight, threatening to wipe out his specimen. He worried the exposure to zombies in pop culture may have bred a new wave of teenager, one capable of slaying the undead far too quickly.

Before he could switch to another group of cameras, an alert popped up on the screen. "Parent's Night: Tonight @7."

The smile spread across the man's face. "It looks like our sample size is about to get bigger."

He eyed the zombie principal, standing in the middle of the room, doing almost nothing except starting the decaying process. "Sit," Mr. Lazarus commanded.

Zombie Rightoff did just that.

Ring. Ring. Ring.

Period 8

"Any better?" Victor asked.

"Our flesh hungry friends are still blocking the door," said David as he plopped down on a crate.

The large boilers continued grinding, making it near impossible to hear. Victor wiped the sweat off his face with his shirt. The others repeated similar gestures, trying to keep the sweat out of their eyes.

Jessica tore at her t-shirt, ripping off the sleeves. The teenager continued ripping the midriff of her shirt until she was left in a halter top. Tying the extra fabric around her forehead, she tried to keep her calm.

"How did you guys do this last time?"

"Is it just me or is it wrong that the zombie apocalypse has a 'last time,'" said David as he shook the sweat from his head.

Victor tried to recall the first time the world nearly ended. Somewhere around this time, the zombie outbreak had reached its apex. Thankfully, the students this time had done a better job of putting up a fight.

"Basically we played a lot of hide and seek," he admitted.

"In the mall this is about the time we had a clothing montage and rallied against the undead."

"You're kidding me," Jessica laughed.

"Nope, then I saved the day." Lauren stared at Jessica, making sure the girl understood who had been the savior during the last outbreak. "I'll see what I can do this time."

"Maybe we'll get lucky and the zombies will go

somewhere else," David tried to reason.

"Not likely. They can smell us."

"You know what I could go for right now?"

Victor rolled his eyes. There was only one thing Lauren ever wanted. "Coffee?"

"Ice cream," she corrected.

Victor raised his eyebrow at the woman. He'd have to remember to mark in his calendar the first time she hadn't crave--

"Coffee ice cream."

"For now guys, we wait. We'll know our cue to bolt," he said lying back on a group of empty boxes.

"If we don't sweat to death first," Jessica said.

"Think of it like a day spa. It's like an academic steam room," he said with a smile.

"Nobody in the steam room ever tried to eat me," Jessica said, settling herself on a seat make of paper towels cases.

"You obviously haven't been in a steam room Xander," he said.

He waited for the laughter at his joke about about Xander's sexuality insecurities. It was those moments he missed Olivia, she'd always be fast to respond. He'd have to save the joke for when he saw Cadence next.

"You make a valid argument, however I believe Jared Leto was never given the chance to be the Joker we all need."

"His inability to fulfill the shoes of Heath Ledger is not because of his limited screen time. His limited screen time is due to his inability."

"Kill me," said Min.

Cadence understood the woman's rage. They had been locked in the pool for the last fifty minutes and already she wanted to use the two members of the debate team as zombie bait. If the undead didn't kill them, she would.

"Does anybody really care?" asked Rob.

Both of arguing boys turned their attention to the goth. "State your case."

"Don't kill me. Kill them. Can I please, Cadi?"

"Maybe."

The double metal doors leading into the pool thumped loudly. Outside the doors, dozens of zombies were trying to get in, and not for their afternoon cardio. The magazine in her gun clicked empty, an answered prayer for the two boys she contemplated shooting.

The only two entrances into the pool were blocked by a dozen zombies on each side. She suspected they could out maneuver them, but not with the kids in tow. The horror writer hated that she had gotten soft.

"Those doors won't hold forever," she said, "we need a plan."

"I'll kill them all." Min snarled.

Her rage was steadily increasing as the boys continued bickering about who played which superhero better. It wouldn't be long before the Asian stabbed them both. Maybe if she was lucky she'd stick the little goth kid too.

"Stop picturing me dead," Rob retorted.

"Calm down, I can't handle another drama queen in our survival pack."

"Ha," Min laughed, "Xander is so gay."

"What's your problem with me?" Rob asked. Through the layers of black eyeliner-- Cadence hated to admit--but it was like looking at a younger version of herself.

"You remind me of myself as a kid."

"Poseur."

She pointed the gun at him and dry fired the gun over and over. "Dammit."

"You were going to kill me!"

"And miss the chance to watch zombies tear you limb from limb? Not likely."

The kid got up, marched over to her seat on the bleachers and put his finger in Cadence's face. "Look, you may have been all that and a bag of chips when you were a kid, but now you're just a washed up wannabe."

He leaned in closer, making sure to accentuate his words. "Queen of the Zombies? You're a has been, a total wash up. I've read your books, and a one-star review is generous."

Cadence grabbed the kid, spinning him about and putting him in a headlock. The two debate kids stopped arguing long enough to stare in disbelief. She clenched her arm around his neck as he struggled to break free.

As his body went limp, she let the unconscious boy fall to the floor. "Do not fuck with my reviews you emo poster child."

Cadence had worried she'd lost a part of herself when she gave up painting and put away the dark clothes and disenfranchised attitude. Now as she stared at the wheezing child, she realized it had only been a phase.

"You strangle a child and have an epiphany?"

Her eyebrow raised, confused how Min knew. "How'd you guess?"

"You get vacant looks sometimes. We leave you alone when we're sure you're not stroking out."

"Thanks, I guess?"

"What are friends for?" The Asian slapped Cadence on the back. "I need to tinkle."

"Over share much?"

Min headed to the changing room, leaving her with a boy passed out on the floor and two young men arguing the finer points of realism in cinema.

"Halle Barry made a good Catwoman," she threw into the conversation.

The shock left both of the boys stunned. "Where do we even begin..."

* * * * *

"Are you going to eat me?"

Mrs. V eyed Tina, amazed that she could easily transition to zombie slaying badass to annoyingly worrisome teenage girl. Both her and Kevin kept their distance, not sure what to do to help her.

"Do I look like a cannibal Aghoris Indian?"

"Uhm," Tina swallowed, "Maybe?"

"What the hell are they teaching you in this school?"

Mrs. V tore at her skirt until she had several long strips of fabric. She wrapped up the bite, making sure to pull it tight enough her arm ached. The jagged teeth marks in her forearm spelled out her future, but hopefully she'd survive long enough to see the mission through.

"Are you going to turn?"

The librarian ignored the question, not wanting to dwell on the inevitable. "We need to check the loading dock doors."

She got to her feet, very aware of how tired her bones were feeling. It was hard to not question what was happening in her body. Did the weariness come from approaching retirement, or from white blood cells combatting an infection they couldn't defeat? Focusing on the here and now, she knew their survival depended on it.

Passing the salad bar and going around the milk cooler, she found herself in the kitchen area. The two students followed, nearly bumping into her as she stopped to grab the meat clever off the prep area. If she was going to die, she'd take as many of the lil' bastards with her as she could.

The dismay as they saw the thick padlocks on the doors was almost as palpable as the smell of tuna fish. Kevin pulled at the locks, confirming they were indeed locked in the room.

"One of the lunch ladies must have the key," he said.

"I didn't see any in the cafeteria," she replied.

Tina tugged on the librarian's blouse. "They're behind us, aren't they?"

"Cadence was right, stating the obvious does work."

The woman in her blue lunch lady uniform didn't have time to attack. Mrs. V swiped with the butcher knife, nearly severing the woman's head from her neck. The zombie's arms continued to rise, preparing to pounce. With a kick, the librarian sent the lady to the ground.

Pulling back her foot, she kicked hard, sending the woman's head flying across the small kitchen. She panted as she waited for another zombie to appear.

"I think that's all of them," she said loudly.

Another zombie appeared.

"Does that always work?" Asked Kevin.

"We can handle one zombie," Mrs. V said louder, excited for a bit of revenge on her killers.

"What do you know," Tina said sarcastically as another zombie appeared near the freezers.

Mrs. V charged the first undead lunch lady. The zombie had time to lunge, but the librarian caught the woman's chomping mouth with the butcher blade. Blood started to course down the lunch lady's face as the blade sliced through her cheeks.

The librarian leaned forward, pushing the corpse backwards until Mrs. V had the zombie pinned to a cabinet. Pushing harder with the knife, she could feel it sinking deeper into her victim's mouth. She slammed her fist on the back of the blade, forcing it cut through bone. Banging the zombie's head against a storage cabinet, she managed to wedge the blade far enough that it caught the zombie's spine, killing it for good.

"Help!" Tina cried.

Pulling the blade from the zombie's lifeless body, Mrs. V spun about and hurled the cleaver across the kitchen. Whooshing past Tina's ear, the blade slammed into the last lunch lady's skull. It took a moment before the zombie's body caught up with the blow, falling to its knees and collapsing on the floor.

"Holy shit," Kevin said.

"I'm hungry," Mrs. V said, heading toward the back of the kitchen. "I wonder if I can find Min's sushi."

Ring. Ring. Ring.

3:43PM

Olivia had had enough of the woman's staring. It was bad enough she was wearing a five year old cheerleading outfit, but the red-haired agent was getting on her last nerve. "What are you looking at, ginger?" Olivia snapped.

Angelica was unfazed. "So you're a zombie, right?"

Olivia secured the plastic explosives to the pillar of the parking garage. They had been at it for hours; if she chipped another nail, she was calling it quits and checking herself in at the spa. "No."

"Are you dead?"

"I was."

"So you died and came back?"

"Kind of."

"Like a zombie?"

"If you call me a zombie, I'm going to punch you in the tit."

Hank snorted at the comment. "I think she's insecure about her living status."

"And you fat man," she pushed her finger in Hank's chest, "if I was dead, you wouldn't be checking out my ass this much."

"She's got you there," Angelica added.

Hank stammered to himself about checking the explosives in the north side of the building. His face was a light shade of red as he turned and ran away from the two women.

"You're like Sonya," Angelica said in a matter of fact tone.

"I think so? That crazy scientist woman said she was the first. Bryce was the second. But let's get one thing straight, I'm the best."

"So there are no others?"

Olivia shrugged. "I don't know. I didn't exactly get the morning memo every day. I just know that jerk of a guy Lazarus was the one funding the whole thing. The crazy scientist chick was the one doing all the science stuff."

"And the daycare?"

"If you were funding an evil operation, where would you hide it?"

"Senior center. Oil tanker. Private--"

"Okay Miss Crazy," Olivia said, "apparently rhetorical questions aren't your thing."

From the exit of the parking garage, she almost had a straight line of sight to school. She understood the important of taking down the corporation responsible for the outbreaks, but as she noticed more and more cars arriving at the school, she had to wonder if something weird was happening to her former classmates.

"Do you notice a lot of cars at the school? It's nearly seven at night, why would there be so many people there?"

Angelica swore. "Parent Teacher Night." The red headed assassin yelled across the parking lot, "Hurry Hank! We've got to go!"

Olivia bent down and secured her shoelaces. "You good here, right?"

"We have a couple dozen more pillars to secure."

"I'm heading to the school."

Angelica's eyes grew wide. "You're going to run?"

"No, I'm going to hijack a car. What kind of cheerleader do you think I am?"

"Help us finish this and we can get there sooner," Angelica tried to reason with the girl.

"It'll be too late," Olivia stared Angelica in the eye. "If I miss my opportunity to save Min, I'll never forgive myself."

"You mean, brag that you saved her."

"Same diff," Olivia said, running to the closest Lexus in the parking lot. It only took a few minutes before the engine was running and the cheerleader peeled out of the garage.

"For Miiiiiiiiiin!"

* * * * *

"Run!" Cadence pushed Rob away from the broken door. Several undead were already crawling around the broken frame, sniffing the air for their next meal.

The pool area didn't offer exits or much room to maneuver. To one side of the Olympic sized swimming pool were a handful of bleachers. Dividers floated in the pool, designating lap lanes. At one end, a diving board and a ladder leading toward the high dive. *I refuse to die covered in the smell of chlorine,* she thought to herself.

Min sliced at the two closest, skulls rolling from their bodies. More started to enter the pool area, and it became obvious they weren't going to be able to fight them all off. They ran, speeding past the two debate team members. She knew there was no way they'd all make it out of the pool area.

"Let me kill them," Min argued.

"Hank won't forgive me if I let you die," said Cadence.

Several of the undead paused as the two debate kids fell to the ground, victims to their incessant needs to argue. "I told you they had counter arguments," Cadence yelled.

"Geek burn," Min laughed.

"We're trapped," Rob yelled. He was right;ss the zombie's had circled both sides of the pool, leaving them near the diving boards. Min held up her sword, ready to start carving them a path to freedom.

"We climb," Cadence said.

"We do not climb things," Min said. "That was our deal this time."

"I said no rock walls," Cadence corrected as she jumped up several rungs of the ladder. "Now climb woman!"

"I'm scared of heights," whined Rob.

Min turned and smacked the kid in the face, smudging his black lipstick across his face. "Pee yourself while they eat you."

Cadence continued climbing; Min followed close behind. She remembered the drill. The undead would act confused for a moment, giving them a false sense of security, then they'd start scurrying up the ladder like they were professionals. Cadence had to wonder if there was a some part of them that retained a sick sense of humor.

"I swear," the boy yelled, grabbing onto the ladder. "When I get to my Aunt Susan's tonight..."

Cadence's back straightened at the name. Standing on the first level of the high dive she turned to see the kid slowly climbing the ladder. "Your Aunt Susan? Susan L? SusanL1778?"

"They're gaining on me!" he said. The first zombie had already started climbing. It looked like in the last installment, a twisted sense of humor was replaced with a need for speed.

"*You* left me that review," Cadence hissed.

"Oh shit." Min backed away, climbing the next ladder leading them up to the high dive.

"What of it?" He asked. "It's just a stupid review."

A member of the undead choir ensemble grabbed onto his leg, trying to yank him off the ladder. "Help me," the boy pleaded.

"Plot twist, poseur," she backed away from the ladder, "I've got nothing but edge left."

The boy struggled to hold onto the railings as another zombie grabbed onto his pant leg. His hands started to slip as they pulled him into the crowd. He didn't have a chance to scream as the undead swarmed over him.

"Harsh," Min said.

"Sure, when Olivia does it, nobody bats an eye. When I let a kid die--"

The stinging from the back of Min's hand brought her back to reality. "We don't have time for rants."

They continued to climb to the top, nearly thirty feet above the cluster of zombies below. The small platform offered little space for the two women. Min guarded the ladder. "I'll stab them when they reach us."

It was a sound plan; they could bottle neck the undead and in no time. They'd be done with the dozens of zombie children. Cadence tried to breathe a sigh of relief, but the sight below nearly sent her into a rage. A teenage goth boy with more than half of his face missing was giving her the finger.

"That little asshole."

Zombie Rob pointed at the diving board. Zombies stopped climbing the ladder, instead throwing themselves against the base of the pedestal holding them up. Cadence grabbed the railing as the entire structure shook. The shaking grew, and it was obvious they'd go down in no time.

"Can you swim?"

Before she could reply no, Min's foot connected with her butt. For a moment it was like flying. The water raced toward her face and she didn't have time to scream as she tucked her legs against her chest in preparation for an epic-level cannon ball.

The water clapped against her ears. Cadence fought to recall the instructions of her grade school swim instructor. "Don't breathe in until you know you're above water." Struggling, she fought to reach the surface of the pool. Air quickly filled her lungs as she broke through the surface.

In a perfect handstand on the edge of the diving platform, Min held her toes pointed toward the ceiling. With a push of her arms she spun into the air; somersault, somersault, somersault, toe-touch, arms straight down into the water. Cadence cursed quietly when only a small splash came from the impact.

A tug on her shirt had her struggling to stay afloat as Min pulled her along in the water. "Pull faster!" Cadence yelled as the pillar holding the diving boards started tilting towards the pool.

Zombies covered the diving board, falling into the pool two and three at a time. Loud groaning echoed off the water and the bare walls as the tower finally broke from of the ground. Cadence kicked with her legs, trying to put more distance between her and the incoming death column.

The wave washed over them. The water pulled Cadence along the bottom of the shallow end of the pool. As fast as she rolled along the bottom, the wave hurled her upward, throwing her over the side of the pool, against the far wall. Min slammed against her in another wave.

When she cracked her eyes, wiping away the chlorine, zombies were spread everywhere in the room. Even the half-filled pool held floating corpses, flailing in an attempt to move.

"They swim like you," Min coughed.

Cadence drove a knuckle into her friend's arm. "We need to run." Zombies tried to gain their footing, slipping on the water and falling back onto the tiled floor.

Across the pool, staring with a sly grin, was the half-eaten goth zombie. With a deliberate motion, the kid raised his hand, pointing at her. "I'm going to kill him," she huffed, "again."

Shoes squeaking with every step, the two girls got to their feet and carefully made their way to the door. Cadence paused long enough to turn, raise her middle finger proudly, and shout, "I'm going after your aunt next!"

* * * * *

"I'm going to die," David said, wringing out his shirt.

Victor ignored the teenager. In the last hour, the Marine had defused three lethal situations between Lauren and Jessica and assured the young boy half a dozen times that they weren't going to sweat to death. For the first time in his life, Victor understood what it meant to be an adult, and he hated it.

"Do you think we should go save the world or something?" asked Jessica. The teenage girl laid on the floor, spread eagle. The coolest spot in the increasingly hot and humid room was reaching a hundred degrees.

"We're not far from the auditorium," he reasoned. "I suppose we should go help the others."

"Leave me to die," David whined.

"Wait," Jessica sat up off the floor, "it's been like ten minutes since Lauren tried to strangle me."

Victor waited for the barista to spring out from a box or from behind an oil drum. It was rare during the zombie apocalypse somebody didn't take a cue when the opportunity presented itself. He sat up from the paper towel throne and scanned the boiler room. He worried an undead teenager was quietly snacking on his friend.

"Lauren, are you there?"

The Marine motioned for the others to sit still while he approached the boilers. Unless she snuck back into the office, the only place she could have gotten to was the far side of the boiler. The massive bins turning steam pushed warm air into the school. With each step approaching the fifteen-foot tall contraptions, the heat intensified. Peering around the side, he noticed a door slightly ajar. Over the hiss of steam being produced, he could hear what sounded like a zombie snacking on a dead barista.

"Jesus, Lauren," he cursed under his breath.

Creeping near the door, he prepared himself for the sight of his friend being eaten alive by the undead. He hoped she had died quickly. If God had been merciful, the zombie would have gotten her in the neck, and she'd be dead in seconds. He feared his friend lay in a puddle of her own blood, frozen in shock as she was being eaten alive, one slow bite at a time.

"Ahh!" He flung open the door, prepared to tackle the zombie to the ground.

"What the hell!" Lauren screamed.

The barista sat on the floor next to a desk. Clutched in her hand, he recognized her favorite accessory, a filled cup of coffee. He glanced at the desk and saw a can of instant coffee knocked over; the glass pot almost empty. Despite the roaring boilers, her slurping was loud enough to hear.

"I thought you were dead."

The barista chugged the remainder of her coffee. "I was," she stood up and thrust the empty mug into his chest. "I got better."

"You're about to go--"

"Okay, everybody," she yelled, "it's time. Right now. We're getting out of here."

"What's her deal?" asked Lauren.

Victor pointed at the coffee cup. "I think she just drank an entire pot."

"Shit," Jessica mumbled.

"Wait, what's happening?" asked David.

"She's caffeinated," Jessica said.

"So?"

Lauren yelled, thumping her fists on her chest. "To the auditorium!"

"Last time this happened, she got a fleet of lawn mowers to kill an entire mall of zombies." Victor explained as the woman charged the door leading into the custodian's office.

"She, *what*?" asked David.

Lauren didn't slow as she threw a palette out of her way, clearing a path into the custodian's office. As she snapped a stray zombie's neck, Victor jogged after her. "Stay close, her caffeine high might be our only hope."

"You people are crazy!" David yelled.

"Dammit," Jessica swore as she followed the rest of them into the office. "She is not going to be the last black woman standing."

* * * * *

"I thought it was a myth."

"It can't be real," said Sam.

Xander reached out slowly, refusing to believe something so luxurious could exist in a suburban high school. The fabric gave under his fingers, soft, plush, a sensation inviting him to relax, close his eyes and slumber. He couldn't resist, he sat down on the couch, surprised by how the firm cushions wrapped around his backside.

"The girls are spoiled," said Sam.

"It's a Tempurpedic," Xander said as he touched a cushion.

Sam tried to ignore the mildly inappropriate moans of the teacher as he explored the rest of the bathroom. The three stalls seemed identical to the boy's bathroom, until he noticed the toilet paper. "Two-ply? What madness is this?"

Xander didn't care about the zombie apocalypse anymore. In that moment, he found himself lulled into a sense of security by the amenities of the east wing girl's bathroom. "Are you surprised? They have three different types of moisturizer by the sinks."

"I'm glad to see where this school's education budget is going," Sam snapped.

"Yeah, let's blame your horrible education on a couch and toilet paper. We won't mention the million dollar security system currently trapping us in a building filled with the living dead."

"That too."

Xander loosened his tie. The red fabric was covered in what he could only assume was blood and brain matter. He couldn't remember if he had killed ten or eleven of the walking dead before they found themselves trapped. If it hadn't been for the kid, he might have been able to make it through the onslaught. Sam was less than useful when it came to fighting zombies.

"What's your deal anyways?" asked Xander.

"My deal? Asks the teacher who seems a bit too at home snapping the neck of students," said Sam.

"Isn't your dad some sort of big deal? Rightoff always mentioned him during those mandatory fundraising meetings," said Xander.

"We're rich."

"I could tell that by your sense of entitlement," said Xander.

"Funny." Sam washed some of the blood off his hands. He gave up as he realized he was covered.

"What's your dad do?"

"He's the CEO of a skin care company." Sam held up the bottles of moisturizer and started pumping copious amounts of the liquid onto his hands. He massaged the liquid in as he returned to the sitting room. "He likes to tell people, 'I'm in the business of keeping women eternally young' or some corporate bull."

The missing piece fell into place. The science teacher. Bryce, Shelley's protege. The cream in the mall being distributed. Xander watched as the kid massaged the moisturizer into his skin.

"Holy shit." Xander jumped to his feet. Sam jumped back, startled by the man. Xander picked up the bottle of hand cream and inspected the label. Provasive. He recognized the company name. One of the primary reasons why the school existed was to give an outstanding education to the children of the researchers who worked for the company.

"What? You look like you had an epiphany," said Sam.

"Want the good news, or the bad news?"

"I think being in the girl's bathroom has turned you into

a drama queen."

"I know what's making the zombies."

Xander stared at the boy's hands. He darted from the bottle to his hands and back again. He tried to wipe off the liquid, dragging his hands across his shirt. "What? No. I'm not going to become one of them."

"Your dad must have a cure."

"How are we going to find my dad? We're stuck in this school."

Attention members of the Boxford High Community. Mr. Rightoff has asked me to speak on his behalf. We welcome you to our annual mandatory Parent Teacher Night. If you can enter by the theater entrance, we will begin shortly. I can promise you, tonight's events are to die for.

The man started to laugh as the intercom ended. Sam's his brow furrowed, his jaw clenched. "I know where to find my dad," he spat in anger.

"You mean..."

"Yeah, that was him."

"If he lets in all those parents, we're going to have far more than handful of undead students."

Sam didn't wait for Xander as he flipped the lock on the bathroom door and flung it open.

"Don't get me killed," Xander mumbled to himself.

7:12PM

"Where is Mr. Rightoff," yelled one of the angry parents. The auditorium easily held three thousand moms and dads. With each passing moment, Lazarus watched them grow more agitated. It wouldn't be long before they started threatening him with lawsuits and defunding of the arts.

"He's dead," Mr. Lazarus said with little grandeur.

"They're all dead on the inside," cried a woman, "that's the life of teachers."

He had been disappointed with the results of the student outbreak. The children were far more savvy than expected; of the two thousand undead, only a couple hundred answered his call. The students were resourceful in slaughtering his zombies; they would make excellent foot soldiers in the future. Of the undead, none of them proved to be one of the chosen, a zombie capable of retaining their intellect.

Of the living, there were a handful he watched through the monitors who seemed more than capable of surviving. While most of the teachers were killed immediately, a small group of them rallied. He suspected it was the same group that had thwarted his previous outbreaks. They must be closing in, if they were able to get this close.

"Mr. Rightoff," he said, gesturing to the curtain, "please join us."

The curtain parted as the principal shambled his way to the podium. As he got closer, the parents watched him on the giant television screens hanging from the cieling. They gasped; they were finally starting to understand.

"What's the meaning of this?" shouted a portly man.

"I don't want to alarm the fine parents of Boxford High School, but you're all about to die in the pursuit of science," said the businessman.

"Not if we have anything to say about it."

Lazarus saw two women standing between the curtain. "You were waiting back there just to say that, weren't you?"

"Maybe," said one of the ladies.

"Wait, aren't you my son's English teacher?"

Cadence smiled. "And he's getting an F."

"You did not just say that," Min shouted.

"Kill them, Rightoff," demanded Lazarus.

Before the zombie principal could step forward, the Asian woman closed the space between them. In a single movement, he caught the glint of steel as she swiped her arm. It took a moment before he realized she was holding a sword. The principal's head rolled off its neck and the body collapsed.

"Wanted to do that for a long time," the Asian smiled.

"Well, let's make it a bit more of a challenge." With a flip of the businessman's wrist, several of the doors in the back of the room burst open. Zombies blocked the exits, standing still, waiting for orders.

"He's like Sonya," Cadence said.

The screams from the audience started in the back and continued to spread. Nobody screamed from the beheading of the school's principal; most of the bystanders were jealous it hadn't been their sword. The crowd started to rise, looking for the exits, trying to push the zombies out of the way.

"Move and they die," said Lazarus.

BANG.

Min jumped as man's head snapped backward, a perfect

circle in the middle of his forehead. She turned in time to see the Librarian come out of the curtain. "Waiting for a dramatic entrance?"

Mrs. V smiled. "Of course."

* * * * *

"Dad?" Sam ran from the side entrance to his father. He knelt down next to the man, cradling his head. "You killed my father."

"We'll probably have to kill him again," Xander said.

Cadence ran over, wrapping her arms around her husband. "Can we try not getting separated during the apocalypse?"

"No promises," Xander said giving her a peck on the cheek.

Sam wailed loud enough even the parents in the audience stopped panicking to stare. "Why would you do this!"

"See what I've been dealing with?" Xander said.

"We killed our teenager," she replied. "He gave me a one-star review."

"Fair enough," he said.

Sam jumped back as his father's eyes opened. "Will you stop your whining? This is why I told your mother we should send you to military school."

"What? But I saw you get shot," Sam said.

Xander nudged Cadence to get behind him. She shoved him to the side. "Don't be pulling that macho crap."

"How are you still alive?" asked Sam.

Lazarus shoved Sam off him and got to his feet. The teenager had tears streaming down his face. He pulled back and punched his dad in the jaw. "You're a wretched father."

"Go kid," Xander said with a whistle.

Lazarus grabbed Sam by the head and hurled him off the stage. "I'll ground you once I'm done killing these fools."

Xander caught Min smiling at him. With a slight grin and a nod, Xander knew his friend was looking for a fight. Xander nodded back. "I'll be right back, Cadi."

"If you die..."

Lazarus watched as the bullet in his skull pushed out, falling to the ground. Xander's fist connected with his jaw, barely turning his head. Min thrust the palm of her hand into the man's family jewels. The zombie fell to his knees, clutching his groin.

She wound up for another punch, but Lazarus caught her fist, twisting her arm until she went to her knees. Xander hopped onto the man's back, grabbing his head and spinning as hard as he could. The body went limp.

"Team awesome," Xander said.

Min gave Xander a high-five as he got to his feet. "Good job, white man."

"We should probably chop off his head or something. You know, the fatal blow or something." Xander pulled the sword free of Rightoff's neck and growled as the businessman got back to his feet. "How many times do we have to kill you."

"You can't," Lazarus hissed.

"About that," Xander said, swinging the sword for the man's neck. Lazarus caught the blade in his hand, gobs of blackish blood splashing across his face. The zombie worked his way to his feet, the sword cutting through his hand, removing a thumb.

With a growl, Xander pulled back the blade and thrust it into his chest. The back of the man's bloody stump smacked

Xander, sending him flying across the floor.

* * * * *

BANG.

"What are you waiting for?" asked David.

"You don't just rush into a situation," Victor said.

Jessica sighed. "He's waiting for an entrance."

"A what?"

She shook her head. "You know, waiting for somebody to set up the perfect line. He wants somebody to say, 'If only we had backup,' and then he'll jump out to save the day."

"Serious?" David's disbelief was written across his face.

"When you're friends with Cadence, you learn to play by the rules."

Through the side entrance to the stage, it was only another twenty feet before they reached the curtain. He held Lauren around the waist, refusing to let go of the growling barista. Her baseball bat was dripping blood from their last zombie encounter. He couldn't tell if it was a caffeine high or withdrawals at this point; either way, she was frightening.

"He's alive," somebody screamed.

Jessica held the door open, rolling her eyes. Victor let go of Lauren. The moment her feet hit the ground, she was screaming, raising the bat over her head.

"You know this isn't a movie," David said.

"Yet," Victor corrected.

They reached the curtain just in time to see Min on the ground with a zombie hovering over her body. The man had a sword protruding from his chest, seemingly unfazed by the blade. Victor watched as Lauren clubbed him with a baseball bat, knocking him down to the floor.

As he got back to his knees, she swung upward, catching

him under the chin and sending him onto his back.

"Mom!" Jessica scream, running to Min and helping her to her feet.

"Did they bite you?" Min asked.

"No," Jessica said, hugging the tiny woman.

"Good," Min said, "I won't need to kill Victor."

Tina reached for the blade, pressing her foot down on the man's chest. Lazarus knocked her backward, causing her to fall on her butt. She slid the blade along the floor to Victor.

"Oh no, scary zombie, don't kill me," she mocked.

Victor grabbed the sword and swung at the man's outstretched hands. Tina screamed for real as the two hands hit the ground and scurried away from her. With both hands on the hilt, Victor swung as hard as he could, the blade wedging itself into the man's spine. Lazarus fell to the ground, his reanimated corpse gone still.

"School's out," David said.

Jessica slapped the boy across the face. "No, David. No."

"Something's wrong," said Cadence.

"What?" Asked Xander.

"The zombies aren't moving." She pointed to the undead horde still holding the parents inside the auditorium. "Something's controlling them."

"He's not the final boss," said David.

* * * * *

"We're missing something," Cadence said as she tried to recall every piece of zombie pop culture.

"What's different in the third movie?" asked Xander.

"This isn't a movie," yelled David.

"Somebody the heroes don't suspect shows up. There has to be a sacrifice. The stakes are higher. The original cast doesn't survive. There's always a weird twist." Every zombie movie she ever watched flashed in front of her. She tried to recall the twists in the plot.

"Not all of us are making it out of this one, Cadence."

Cadi saw the bandages on Mrs. V's arm. The blood had already soaked through and the veins in her arm were already swelling. The librarian didn't make eye contact, instead, she stared ahead, trying to keep a stoic expression on her face.

"No..." muttered Cadence.

"I'm going to kill you all,"screamed Lazarus.

"Seriously," Cadence yelled as Lazarus struggled to pull the sword out of neck. "Why won't you stay dead."

"Cadence," Mrs. V whispered, "you need to get the rest to safety. I've got him."

"We're not leaving you."

"You said it, not everybody makes it out this time."

Cadence bit back the tears. The woman had been like a surrogate mother to their wayward band of degenerates. If it wasn't for her sagely wisdom, they'd have died during the first zombie outbreak. The former goth didn't want to start ugly crying.

"Beau would be proud."

"Keep them alive, Cadi."

Hello terrified parents and zombie slaying faculty. It has come to my attention that you think you'll make it out alive. Let me assure you, there is absolutely no chance you'll survive. I appreciate your cooperation in my well-executed revenge.

"Fannie!" Lazarus cried out.

Mrs. V grabbed the bat from Lauren.. "Kids, get away,"

she said as she choked up on the bat. Kevin grabbed Tina's hand and backed away with David and Jessica. "This is going to get messy."

In the back of the room, zombies started jumping into the crowd of parents. Screams filled the auditorium as parents tried to flee the massacre. The horrific scene in the back of the room distracted her long enough that a single zombie made it onto the stage. The boy Xander had arrived with lunged at Kevin. As the boy grappled with the undead student, he stepped into a lever just off stage. A trap door opened underneath the teenagers, dropping them somewhere underneath the stage.

"Victor, get them!"

Kevin fell backward with the zombie still trying to chomp at his face. As the trap door started to shut, the Marine ran and skidded across the floor, falling into the trap. The door shut, cutting them off from the kids she was determined to protect.

Xander pulled at her arm. "We need to leave, Cadi."

"I can't," she said as she watched Mrs. V club Lazarus in the head with the bat.

Lauren stumbled past them, her eyes darting back and forth. "Where am I? How'd I get here?"

Xander pulled Cadence behind the curtain as parents tried to climb up the stage to get away from the zombies.

"We can fight," Min said, breaking her from her stupor.

Cadence shook her head, trying to hide the tears. "No," she said. "We have a final boss that needs to die."

7:58PM

Cadence exited the side door into the quad next to the auditorium. Typically, this space was filled with the noisier students, the theater kids, and their arch-nemeses, the band geeks. Stairs all around led down to a "pit" where the students would lounge and relax between classes.

The only exits were the hallway near the half a dozen glass doors--leading into the courtyard and parking lot--or a narrow doorway near the base of the pit, leading into the music performance space. Zombies blocked both of them.

"We need to pick a direction," Xander said.

"I'm out of steam," Lauren said. "Unless you're hiding chocolate-covered espresso beans, I'm tapped."

Cadence contemplated running down the narrow hallway, hoping they could push back the zombies until they reached the band room. If they made it that far, they could escape into the main corridor. It was a Hail Mary; the chances of them making it out alive were slim.

"We're surrounded," Xander said. "Min, you go left, I'll go right."

"It's a good day to die, white man."

A screeching from the parking lot made the zombies turn. Cadence pushed Xander. "I don't care what it is, run."

"What she said," Min said, following them down the stairs toward the center of the pit.

"Everybody down." Xander pulled the three to the ground, covering their heads the best he could.

* * * * *

"I can tell you're turning."

"I can't tell you're a cretin," Mrs. V dodged a parent running across the stage. Her arm had gone from hurting to almost numb. In all the years she had been hunting down zombies, she still didn't know what to expect. How long before the infection killed her? How long after that till it brought her back?

"When you die, you'll just be another one of my puppets."

The screams from the audience was already starting to subside. With so many people packed into a tight space, there was no avoiding the undead. She trained the others to lure them into open areas when fighting. Zombies thrived in confined spaces. If they were any other humans, she'd have felt remorse. No, the parents of suburban high school students were some of the vilest creatures. Their attitude would be improved as the living dead.

Lazarus threw a parent to the side as he stomped toward her. The bat cracked against the man's head, throwing him along the ground. "Doesn't look like they're puppets anymore," said Mrs. V.

The man's skull dented inward. Despite his damaged brain, he shook it off. "Of course, leave to that Fannie Shelly. You probably remember killing her twin. She's not quite the scientist her sister was, but she was always easier to work with."

"It appears she isn't a fan of your management style."

"I'll kill her once I'm done with you."

"With bad lines like that," she stalked over to the man and swung the bat again, hurling him across the stage, "I can see why she hates you."

* * * * *

Glass rained across the quad. Steel beams gave way as the car swung around, skidding through doorways. Dozens of zombies were thrown across the quad. Cadence lifted her head just in time to see part of the roof collapse over the doors, making it impossible for zombies to escape.

"What the hell," she said, shaking glass out of her hair.

"The cavalry is here," Xander said.

"Too late to set up the joke," Lauren said.

"Did somebody say they needed the cavalry?"

Cadence's eyes went wide as the door of a Lexus creaked open. "Follow me if you want to live."

Cadence ignored the zombie crawling toward her, stepping on its hand, then its back as she approached the cheerleader. "I saw you die."

"I got better."

"But you..."

"You're ruining my save," Olivia whined. She punched a zombie, sending it flying backward. "Oh yeah, Bee Tee Dubs, I'm even more awesome now." She kicked a zombie. Her sneaker caught it under the jaw, removing the front of the dead parent's face.

"I already want to kill her," Min mumbled.

* * * * *

The zombies on the stage ignored her. It couldn't be a good sign that they no longer saw her as food. If anything, that terrified Mrs. V more than being eaten by the lower middle class. Before the infection killed her, she was going to finish this last fight.

Lazarus' head already started to reform, expanding like a balloon until the dent was almost impossible to see. She was starting to understand how Sonya kept appearing before. It was going to take more than a baseball bat to kill this man.

"We're so close to finding the cure for aging."

"You've killed tens of thousands of people just to make a designer hand cream?"

"We had to find a large enough trial group."

"You decided to infect people for your experiment? Instead of a controlled, double blind experiment where you give your data to the FDA's Center for Drug Evaluation and Research, you decided to skip to the end?"

The man cocked his eyebrow, surprised at her knowledge of the drug approval process. "While I'm impressed--"

"You shouldn't be. I'm a librarian."

She drew the bat back, and took one last swing. Her hands could barely hold onto the piece of wood. Lazarus held up his arms, blocking the blow. Pain raced through her limbs, and she realized the bat had already fallen out of her hands.

"You can barely stand, librarian."

She started to laugh. It had been a long journey, but she was ready for it to finally end. "I'm coming home, Beau."

The librarian tore at her blouse, until the black kevlar underneath was visible. Wires crossed her chest, connected to a single pin near her right breast. With the pull of the pin she wrapped her arms around the businessman. "You don't fuck with the librarian."

* * * * *

"So, are we going to run and save the day? Or did I show up during the part where I deliver a lengthy monologue about how I got here?"

"Part of the movie where we run and you try to keep up," Xander said as he kicked a zombie in the face. He pointed to the closest doorway. "Keep up."

"Thanks, Olivia. I'm so glad you could save us, Olivia. My, you're looking even more beautiful than normal, Olivia."

"Shut up, cheerleader," Min said as she trotted toward the door.

"You didn't by chance think to bring some dark roast?" Lauren asked.

"Sorry we didn't search for you, Olivia. We hope you're okay, Olivia."

"I said shut up!" Min yelled.

BOOM.

An explosion erupted from inside the auditorium. Olivia ducked and covered her head, waiting for the roof to come falling down. Cadence stood frozen, staring at the wall shared by the auditorium, oblivious to the zombie shuffling toward her. The goth girl took a small step forward, holding up her hand as if she reached toward an invisible object.

Olivia jumped down the stairs. The palm of the cheerleader's hand caught the zombie under the jaw, ripping off its lower mandible. The zombie continued trying to gnaw at the woman, it's tongue slathering her shoulder in spit. With another punch to the head, the zombie stopped moving and collapsed on the ground.

"Cadence, this is when we're supposed to run."

The cheerleader's friend hardly acknowledged her. Shaking the girl, Cadence's eyes focused on the girl. "What's wrong you--"

"Mrs. V is dead."

Olivia deflated a little at the words. "Oh."

"She--"

"Tell me about it when we're safe."

Cadence didn't make any attempt to run.

The cheerleader grabbed Cadence and slung her over the shoulder in a fireman's carry. The lights flickered and shut off, leaving the room in near pitch darkness. "Thanks for keeping me alive, Olivia."

Olivia stepped over a crawling zombie and spun, using Cadence's feet to knock another zombie to the ground. She caught up to Xander and Lauren, and followed them through the hallway.

"She died a warrior's death," Min said as she followed.

"Save the cheerleader, save the world, my ass!" Olivia bellowed as she ran.

8:33PM

Jessica ran her hands over her neck and down her body, inspecting for broken bones. Her eyes opened to a dim red glow shining from an emergency light overhead. Half her body rested on a soft pillow top, a cushion of some sort.

"I knew the senior talent show had a trap door," Tina mumbled.

"Thank God," Jessica said. "Kevin, are you okay?"

She waited for a response, but could only make out slight growling. "David, please tell me that's you growling."

"My head hurts," David groaned.

She couldn't see him, but she was thankful the little dork had survived the fall.

Victor stood over her, holding out his hand. "We had company, I took care of it."

Getting to her feet, she squinted, barely able to make out the source of the noise. A snarl startled her. Sam. Suspended in the air with a spear through his chest, the annoying classmate growled, swinging his arms in hope a meal got too close. She touched the end of the spear, making it vibrate with a twang.

"I'm not going to ask why the theater company has actual spears," Tina said.

"Authenticity," Jessica said in disbelief.

"You know, this school had problems before the zombies,"David said.

Jessica couldn't argue with his logic. Another groan filled the basement. She and Victor spun around, ready to lunge at the first thing that moved.

292

"You've got your mom's reflexes," he said.

"Lot of good they've done me so far."

"It's Kevin," Tina said.

Jessica waded through a sea of clothes littering the floor and reached the boy. The moment she got close, she could see the awkward angle of his leg. Tina was already moving, searching for something in the sea of mannequins.

"We're going to need to make him a splint if he's coming with us."

It was the first time Jessica had dealt with Tina since their quad death match. There was a sigh of relief that they wouldn't have to fight again. "Kevin, Tina's going to get you bandaged. We'll be out of here in no time."

"No, leave me behind."

"We're not leaving you behind," Jessica said, annoyed he'd even suggest it.

"You won't make it, I'll slow you down."

"The kid has a point," Victor said.

Kevin shot up, hissing from the pain. "Wait, you can't do that."

"He has a point," Tina said.

"What?"

"Maybe we should put him out of his misery now," David said.

Kevin's face gave away his shock. His mouth hung open, stuttering as he tried to find something to defend himself with. Jessica started laughing at the expression. "We're shitting you. We'll get you bandaged up."

"You're all jerks."

"You have some pain killers? Cause this is going to hurt." Tina started tearing strips and breaking pieces of wood to make a splint. "It's going to hurt a lot."

Jessica turned to Victor. "We need to get back to the others."

"I know," he said. "There are a lot of zombies and we have no weapons."

"What do you think we should do?"

Jessica eyed the Marine. They had done everything they could to survive. They made it to the auditorium. They were supposed to kill the big bad and be done with this nightmare. Nothing seemed to be going according to plan.

"Jess, we're not exactly ready for a fight. I don't think we're in any shape to help the others."

"No," she said, determined to help her mother. "What would Cadence do in this situation?"

"She'd give a speech or something. She might rally the troops and talk about how we could be humanity's last stand."

"Sounds inspiring."

"Or they'd have a clothing montage?" Victor suggested.

She laughed. "You're kidding me."

The Marine slowly shook his head. "I don't joke about a clothing montage."

"Oh dear..."

* * * * *

The dim red emergency lights made it more terrifying. In front of them, a long stretch of hallway. Behind, a wall of zombies clawing at one another to get a chance at fresh meat. Cadence was starting to get tired thinking of herself as meat.

"They're catching up," Lauren said.

Runners didn't tire.

The muscles in her legs pushed harder. She passed Xander. Grabbing onto a door handle, she caught him around the waist, snapping him backward. "We can't outrun them." She shoved the door open to the suite of rooms that served as the guidance department and shoved him inside. Olivia hip checked Min, knocking her into the room as she shoved Lauren into the doorway.

"Keep running!" she yelled.

The zombies were fresh. It meant they'd be more agitated, lively, and more determined to reach food. Cadence bent down. As a zombie charged her, she grabbed its waist, hurling it onto its back. Xander grabbed her by the shirt and pulled her into the office.

"You guys were way more fun last time this happened," Olivia said panting.

"Do you even breathe?" Min asked.

"Funny story--"

Cadence pulled the handle of the door, a zombie arm stopping it from shutting. She held onto the handle, Olivia helping hold it shut. Xander wedged his gun through the crack and pulled the trigger, sending zombie brains flying through the air.

"One bullet left."

Cadence opened the door enough to let the zombie fall backward and slammed it shut. She reached for the lock and realized there was none. "No fair."

Fear. It had been material for a novel, but now, with Mrs. V dead, the reality of dying made the zombie apocalypse a lot less fun. She let go of the door and turned, pushing Xander and Olivia to follow Min and Lauren down the long hallway. Her shoes fought to find traction on the industrial carpet.

Hundreds of zombies forced the door to collapse into the guidance suite. Stealing a glance over her shoulder, she watched as the undead fought to free themselves from the tangle of limbs and pursue.

Doors lined the hallway, leading to the individual offices of school psychologists. Whipping open one of the doors, it caught a zombie, forcing it to stumble and create a mound of bodies.

Cadence repeated the motion. Again. A third time. Zombies tripped and fell. Their tenacity was only overshadowed by their lack of coordination. She focused on the length of the hallway and saw Min holding a fire extinguisher. Cadence ran past as Min was already filling the hallway with white powder.

Cadence sped past Xander, who had his gun out. His .45 fired. The force of the explosion nearly knocked her to the ground. She barreled into the door at the end of the suite that would lead them back into the main hallway. The sound of growling in the mist of white made her throw caution to the wind.

She opened the door.

"No zombies out here?" asked Olivia.

"No."

"Good," said the cheerleader.

"We're not done running," Xander said, pointing down the dark hallway.

Min whooshed past them. "No Asian buffet tonight."

Cadence followed the tiny woman into another long dark hallway lined with lockers. She hoped Victor was having more success hiding than they were.

* * * * *

"Victor, you look ridiculous," Kevin said propping himself up on a bench. Pain radiated through Kevin's leg, but thanks to Tina's brace, he could at least move a little.

The Marine inspected the ruffles of his Victorian doublet. "Says you." He straightened his vest and rolled his neck to the side cracking it. Fastening the top button, the collar completely covered the skin up to his face. "Practical for the zombie apocalypse, and dashing if I do say so myself."

"Yeah, this is not going to work," Jessica said, staring down at her brown bra and Native American inspired skirt. "This is too many forms of racist."

Kevin's eyes lit up as she stepped into the light. He remembered seeing the school's production of Peter Pan, and the girl who played Tiger Lily did not look this hot. The woman's abs were more than visible in the light. Her hips shook enough that the tassels of her skirt danced back and forth. "Yeah," she said, "so racist."

"At least I'm zombie bite proof." David hopped out from the mannequins. With each little jump, the thousands of little metal links in his chainmail vest jingled. "What play were they putting on?"

"Good news," Jessica said, holding up a sword, "the props department spared no expense." She swung it back and forth, slicing through the air. "Not quite balanced, but it'll do in an apocalyptic pinch."

Victor pulled a sword off a rack of weapons. He held it up to the light, testing the weight. "Yeah, this will do nicely."

A thump from above reminded them that zombies weren't too far away. Victor slid his sword into a sheath he had tied around his waist. He started for the door and paused. "Wait, where's the blonde?"

"Tina?" Kevin called out.

"Clothing montage worked," came Tina's voice.

In the middle of a poorly painted backdrop for *Cats*, Tina pulled the tie off her hair, letting it cascade down onto her shoulders. Kevin was thankful the dark room hid his expression. Her torso was covered in a tight metal breastplate inspired by Roman gladiators, shrinking her waist and emphasizing her breasts.

"Holy shit," Jessica said.

"Oh this?" Tina said, adjusting a gauntlet. "Glad they had something in my size."

"What the hell kind of play did that come from?" asked Victor.

"Ben-Hur, the musical," said Jessica.

"We ready?" asked Victor. Kevin ignored him, instead focusing on Tina running her hand up and down a six foot spear. The teen boy found himself growing increasingly uncomfortable.

"Let's go," Victor repeated. "Now that blonde gladiator has won the award for least practical costume, we're ready to face the dead."

"Damn straight we are," Tina said, stomping past Victor and flinging open the door. "Brutus, keep up while I go Holy Roman Empire on these bastards."

9:11PM

"Being tied up to a table for five years does not make for good cardio."

"Shut up, cheerleader," Min said.

"I'm glad to see nobody has tamed Min."

Xander was happy to find out Olivia was alive. Sort of. While the zombies might not try to tear her limb from limb, they wouldn't be so kind with the rest of them. He kept to a slow trot behind his wife, but he found Olivia was continuing to slow. He jogged alongside her. "You doing okay?"

"I'm going to die," Olivia gasped, panting for air. Sweat poured down her forehead, soaking the collar of her shit. "Remind me to get one of those treadmill desks if I survive."

"You're doing fine," he lied. "Besides, if you lost any more weight, I'd miss--"

"Nothing you're about to say is a compliment," she barked.

Bodies littered the ground. If zombies only chewed here and there, the victim came back to life. No, these dead students had had their heads removed by starving zombies. Every so often, a zombie lay on the floor with a hole in its forehead, or missing its skull. The students fought back, but even exposing them to the realities of the zombie plight hadn't prepared them for this. A sophomore from his government class laid on her back with an arrow sticking straight up from her eye socket. *Maybe some of them survived,* he thought.

"We need some weapons," Xander said.

"And coffee," Lauren added.

"I'll kill them with my bare hands," Min bellowed.

"Why are you running then?" Olivia asked.

"Low chi."

"Sure, I believe that."

Xander stopped as he came to the thick wooden door leading to the chemistry lab. "Hey, in here."

"Shouldn't we be going after the villain?" asked Olivia.

"We need weapons."

"I'm not sure a scalpel and frogs in jars are going to help."

Xander ignored Olivia's cynicism as he opened the door. "Everybody in."

There weren't as many running zombies following them. Other than the stroller-jogging moms of Boxford, it seemed the rest were typical slow crawlers.

As a hundred more zombies entered the long stretch of hallway, a sense of dread washed over him.

"Oh shit," he said.

* * * * *

It had only been a week since David had arrived at the school. His parents would be glad he was making friends. Pushing the zombie back with his arm, he gave Jessica a chance to finish off the two already attacking her. As the freshman plunged a small dirk into the zombie's skull, he couldn't help but think, his parents would be proud.

"Chainmail win," he said as he pushed the twice dead zombie off him.

Victor brought down his sword, cleaving a zombie down the middle of its skull. He braced his foot against the parent's chest and heaved, pulling the sword free. "In the classroom; we can bottleneck them in the doorway."

David stood in the middle of the hallway, eyeing the doors on either side of him. To the left, the math lab; to the right, the engineering development lab. He was torn between his love of advanced mathematics, and his desire for artificial intelligence. Kevin robbed him of the choice as the crippled student opened the door to the robotics lab. The other's followed the kid into the room.

His heart jumped into his chest as a score of zombies filled the end of the hallway. He darted into the lab and slammed the door shut. "There are too many to bottleneck. We need to barricade the door."

Tina and Jessica were already pushing a giant lab table toward the door. The men jumped out of the way as the girls flipped the table, blocking it off. David ignored their yelling to help rig a stronger barrier. The room held two dozen work benches covered in pieces of robots yet to be finished. The variety of robots sitting on the tabletops reminded him of why he had been excited to join Boxford High. Tracing a conspiracy had kept him busy in his free time, but the school did have a reputation as being the best in the state.

David poked at one of the drones on the table, impressed with how durable the students had managed to make it. He recognized the base model. "This is military grade equipment," he mumbled.

A little green light signaled the drone's battery held a full charge. David pushed the on switch and the motors started to power up, lifting the drone a few inches up off the table. Next to the machine, a tablet screen turned on, showing images from the drone's camera. With a few tentative clicks, the drone rose into the air. He eyed the glass window above the door.

"Guys," David said with a smile, "I have an idea."

* * * * *

"Do you honestly think this is going to work?"

Xander shrugged his shoulders. "Honey, I know you're not a fan of me blowing things up, but unless you have a better idea..."

They had spent the last ten minutes ransacking the chemistry lab. Other than a few vials of sulfuric acid, a couple of bottles of alcohol, and some good scotch hidden in the teacher's desk, there wasn't much. Xander resorted to more explosive ideas.

The chemistry lab had two entrances. The one they came in through, and the one they all stood near. Between the two were stacks of desk and chairs, acting as a barricade.

Xander wanted to flood the room with zombies and lead them to a fiery death. She loved the man's creative thinking, but even this was getting crazy.

"He just wants to blow something up," Olivia said.

"Not enough fire in the bedroom?" asked Min.

"Burn," Olivia said, giving the Asian a high-five.

"I hate you both," Cadence sighed.

"This is where it started," Olivia said with a sense of nostalgia. "I mean, Mrs. Shelley and her coke bottle glasses, she made the formula right here."

Cadence hadn't thought about it. Ten years ago, this is where they first feared something crazy was happening. It wasn't much different now, crazy scientist, school full of zombies. At the rate they were going, Cadence feared she wouldn't make it out alive, and then her publisher would be *really* mad.

"You ready?" Xander called from across the room.

The moment she nodded, he flipped the lock on the door. He hesitated, watching the handle. The zombies managed to tear it open.

Cadence screamed for him to run. Her fists clenched. She held her breath as he spun and started running down the zig zag of tables placed to slow down the zombies. The odd smell in the air was getting thick; at any moment it'd mix with the stench of rotting corpses.

Xander jumped over a stack of overturned bench stools. Cadence gasped as woman in a business suit nearly caught the back of his shirt. Her husband jumped, arms outstretched, sliding underneath a stack of desks. Pulling his legs through, he kicked at the chairs, sending them falling over the oncoming zombies.

"Do we go now?" asked Lauren.

"Not till he's here," Cadence said.

"We should go now," Olivia said.

"No," Cadence growled. "Not till he's here."

Zombies poured into the room, already forty were shoving at the barriers, determined to reach their food. Skidding around the teacher's demonstration table, he nearly reached them. Cadence nodded to Lauren. "Get it ready."

The barista held a large bottle of clear liquid, giving a thumbs up. Cadence rested her hand on the door handle, ready to throw it open. The thumping in her chest reached a crescendo as a zombie got between Xander and his escape.

"Fine," Olivia said grabbing scissors out of a coffee cup. The cheerleader pinned the zombie to the wall as Xander ran past. With a jab, the metal sank into the zombie's skull. "Don't say I never did anything nice for you."

"Go!" Cadence screamed.

Cadence threw the door open as Lauren started pouring the contents of the bucket on the floor. She pushed Min and Lauren out the door while Xander and Olivia followed. The writer had a moment to notice the two hundred zombies gathered at the far door, trying to shove their way to the front of the dinner line.

"Shit," Lauren said letting the contents of the bucket continue pouring onto the floor.

A man in flannel and jeans spotted the survivors. Ignoring the group trying to force their way in the door, he started toward the group with a dozen zombies, following suit. Cadence ignored the impending chase as Xander pulled out his zippo and flipped it open. He struck the flint and tossed it into the liquid.

"We're supposed to run, right?" asked Lauren.

"Run!" Cadence yelled.

She didn't need to see the flame creep along the trail of alcohol. The sound of flames whipping back and forth was audible. They only made it the length of another classroom when the fire reached the chemistry lab.

Olivia stopped and turned around. "I expected more bang." Cadence pushed the cheerleader forward.

VOOSH. BANG.

* * * * *

David watched the screen of the drone. He ran his finger along the tablet, forcing the flying robot to turn a corner down the hallway. Slowly, it pushed forward. Swiveling the camera under the drone, he could see the horde of zombies being led away from their location. Tapping a button on the screen, the small craft flashed its lights and let out a buzz, attracting more zombies.

"You're a genius," Jessica said.

"I've been told."

Victor lifted a long piece of reinforced PVC pipe and inspected the two tanks of gas attached to the top. Shaking the device, he noticed the jar funneling marbles into the contraption. "Is it just m,e or did somebody make a potato canon that uses marbles?"

David looked up for a moment. "Careful, with that much pressure, those marbles could punch through steel."

"Good," the man said spinning the gas valves. "We ready to get out of here?"

The building shook. Everyone grabbed the closest piece of furniture yo steady themselves. "Holy shit," Tina said. "What was that?"

Victor couldn't hold back his smile. "That was the sound of Xander blowing up the chemistry lab."

"Why would he do that?" asked Kevin.

"It's not an apocalypse until we burn down the school."

* * * * *

Xander held onto a locker as he made his way to his feet. The wall between the chemistry classroom and the hallway was missing. The roof of the building was collapsing, burying hundreds of zombies. Even the closest living dead were dragging themselves along the floor, their lower halves torn away.

"That worked better than I thought it would," he said.

"Are you happy?" Cadence asked.

The ringing in his ears nearly drowned out his wife. "I just blew up a chunk of the school."

Cadence sighed. "Your need to blow up the school was one of the reasons I fell in love with you."

305

"White people are bad at foreplay," Min said.

"Amen sister," Lauren said.

"Preach it," added Olivia.

"No," Min pointed at the cheerleader. "This is minority time."

"Harrumph." Olivia pushed out her lower lip, pouting.

The first zombie emerged over the pile of fallen debris. Its howl sent shivers down Cadence's arms. "Okay, I'm starting to get annoyed."

"Zombie Queen," Xander smiled.

"I'm going to start writing *science-fiction*," she snapped at him.

"Through the gym and we'll be near the office," Min said.

Olivia raised a perfectly sculpted eyebrow. "Does this mean we have to climb a rock wall?"

"Uhm," Cadence said starting to jog toward the gym. "Maybe. A little."

"*Ugh*. I wish I'd stayed dead."

* * * * *

"Did you hear something?"

Angelica ignored the question. Shifting the van into drive, she started to pull out of the parking garage. "We're going to need to be far away from here when this place blows."

As the van blew through the ticket taker's lowered arm, they both gasped. Off in the distance, a bright light flashed. She slammed the breaks near the base of the underground garage, in plain view of Boxford High.

"Xander finally got to blow up the school," Hank said.

"It's about time," Angie said.

"Think he'll stop talking about it now?"

"God no," she said. "Now he's going to be all like, 'Remember that time I blew up the school?'"

"So true," agreed Hank.

"We should probably go save them," Angie said, slamming down the gas pedal.

"They'd be so screwed if we weren't around," said Hank.

"Let's go save the day," she said peeling out of the garage.

10:21PM

Tina used the butt of her spear to knock a parent to the ground. With a spin, she slammed the point of her spear into the man's face. Victor hated to admit it, but these kids weren't half bad. They exhibited teamwork, tag teaming zombies until the hallway was clear.

"Great job," Victor said.

"We appreciate your approval," Tina said.

"I'm detecting sarcasm."

The gymnast gave him a dirty look. If he didn't know better, he'd have thought Olivia had been reincarnated as a blonde. Victor hated to admit it, but he missed the cheerleader. She made the end of the world more exciting.

"So when we defeat this super villain, how do we get out?" Kevin asked.

"Doors are sealed tight," Jessica said. "When she dies, will the zombies die?"

"No," Victor replied. "Even if we stop her, there's still a few thousand zombies that need to get killed."

"How'd you do it last time zombies broke out in the school?" asked Kevin.

"We kind of burnt down the entire school with them in it."

"What about the mall?" asked David.

"Special forces showed up and killed them all."

"Do we have a plan to burn down the school again?" asked Tina.

"Nope."

"Can you call special forces?" she asked.

"Nope."

"So basically we're all stuck here. Trapped. Well, you know, unless we kill two thousand zombies and defeat an evil scientist."

Tina had a point. Victor thought about it for a moment. Tactically, they might be able to take out a few hundred. It had been hours since they had last ate. It had been hours since they had had a chance to rest. It had been hours since they had had access to Facebook.

No, they wouldn't make it.

"I might be able to get the doors open," David said.

* * * * *

"NOOOOOOOOOOOO!"

Cadence admitted, Olivia was screaming what she was thinking. As they burst through the doors into the gym, the two basketball courts seemed like a vast space to cover. Even if they made it across the rubber wasteland, at the end a rock wall awaited.

"Why the hell did you have them install a rock wall?" asked Xander.

"I'm going to let a zombie eat me for dinner," Cadence added.

"Too tired to climb," Lauren groaned.

Xander grabbed a baseball bat from a row leaning against the wall and shoved it into the door handles. The first zombie hit the door, slamming it's bloodied hand against the little window slit. The doors weren't meant to be secure, it'd only take a couple of zombies to jar it open.

"What do we do?"

Min smiled at him. "Get to the wall; I need to reach the supply closet."

Cadence could see the equipment lining the side of the gym. It looked like they were starting to prepare for unit in baseball. Her husband gripped another metal bat, taking a practice swing. "You heard her folks, more running."

Cadence hated him so much for saying it.

The door cracked, threatening to come off its hinges. She only had a split second to decide: endure the most painful suffering of her life, or be eaten by zombies. As the bat burst from the door handles, she decided to run.

"I hate you all!" she yelled.

The zombies were close on their heels. If she slowed, reaching hands would grab onto her shirt, or worse, her hair, and she'd be dinner. Cadence prepared to yell at Min for coming up with this stupid plan when she saw the petite woman reach into her gui and produce a remote control.

Min screamed, "Duck and roll!"

Cadence turned to see a break in the floorboards. A volley ball net was rising up out of the floor. It stopped at chest height. Cadence dove to the floor, sliding harmlessly underneath. Xander grabbed her by the hand and hoisted her up, pushing her to keep running.

"One more time!" Min yelled.

"So that's what our taxes have been paying for," Xander huffed.

Another net rose up from the floor, this time stopping at waist height. Cadence jumped, amazed that she cleared the mesh screen. With a glance over her shoulder, she was surprised at how many zombies were caught in the net.

"Keep running," Min said, veering right. Bleachers lined the wall. In the middle of all the seating was a narrow break leading to the supply closets. Cadence hoped Min was making the right call.

"We're almost there!" Olivia shouted.

The first net snapped under the weight of a hundred zombies. "Once this is over, sweetie, we're moving to the country."

"Deal," her husband said.

Olivia reached the wall first. The cheerleader fell to her knees, screaming with her arms raised toward the Heavens. "I am not climbing another wall. No. I swore. On a lab table for years, and this damned wall haunted me."

"Do we go up?" asked Lauren.

Cadence reached the room, gasping for breath. Shaking her head, she tried to catch her breath. "Not." Breathe. "Without." Breathe. "Min."

"She's going to have problems," Xander said, pointing toward the mass of zombies flooding the gym. They had almost reached the door. Even if she could get out, she'd have to climb the bleachers to get away.

"We need to help her," Cadence said.

"Bitch is on her own," Olivia said.

"Stop kidding yourself," Xander said. "You free yourself from an evil scientist and first thing you do is come back here. We all know you have a lady crush on Min."

Olivia began to swear, then stopped when she realized it was futile. "I hate you all."

"I have an idea," Cadence said. "You too, Olivia."

"Fine," the cheerleader spit. "But it's because we need her, not because--"

Xander put up his free hand. "We'll discuss your lesbian tendencies later."

* * * * *

"There is absolutely no way I can open the doors."

Jessica patted David on the back. "What about windows? Alarm? Can you get us access to our phones?"

The geek typed quickly. She couldn't figure out what he was doing. His fingers moved in a blur, launching one command after another. Each time David paused, he let out a low growl. It was almost amusing how angry he was getting at the machine.

"Windows, no. Alarm, no. Cell phone jammers, no."

"So what *can* you access?" Tina asked. "This is starting to look like a waste of time."

Jessica wanted to hit the girl. "Leave him alone; he's trying." She wanted to applaud her self-restraint. Mentally, she had the popular girl on the floor and was banging Tina's head off the ground. If they survived the zombie apocalypse, she'd kill the gymnast then.

"Guys," Kevin said at the window, "somebody's coming down the driveway."

"Keep trying," Jessica whispered to David as she shuffled toward the window. From the second story, they had a view of the parking lot, crammed beyond capacity with cars. Down the long driveway, a single vehicle shining its high beams approached the school.

"Maybe it's the cops," Kevin suggested.

"Somebody must think it's weird that parent's night is still going," said Victor.

A white van turned into the parking lot, slowing down to a crawl. The side of the van read, "Extreme Exterminators." Jessica started pounding the glass. "It's Angie and Hank. That's their undercover van."

"The glass is too thick, they'll never hear us," said Victor, grabbing a chair to smash against the window.

"Even if they can hear us, what can they do?" asked

Tina.

"Call for backup?" said Kevin.

"And how long until backup shows up? We kind of need heavy firepower now."

Victor grabbed Kevin and dramatically kissed the teen's forehead. "Kid, you're a genius."

"Uhm. I'm going to report him for inappropriate touching."

* * * * *

"Why the hell are cars lining the driveway?" asked Angelica.

"Didn't Jessica say something about Parent Teacher night?"

Angelica let out a low growl. "Of course. Two thousand undead children isn't enough of a challenge. Let's throw a couple thousand irate parents on top of it."

"It is the third movie in the trilogy," Hank shrugged.

Angelica slapped him. "No. You are not turning into Cadence. Stop that shit."

Hank rubbed the spot on his face, and returned to examining the hundreds of additional cars. It didn't shock him that the average cost of the cars in the parking lot were more than he made in a year. With the second cleansing of Boxford, there was a good chance the town would plummet into an economic depression. Hank sighed; his taxes were going to sky rocket.

"Do you think the doors are unlocked?" asked Angie as she coasted through the circle leading to the front door of the school.

Popping the car into park, they both got out. Angie opened the back and handed Hank a rifle. She slung a strap over her shoulder, loaded two more guns into her holsters, and mounted a gun on each thigh.

"Worried about zombies?"

She shook her head. "Teenagers."

Hank reached out and grabbed another gun. "Point made."

Hank walked up to the front door, grabbed the first door handle, and shook it violently. He moved down to the next set, and the set after that. Convinced all the doors were locked, Hank pressed his face to the glass looking inside. After a few moments, a zombie ran through the lobby, jogging toward the other end of the school.

"Yup, they're all definitely dead."

Angie shrugged. "At least Cadence can't drag us to another awful school play."

"Seriously," Hank said. "I was going to walk out."

"I was going to shoot the lead."

Hank rolled his eyes. "When we're done with this, I'm recommending you go back into anger management."

"I'm angry thinking about it."

Hank jumped at the sound of gun fire. He stepped back from where Angie shot. With two more bursts, they were both amazed that the bullets barely scratched the glass. He ran his finger over the spot, impressed. "That's half inch bullet proof glass. A rocket launcher wouldn't shatter that."

"I have things bigger than a rocket at the house."

Hank shook his head. "That'll take us an hour to get there and get back."

"What do you suggest, mister?"

Hank paused as the lights above the door started flashing on and off, flickering again and again. He checked inside the lobby and saw the lights weren't flashing inside.

"Is it morse code?"

Angie shook her head. Another wave of flashing started. She started counting each time the lights came on and went off. "Jesus, it's binary."

"You know binary?"

"Shut up, I know everything."

"What's it saying?"

She continued staring at the light. "S. O." Her eyes grew wide. "It's an S.O.S. Somebody's alive."

Angie walked into the parking lot and started checking out each of the classroom windows. "Hank, you're going to want to see this."

As he joined her in the middle of the traffic circle, he saw the lights on the side of the building lighting up to spell "help."

"How the hell are we going to help? We can't even get in," Hank shouted.

All the lights in school turned off except for one. Hank could see a man outlined in the glass. Squinting, he couldn't tell who it was, but he could see the man pointing to the left. "Are they telling us how to get in?"

"Just do what he says, I'll relay."

Hank started walking down the parking lot far enough he couldn't make out the figure anymore. Angelica yelled, "Stop." He waited for instructions. "Go back, I think?"

Hank worked his way through the cars, careful not to scratch any of the dozen Prius's parked in the lot. As he worked his way past the third Mercedes, he brushed up against the door, his gun scraping the paint. "Because I can."

"Stop."

"What the hell?" Hank yelled back.

"Go right," she yelled. He followed her directions.

"Stop."

Hank turned around to face the school. He was nearly half way across the parking lot and could barely make out the light in the window. "What am I doing?" he yelled.

"I have no idea. They're jumping up and down now."

Hank faced a Hummer in the parking lot. "Do they want me to drive through the school?" The smile spread across his lips as he figured it out. Quadrupled parked was a large U-Haul trailer.

"Angie, you're going to want to see this!"

* * * * *

Her body ran through the motions. Despite the growling outside the door and the scraping of nails, Min pushed aside the distractions. In the middle of an open field, she imagined a well. As her arms flowed through well-rehearsed moves, she imagined the well filling with water.

The supply closet was huge when not filled to the brim with sports equipment and mats for the cheerleaders. But in the center, there was enough space for her to move without hindrance. It only took three minutes for her to move through the entire sequence. The apocalypse outside could wait while she recharged her battery. Since the outbreak, she hadn't had the chance to unleash the carnage she knew she was capable of. That was going to change.

Min neared the final position and the well in her mind was overflowing with the clearest water. Her imaginary self reached into the pool of water, cupping her hands together, and brought the cool liquid to her lips at the same moment her body finished the final position.

Min opened her eyes; a golden ring glowed around her eyes. "Cadi's last book will have an Asian saving the day."

The T'ai Chi master removed a long slim, blade hanging on the wall, and slid it into her belt. She placed a quiver of arrows on her back and slid a bow over her shoulder. Pulsing in every limb of her body was the confidence granted to her by mastering her chi. The water of the well moved down her arm and reached her hand. Drawing back her arm, she focused on her breathing as she lunged her palm forward.

As the heal of her hand hit the center of the supply closet door, the wood splintered. The power of the punch sent the door flying backward, launching zombies in all directions. Emerging from the closet, her body moved with grace and a fluidity taught to Min by her grandfather. Each strike imploded a zombie's chest or decimated its skull. Each hit dropped another undead parent.

Scanning the area, she knew she was trapped. Even wielding this level of chi, she would never made it through the hundreds of zombies. Kicking a zombie in the chest launched it backward. With bleachers towering on either side of her, she started climbing. A woman in mom jeans grabbed her ankle. Min tried to smash her heels into its face, but found the zombie dodging her.

Her fingers started to slip when something smashed into the zombie's skull, sending it to the ground. Min pulled herself up until she reached the top of the bleachers. Near the rock wall, Xander and Olivia pointed the automatic pitchers in her direction. Another volley of baseballs launched at a hundred miles per hour, knocking several zombies to the ground.

While Cadence and Xander taught the students of Boxford all about zombie culture and how to spot zombies, Min had prepared the students. While Mrs. V filled the library with the latest zombie novels, Min diverted the school's budget. Unknown to the principal, the gym teacher was behind the budget shortage. It started with a few weapons, then an automatic volleyball court. During Christmas break, she had managed to requisition enough money from the turf field to build a second pool in the school.

Min reached into her gui and pulled out the remote and pressed a large blue button. The gym started to shake as the middle of the gym started to lower and separate. She hadn't figured out a way to fill the pool with water without being discovered. As zombies toppled into the huge pit, she found herself thankful she decided against using a hose from the locker room.

"Who the hell are you?" Olivia screamed across the gym.

Min ignored the cheerleader's heckling. Running along the top of the bleachers, she grabbed onto a rope used to test students' core strength. Pushing off from the wall, Min soared through the air, drawing her blade. Wrapping her leg around the in the rope, she let go, hanging upside down as she neared her friends.

The blade, forged by her great great grandfather, slid through the neck of three zombies without resistance. She reached the height of her ascent and grabbed the rope, preparing to send her spectators into a state of shock and awe.

Min let go as she neared her friends. Rolling along the ground, she jumped into the air. Punching with one fist, Min obliterated one zombie and severed the head of another. Turning slowly, she took satisfaction in the slack jaws.

"Time to kill a scientist," Min said with a steely gaze.

"I'm not climbing this wall," Olivia said.

Min walked over to the wall and twisted one of the small rock climbing grips. Part of the wall pushed in. "Coaches' offices."

Cadence stared in disbelief at the small warrior. "So you're the reason Rightoff was always complaining about budget problems."

"Didn't see that coming?"

Cadence shook her head. As the writer walked through the door, she pointed at the frame. "Did you get reinforced steel doors?"

"Admire when we're safe," Xander said pushing her in.

Min stared at her handiwork. A sea of zombies filled the empty olympic pool, while several hundred were walking around the edges still pursuing them. A toothy smile spread across her lips. Yes, they'd remember her machinations this day.

"Oh coffee!" Lauren said.

Or not, Min thought.

11:27PM

"We haven't even had a clothing montage," Cadence said.

"We are not stopping so you can change your clothes," Xander said.

"Min got a rally moment," Cadence argued. "Even Lauren got more coffee."

"Coffee. I have lots of coffee. Lots. Delicious coffee."

Xander smacked his forehead. "Don't use Lauren as an example."

Min held up her arm, signaling for them to stop at the corner of the hall. With a right turn, they'd be in the massive lobby of the school. High above them, a skylight let in light from the moon. It had been modernized, but it was the only part of the original school that was left standing from the last time zombies ravaged the school.

"The principal's office is the only room with a PA system," Xander reasoned.

Cadence peeked around the corner. She could make out the door to Mr. Rightoff's suite. Just beyond the door, housed in a small office, she expected another evil scientist to wait for them. Ten years ago, it had been a maniacal woman gone wrong. It only seemed fitting it be a craze relative bent on revenge.

The writer noticed the one thing missing in the lobby--a horde of zombies. Ms. Shelly had had a hoard of them surrounding her at the end, and even Bryce made them wade through a swarm of them for the final battle. Now, the only zombie in the middle of the hall was...

"Jesus," Cadence cursed, recognizing the boy she watched die earlier. "I'm done. I quit. No more discretion." Cadence grabbed the bat from Xander and walked into the lobby. The boy's smile remained plastered across his face, made even more disturbing by the missing chunks of skin around his neck.

Rob. It hadn't been enough to watch the jerk die the first time. Now, now Cadence got to exact her revenge. The zombie spotted her and shuffled its way toward her. The first swing connected with his shoulder, sending him to the ground. She drew the bat high above her head, waiting for him to get in position.

"This is for my one star," she muttered as the bat came whooshing down, crushing the zombie's skull. She didn't understand people who said achieving revenge left you feeling hollow inside. Right now, a sense of satisfaction coursed through her veins.

Clap. Clap. Clap.

"We're going to skip the monologue this time," Cadence laughed at the elder woman in a lab jacket. Charging, she brought the bat over her head, ready to club the living zombie to death.

Ms. Shelly's hand shot up, grabbing Cadence by the throat and lifting her off the ground. Cadence tried to swing the bat down, but the woman caught it, tossing it to the side. "No, I don't think that's how this is going to go at all."

* * * * *

"We need to get going!" Victor yelled. He held up the makeshift gun and pulled the trigger. Three marbles whipped through the air, striking two zombies in the head, burrowing in their skulls.

"Almost done," David said.

David snatched Jessica's iPod and slipped a cord into the auxiliary port. With a few more strikes of the key, he was done. "We're good," he said, grabbing his tablet. He smiled at Jessica's confused expression. "You'll see later."

Kevin's weight on his shoulder made it difficult to move. Struggling with each step, they made their way down the hall. As a zombie appeared, Jessica and Tina stabbed and swiped, removing heads and puncturing brains. Thankfully, the drone directed the zombie masses away from them.

"If we can get to the principal's office, I can open the doors." He hadn't been trained by a T'ai Chi master, nor was he a highly-skilled gymnast. Other than Kevin, David felt he was nothing more than dead weight in their band of teen survivors. At least he could lie. Whether or not he could open the doors, at least he could give them some hope.

Victor held his finger to his lips, urging them to be quiet. In the distance, David could see a line of undead just beyond the door. They needed to make their way to the first floor. The dozen undead didn't seem to be moving--just shifting their weight from one foot to the other, waiting for stimulus.

Tina's feet made no sound as she tiptoed to the door. Quietly pushing on the handle, she froze as the door made an audible *click*. Victor raised his marble cannon, ready to fire if they turned around.

With the door open, the student council president waved them in. Jessica snuck past, while David tried to help Kevin hobble his way to safety. The boys froze as one of the splints on Kevin's leg dragged along the ground. David held his breath, watching the back of the zombie's head only a few feet away. For a moment, he thought they had gotten lucky. One of the zombies appeared to be sniffing the air, turning in their direction.

A marble sized hole appeared in one head, then another. Victor shoved them both into the doorway. Jessica and Tina were fast to slam the door shut and braced themselves, using their weight to keep the mass at bay.

"We're too close to die now," Kevin said, using the stair railing to get back on his feet.

"I have a plan," Victor assured them.

"Is it a good one?" asked David.

"Did I say that?"

Victor unscrewed the container on his gun holding the rest of the marbles. He pressed his back against the doors, bumping back and forth as the zombies tried to push their way into the stairwell.

"Head to the lobby, I'll be there shortly."

David let out a long sigh. Today was as good a day to die as any. He shoved Tina out of the way and braced himself against the door. "You two take Kevin, I'll help Victor."

Jessica gave him a quick punch in the arm. "Don't die, hero."

"I'll take your advice under advisement," David said, feigning a smile.

"You're going to get us killed aren't you?" he whispered to Victor.

"I'm not making promises."

"If I die," David hissed, "I'm eating you first."

"If?" Victor's eyebrow raised made David question this decision.

"When," he grumbled.

"You ready to run?"

David nodded.

"Go."

David jumped away from the door and started for the stairs. He held onto the railing, jumping two and three stairs at a time. As he hit the landing half way down the stairs, he could see the barrage of marbles rattling around, falling down the steps. Victor grabbed onto the railing and jumped over, landing on the next flight. The zombies barreled onto the landing, stepping on the marbles and sliding along the cement floor.

David continued jumping down stairs as a zombie flew head first down the stairs. He caught up to Victor and another set of doors. Before Tina could close the doors to freedom, a zombie tackled David, sending him skidding along the floor. Clawing to get away, the zombie rested firmly on top of his legs, pinning him to the ground.

"Help," David yelled. "It's going to eat me. Help!"

His life hadn't been long, but it had been good. He thought about his mother and how she'd leave a plate for him at the dinner table at first. Then she'd start packing up his room until he was just a picture on the mantle. He'd want her to move on, to start a new life. David hoped heaven existed.

"Somebody get him," Tina said.

David opened his eyes and saw Jessica holding a bow. "We found our missing weapons."

"Oh," David huffed.

"Come on," Victor pushed the zombie off with his foot. "Stop praying and let's go save the others."

"How do you know they need saving?" asked Jessica.

"It's a trilogy," Victor finally admitted it; Cadence had rubbed off on him. "It's always up to the new cast."

Cadence fell to the floor as an arrow *thunked* into the side of the scientist's head. The mad woman pulled at the arrow, finally breaking off the shaft. Ms. Shelly roared as she brought up her sensibly-selected shoe to stomp Cadence.

"Can't a woman get revenge for her sister," she ground her on Cadence's chest. "I'm not asking for much, am I?"

Cadence tried to push the woman's foot off her chest. The writer could feel her lungs refusing to take in air. If her friends didn't move faster, she'd be sure to devour them all when she rose from the dead.

Lauren. Of course, it would be the barista from hell who came to her aid. Cadence contemplated dying, anything to not owe the woman a favor. If Lauren rescued her, Cadence would be buying her dark roast for the rest of her life.

Lauren's fist was drawn back as she lunged at the scientist. One punch, two punch, an upper cut, a volley of jabs; each round of punches did little to move the zombie. When Shelly swung the back of her hand, connecting with Lauren, her foot moved just enough for Cadence to roll away.

Blood burst from the zombie's neck, a dark gray goop. One arrow in the neck, another in the forehead, and with her last arrow, a shot directly into the eye.

Cadence scrambled to get to her feet. Xander picked up the bat, letting it bounce on his shoulder. They weren't new to the world of street-thug-worthy zombie slaying, but Cadence knew that without a plan, taking shots at Shelly wouldn't do anything but make her drag out her final monologue.

It happened exactly as Cadence predicted. Xander swung; Shelly ducked. He tried again, she knocked the bat away harmlessly. With a palm to the chest, Xander flew backwards. Cadence tried to scream, but found her voice caught in her throat as she struggled to breathe. The professionals were looking as if they had never done this type of thing before. Five on one, and Cadence and her friends were acting like amateurs.

"Which one of you killed Miss Shelly?"

Olivia raised her hand, then Min, even Xander followed suit. Cadence raised her hand out of obligation.

"I would like to point out, I, Lauren, am the only person who had no involvement in killing Miss Shelly." Lauren said.

"You killed Bryce," Olivia yelled.

"Bryce?" The Shelly sister barked. "You killed my dear, sweet, innocent--"

"I'm gonna cut you off right there," Olivia said. "Dear, maybe. Sweet, not really. *Innocent?* That psycho killed me."

"Weird when you say that," Min added.

"I will kill you all, one--"

"Yeah, gonna have to cut this short. Can we skip your master plan and just fight to the death?" Olivia asked.

"No more. No monologues. No zombies. Death. Death. Death," Lauren rolled her eyes.

If they survived, Cadence swore they would get Lauren into a rehab program. But with five on one, Cadence was feeling pretty good about their odds.

The writer cleared her throat. "You're trapped with us."

"Is she," came a voice from the second floor balcony.

* * * * *

Jessica could barely make heads or tails of the scene playing out in front of her. She reached the lobby just in time to see the teachers--the original class of the apocalypse--waging war on their villain. Both of them?

Xander, Cadence and Lauren were trading blows with a woman in a lab coat. They ducked, side stepped, and leapt out of the way of her wailing arms. Each punch they landed, every kick, it seemed nothing moved the scientist. Even as Xander snapped the woman's arm at the elbow, she only laughed in response.

"Olivia?"

The moment Victor said it, Jessica recalled all the stories they told around the table about the annoying cheerleader. They complained about the woman frequently, but it was obvious by how often her name came up, even her mom missed the woman's ramblings.

"Didn't she die?" asked Jessica.

"It's the zombie apocalypse, dead is a relative term," Victor said. "Kick some ass, cheerleader!" he yelled.

A red-haired woman with far more grace engaged Olivia and her mom. The woman moved like her mom, knives in each hand, deflecting each of Min's jabs. Jessica gasped as the woman lunged at her mom. Min skillfully pushed the blade aside, sidestepping the woman, sweeping to the ground, and knocking her attacker's legs out from under her. Jessica swore if they made it out alive, she'd take her mom's training more seriously.

"There's only room for one hot chick," Olivia said, jumping into the air and kicking the redheaded woman in the neck. Olivia dropped to her knees, cupping her hands as Min charged. Launching the T'ai Chi master into the air, Min flipped until her legs landed on her assailant's shoulders. With a precision strike, Min brought the blade down, driving it through the woman's skull. Jessica almost jumped a little with glee at her mom's victory.

"Bad ass bitches are back in action," Olivia smacked Min on the butt. "Glad I'm back yet?"

Jessica's jaw dropped as the woman her mom impaled sat up, pulling the sword from her skull. "Mom," she pointed.

Min turned around and started stomping her feet in a tantrum. "How many times do I kill you?"

"Not enough," the woman said.

Jessica watched as the gash on the woman's head vanished, stitching itself back together. It was obvious that they weren't going to win just stabbing the living zombies.

"Zombies," Jessica said, giving Tina an elbow. "Ready for a team-up?"

"Going to apologize for the fat lip?" the girl asked.

"No."

Jessica pulled up the bow. The first arrow soared across the lobby, landing square in the forehead of zombie. Practice arrows would have simply impaled themselves on the zombie's skull; she understood why her mom had gone the extra mile.

"Behind you," David yelled.

Spinning around, Jessica dropped to a knee and in a fluid motion pulled another arrow from the quiver, cocked it, and drew the bow. Towering over her, a zombie prepared to descend, it's jaw already stretching, preparing for a meal. With a twang, the arrow flew the two feet, shoving through the jaw of the zombie, into its skull.

Tina moved onto the next. The gymnast slammed the spear into a zombie's mouth and then kicked, knocking it off the end. With another couple of jabs, she dropped two more.

Jessica considered complimenting her, until Tina looked

over her shoulder with a smug smile.

"Oh, it's on," Jessica said.

* * * * *

"You were a model?" Olivia gave a disgusted look. "I mean, you're hot, but not model hot."

"So *you're* a cheerleader?," Sonya sneered. "Didn't realize they let uggos on the squad."

Olivia balled up her fist. Sonya ducked under the punch. The cheerleader's hand hit the brick wall, breaking the cement. Bones snapped and she started to cradle her hand, but stopped. Examining her fingers, the cuts on Olivia's knuckles had vanished; the bones popped back into place.

"I'm a superhero," Olivia whispered to herself.

Olivia stalked toward the redhead. The knife hit her torso and she flinched, expecting pain to run through her body. Sonya looked up from the blood pouring out of Olivia, and the cheerleader was smiling. "Looks like there's another undead super bitch in town."

"Oh no," Sonya laughed. "Too bad you can't do this..."

Dozens of zombies filled the exits of the lobby. Even with the teenagers stabbing and breaking necks, it'd only take seconds for them to be overrun with undead. Olivia was impressed with Sonya's ability to command zombies like the b-string cheerleaders.

"Let them go," Olivia said.

"You know that's not going to happen. Matter of fact, maybe I'll let you watch me kill them."

Movement behind Sonya caught Olivia's attention. Beyond the undead model, something large was outside the doors to the lobby. "Don't say I didn't warn you."

"I have an undead army. What do you have, second-rate

329

cheerleader?"

Olivia's smile widened. "I have batshit crazy friends."

* * * * *

It wasn't so different than the video games Hank played in the backroom of the dojo while Min taught classes. With both pedals floored, the legs of the exoskeleton powered up, sending him running.

There had been dozens of weapons in the back of the U-Haul, but he'd be a fool for not taking the biggest one for a ride. Hank fit snugly into the pilot's seat. With the cockpit closed, the eight foot tall robot looked like a wide stocky human with arms that almost touched the ground. With a flip of his right thumb, the rocket armed. The readout on the screen showed the glass doors as the target.

VOOSH.

The rocket hit the bullet proof glass. The doors tore from their hinge. As the mech slammed into the glass, he managed to scrape his way into the lobby. The moment he cleared the doors, the screen identified the undead. He clicked the automatic button and a gun on his shoulder spun to life.

The bullets flew, striking zombie after zombie. "Sorry," he yelled as Xander grabbed Lauren, pulling her to the floor. Heads exploded in every part of the lobby, sending bodies to the ground left and right. A light started blinking on the screen, warning him the machine was going to overheat.

He panicked and slammed the power button. The entire mech powered down and the cockpit doors opened. The remaining survivors blinked in disbelief. "Uhm. Get away from her you bitch?"

11:59PM

Jessica watched David, huddled on the floor, pull out his tablet. He pointed at the redheaded woman. "Go get her."

"Uhm, sure Mr. Bossy pants."

"I've got your back."

"How?" she asked, pursing her lips to emphasize her disbelief.

"This." The boy pressed an image on the tablet's screen. The familiar tone of the school PA speakers sounded. Usually it would be followed by a sports announcement or the football team participating in another shirtless carwash. Music pumped through the speakers.

Jessica recognized the song from her iPod. The heel of her moccasin boots tapped to the beat of techno music. Her mom described it as chi, but Jessica could only explain it as reckless abandon when music rolled through her body. In the depth of her chest, her heart beat in time with the music.

The redhead holding her mother's sword raised an eyebrow. "You think the B-squad can beat me?"

"Tina, sorry I punched you in the lip." Jessica said.

"About time," the gymnast leveled her spear at Sonya. "Sorry I didn't win."

"Oh no," Sonya mocked, "two kids think they--"

Jessica ran at the woman, ducking the swipe of the blade. In a well-choreographed dance, she moved just fast enough to dodge each thrust from Sonya. The smug look on Sonya's face started to fade, replaced but a sneer. The angrier she got, the more often Jessica managed to sneak jabs.

The music pumping in the school lacked the rich bass

typically seen at raves. If somebody pulled the fire alarm and the lights started flashing, it wouldn't be much different than the low budget basement parties she attended. Jessica snapped back to reality as Sonya's sword crashed against a metal spear.

"Saved by the cute chick," Olivia cheered.

"Use your chi!" Min called.

"Your mom sounds like Yoda," Tina said.

Tina pulled the spear back and Jessica was already in motion. Sonya shoved the blade forward, the edge grazing the black girl's shoulder. With a punch to the elbow and a twist of Sonya's wrist, Jessica forced the blade out of the woman's hand. Min had trained her well. Jessica caught Sonya's elbow in the chest and slid back along the floor.

Gasping for breath, Jessica realized her mom had been training her, not for the sake of discipline, but for this very moment. Tina couldn't move the spear fast enough. In seconds, Sonya had managed to wrangle the weapon away and with a heel to the chin, Tina flew backward, her back slamming onto the floor.

This moment. Her mother had known it would come down to the next generation to save them. The burden of being chosen washed off her shoulders as Jessica pushed herself upright. Climbing to her feet, Jessica knew that if she couldn't stop Sonya, nobody would be able to.

"David, track forty-seven."

The track changed. The speakers in the lobby had reached their threshold and at any moment, the bass would render them useless. The thumping of the bass matched the tempo of her heart beat. For a moment, Jessica reached her rave nirvana, the happy place where she stopped existing and there was only music.

"The chi," her mom said.

To Jessica, Sonya looked like she was moving in slow motion. Jessica caught the woman's leg. Elbow down, she drove it into the woman's joint. The crack was loud enough, even Tina turned her head in disgust. Sonya tried to drive two knuckles into the teen's neck, but Jessica rolled backward, putting distance between her and Sonya.

With a snap kick, Jessica hurled Sonya against the wall. She grabbed the woman by the back of the head, and continued slamming it into the wall again and again. On the third smash, blood started to smear along the tiled wall. Jessica let out a groan as the woman's broken elbow hit her in the stomach.

"You're not half bad," Sonya gasped.

"Shut up," Jessica said.

Sonya raised the spear, ready to lunge, when a red dot appeared on her head. The bullet pierced her skull and the right side of Sonya's skull exploded, showering Tina in blood and gray matter. Jessica had a moment of satisfaction as the girl's face looked like a crime scene.

"I told you to stay dead, bitch." Angelica held a rifle against her shoulder, smoke smoldering from the barrel. Jessica made a mental note to include Angie on the Christmas list this year. She had never connected with the woman; far too serious for Jessica's taste. Now, Jessica planned on talking the woman out to dinner.

Sonya laughed.

The energy pulsed through Jessica's body. She pushed it into her hand until it felt as if it might pop. With a deep breath, Jessica put all her body weight into the move. As the heel of her palm connected with Sonya's sternum, she felt the explosion course through her body. She followed through like her mom taught her. Bones snapped, crushed, and pulverized as Jessica extended her arm.

"Holy shit," Tina yelled.

The energy intensified as Jessica gripped Sonya's spine. Pulling, the bones snapped, unable to resist her iron will. Jessica brought up her foot, pushing the woman backward. The sound of wet smacking flesh halted as she raised Sonya's spinal cord for all to see.

"Not half bad my ass," Jessica whispered to the woman.

* * * * *

"Olivia," Xander reached into his pocket, pulling out several small vials. "You need to figure out that Jedi mind trick and control the zombies."

"Yeah, I'll get right on that," Olivia snapped.

"Two living dead are mopping the floor with us. We already exhausted our T'ai Chi masters. We don't exactly have much for round three."

"So much pressure," Olivia grumbled.

"How is it any different than being a cheer captain?"

Olivia's head snapped upright. "I *am* the cheer captain."

"What have I done," Xander mumbled.

Olivia stood, taking scope of the room. Angelica was trying to knife yet another scientist to death. As Jessica held up Sonya's spine, Olivia was very aware of the family resemblance.

The rest of the group had started to huddle in the middle of the lobby as zombies threatened to descend upon them. Olivia couldn't have her friends be bitten by the dead. She feared one of them would come back, and then she'd have to spend eternity with them. With her luck, Lauren would be her zombie companion for life.

334

"No," she whispered. The word spilled out across her lips. Olivia expected the zombies to stop, to obey her every word. They continued closing in.

"Augh!" she growled. If this happened on her squad, she'd have made sure every person know her displeasure. The first time she slapped one of the girls, Olivia knew she was destined to rule with an iron fist. There would never be room for those not willing to fall in line.

"No!" she screamed. "No. No. No. No." The cheerleader stomped her fist and screamed. When they continued moving, she let out a wail loud enough that even Xander covered his ears.

The horde stopped.

"Who's the zombie queen now, Cadi?"

"Good girl," Xander said. "I knew there was a reason I didn't put a bullet in your forehead."

"You always say that," she gave a slight giggle.

"Tina," he slid the vials along the ground.

The girl slid across the ground, snatching two of the vials. She jumped up, popping the corks. Jessica tossed the woman's spine on the ground. Emptying one vial on the zombies vertebrate. The hissing started. The other vial she poured in the gaping hole in Sonya's head. Both parts dissolved in puddles on the ground, leaving little chance for recovery.

"Is she like dead, dead this time?" asked Olivia.

* * * * *

"I told you to stay dead, bitch!" Angelica yelled over the blaring speakers.

The moment Angelica took stock of the characters still fighting in the room, it became obvious a star player was

335

missing. The moment she made eye contact with Cadence, the pained look on the girl confirmed her worst fear. Five years ago, the machinations of a greedy corporation stole her father. Now, it robbed her of a surrogate mother.

The woman in a lab jacket screamed for all to hear. "None of you will make it out alive! I'll make you suffer for killing my sister."

"You!" Angelica threw her rifle to the side and reached to her hips, removing bayonets from their sheaths. Stalking forward, anger fueled every step. It had been hard enough to lose her father, but he had died in the line of duty, a warriors death. Renee on the other hand, she didn't deserve to die in a high school at the whims of a science project gone horribly wrong.

"She only wanted to keep the world young," the scientist said.

Angelica didn't have pithy words for the woman. There were no comebacks or sly retorts that would make this go any smoother. She wanted to watch the woman die, slowly and painfully

Without fanfare, the blade in her right hand jammed up through the scientist's jaw and into her brain. Angelica gave the knife a slight turn as she pulled it out, letting the serrated edge cut bone. She prepared to cram the other knife in the woman's temple when the scientist grabbed her arm.

"Haven't you learned," the woman hissed, "I can't be killed."

The high pitch nasal-y sound of the woman's voice enraged Angelica. From battling Sonya so many times, Angie knew the moment she swung at Shelly's forearm, the knife would pass through as if Shelly were cutting butter.

"Hey, I need that," cried Shelly.

Angelica stepped outside the woman's swinging stump. The moment the punch cleared, Angie sliced along the woman's back, severing the muscles used to lift the arm. Half paralyzed, Shelly growled, lunging with her remaining hand.

Grabbing the woman by the trench coat, Angie rolled backward, taking the scientist with her. Kicking off against Shelly's stomach, she flipped the woman, sending Shelly onto her back. Angelica scurried to climb on top of her. Shelly's stump slammed Angie to the ground, knocking the wind from the living woman's lungs.

"You think you csn win?" Shelly climbed on top of Angie. The stump had already started to grow, repairing the damaged tissue and forming a hand from the tip. "I have an army. What do you have?"

Zombies had circled the group, forcing them into a tight circle. Had they each had guns, they may stand a chance against the hundred living dead. Without the appropriate amount of fire power, Shelly was the only thing standing between them and certain death.

"Let them go," Angelica said.

"Why would I do that?" Shelly asked.

"Good sportsmanship," yelled Hank.

"We wanted to invent the fountain of youth, but what we found is so much better. My children," Shelly gestured to the crowd. "They are all my children."

"Your kids are ugly," Min shouted.

"And now, they're going to kill your family."

"No. No. No. No. No."

Angelica had nightmares about the cheerleader. The obnoxious girl had haunted her since the mall. The sound of her voice should have been nails on a chalkboard, but when

Shelly's face flushed with anger, Angie smiled.

"Looks like your kids hate you," Angelica said.

"Who's the zombie queen now, Cadi?"

"No!" yelled the scientist. "I am your maker! You obey me. You can't--"

The moment the woman removed her weight from Angelica's chest, Angie reached down to her belt and pulled off a small cylinder. "Insert witty comment here, bitch."

Angelica crammed the object into the woman's mouth, breaking teeth as Angie wedged in between Shelly's jaws. Shelly clawed at the object in an attempt to pull it out. Angie rolled away along the ground. As Shelly turned to her, Angie raised her hand, holding a small pin.

The grenade didn't explode, instead starting with a low hiss. As the material inside mixed with the surrounding oxygen, the red flame turned blue, then white. Shelly's mumblings faded as the grenade vaporized portions of the woman's face and neck. Within seconds, Shelly appeared to be melting to the ground, her body nothing more than an oozing mess.

* * * * *

"Hardcore," Cadence muttered.

With each breath the writer sucked in, it became more and more apparent she had a cracked rib. The baseball bat was just beyond her reach. If the zombies around her decided to lunge, she might be able to grab it and kill one or two before the pain overwhelmed her.

"What now?" asked David.

"Don't eat us. Don't eat us. Don't eat us." Olivia continued repeating the mantra with her eyes clenched shut. The cheerleader held up her hands, pushing the air as if she were physically keeping the zombies at bay.

"If I can get to the mech," Hank said, "I can mow down the room."

The first zombie's head exploded. In between tracks on the intercom, the lobby filled with the familiar sound of whizzing bullets. A red dot appeared on a nearby zombie's head, a moment later it fell to the ground.

Cadence kept her head down as bullets flew past the hole created by the exoskeleton and pelted the undead. The music stopped. "What's happening?" David yelled.

"The cavalry," Hank said.

Gunfire filled the room as men in black vests walked in the door in a tight formation. The thick black collars around their necks gave away their membership to the anti-zombie unit Cadence and her friends worked with. Cadence reached out for Angelica to try and pull her out of harm's way. With her shoulder's slumped, her friend walked toward the door looking completely and utterly defeated.

"Good luck, Angie," Cadence muttered.

Within the hour, over a hundred armed men had stormed the school. They sat outside on the landing the students had to climb every day to enter Boxford High. The adults sat to one side, while the four remaining students circled around Kevin in the ambulance.

A man in black barking orders into his phone approached them. Cadence assumed he was in charge of their rescue. "How did you guys know to come here?"

"V called my commanding officer. She declared a Code Z."

"But the phones--" Xander started.

"She said the mini boss had a satellite phone? Any idea what she meant?"

The group started laughing at the statement. "Inside joke."

"Once we're done here, we'll be moving onto the research done by the Shelly sisters and Bryce."

"Thanks," Cadence said.

Once the man left, it was finally Hank who spoke up. "So, we saved the world again? Shouldn't we be happy or something?"

"Not us," Victor said, pointing to the kids. "Them."

"Your kid is a serious bad ass," Olivia said.

"I know," Min reassured the cheerleader.

"And think about her college options. She's black *and* Asian. Dude, she'll be set for Harvard."

Min slapped the cheerleader. The crowd froze at the sound. Olivia gave the small woman a hug, squeezing her. "I've missed you too."

"I hate you," Min said.

"So, looks like you and Jessica survived," Victor said.

Lauren's eyes darted back and forth, scanning the area. "Shhh. It might not be over. A stray zombie could show up. No, I will not sleep until--"

"So," Cadence interrupted the woman's coffee-fueled rant. "What do we do now?"

"So," Olivia started, "When I was driving here to totally save your asses--"

"To gloat," Cadence corrected.

"Can we trade her in for Dione?" asked Victor.

"Shut up, spank monkey," Olivia snapped back. "I saw a sign. Did you know that King David Mall is having its grand reopening?"

They all got quiet at the mention of the mall. Cadence and Xander stood, ignoring the woman. "We're going to get going."

"But..." Olivia said.

"Hey mom," Jessica said walking over with Tina and David. "I figure since we saved the world, could I get an advance on my allowance?"

"We want to hit up the mall," Tina said.

Min started in a rant. The little woman's voice continued as Hank jumped up, reaching into his pocket. Fumbling about, he pulled out a small gray box.

"I almost forgot!"

Before anybody could ask, he pressed the button. Cadence sighed. "What are we waiting for?"

Several blocks away, the sound started as a low rumble. The ground under the writer's feet started shaking. Smoke rose above the trees, and an explosion started, large enough that the heat reached their perch. They watched in silence as something in the center of town blew up in a blaze of glory.

"I think that's our cue to go home," Victor said, standing up.

"End of the story?" Xander asked Cadence.

"I think it's time to write 'The End' on this one."

"Wait," Olivia said, pointing at the start of the driveway. "Who's that?"

One of the soldiers in black put his hand to his eyes, blocking out the sunlight. "Oh, that's our commanding officer."

A small two-door sports car weaved its way through the parked cars. The engine roared loud enough that they could hear it as it entered the parking circle. The engine died and a man stepped out of the vehicle and started walking toward them.

"Oh shit," Xander said.

"It can't be," Min whispered.

The man walked up the stairs with a toothy smile. "Hola, mi amigos. If you're ready, I have your next mission."

Epilogue

The knife on the cutting board moved swiftly, slicing through the carrot before moving onto the onion. Xander whistled while he poured the ingredients into the large pot filled with water. He flipped on the burner, taking a deep whiff of his latest concoction.

"Xander!"

He grabbed the handle of the knife and tiptoed through the kitchen, into the study. Cadence had jumped up, knocking her chair over. She pointed at the computer screen, her hands shaking.

"What happened?"

Xander creeped closer, prepared to stab his wife if he discovered she had been possessed or taken over by a body snatcher. He leaned in, inspecting the computer screen. The browser window was open to Amazon. Living with the woman long enough taught Xander to inspect the book ranks each morning to determine his wife's mood.

#1.

"Congrats," he said, proud of his wife. "You are officially the Zombie Queen. Don't listen to anything Olivia says."

"I won't be the Zombie Queen much longer."

"What?!" Cadence had slaved for years writing books to achieve the title; each novel had reached the best seller's list. Xander couldn't imagine her quitting now. Cadence basked in the glow of her fans wherever they went.

"I've been thinking," she admitted. "Now that we've saved the world, maybe its time I branch out."

"Oh?"

"Vampires," she said. "I shall be the Queen of the Undead."

"Uhm," Xander started. "Do you think that's wise?"

"Why's that?"

"You've always written what you know. It's not like we've fought any vampires before."

She sat down at the computer, opened a word document, and started typing the first line of the novel. "Yet," she said.

They both froze at the statement. The hair on Xander's neck stood on end, goosebumps raced down his arm. "Dammit," he said. "Look at what you've started..."

* * * * *

Jessica pulled the headphones off her head as she entered the Dojo. A class of "Wee Warriors," were moving in unison with their instructor. At the front of the classroom, demonstrating each movement, was her arch nemesis.

Jessica caught Tina's eye and they exchanged chin nods. Jessica removed her shoes and placed them in a small cubby. While she walked across the floor behind the class, she admitted to herself that Tina's forms weren't amazingly accurate. If the clock on the wall was correct, they'd be going for another forty-five minutes before she took over with the older kids.

"Hey honey," Hank said as she walked into the backroom.

"Hey dad," she gave the man a peck on the cheek. "Is mom around?"

"I hate you!" Min yelled.

"I hate you more," came another voice.

"Aunt Jin in town?" asked Jessica.

Hank nodded. "You are so screwed."

"You're telling me. I might need you and Tina to defend me."

"Ain't enough rice in China," Jessica said.

Jessica sat down at her mom's desk and pushed aside a stack of paperwork reading, "Sword Insurance," and set up her laptop. David had smuggled her one of the best computers available on the open market, far more powerful than she needed to mix her own music.

"Chinese food tonight?" asked Hank.

"I still can't tell if that's racist or not," Jessica said.

"I know," he smiled. "That's why I like ordering it."

Min appeared out of the supply closet. Next to her, a nearly identical woman stepped out. Both the woman and her mother wielded a scowl known to make men cry. Jessica could tell by the way her mom stomped toward her that she had done something wrong.

"I didn't do it," Jessica said out of habit.

"What is this?" Min shoved the laptop shut and placed an envelope on top.

"Uhm," Jessica inspected the envelope. There was no return address. "A letter?"

"Open it," Min said. "From your boyfriend?"

"Leave her alone," Hank said.

"No Chinese food for you, racist."

"But--"

"Dear Jessica Li," the letter started. "We would like to congratulate you on your acceptance into the Music Composition and Marketing major..."

Jessica looked up from the letter to her mom and dad, both smiling from ear to ear. Jessica returned to the letter, rereading the statement several times before looking up.

"I got into college!"

"Of course you did," Min said flatly.

"When Olivia mentioned Harvard, I just thought, why not?" Jessica beamed.

"We have a Harvard girl in the house," Hank's smile wouldn't let up.

"Now," Min started, "go help Tina with class. College ain't going to pay for itself."

"Yes, ma'am."

"Start the Wee Warriors with swords," Min paused. "No, no insurance yet. Be safe, start with daggers."

* * * * *

"Dude, you almost shot me!"

David peaked through clenched eyes to see the bullet hole just to the right of Kevin's head. "They recruited me to work on computers," said the kid. "Why do I have to know how to shoot a gun?"

"It's called basic training," Kevin said, taking the weapon from him. "Everybody has to get trained."

Kevin released the magazine, counting the remaining bullets. He jammed it back in with a click, loaded a round in the chamber, and took aim at the target thirty-five feet away. Inhale, exhale, inhale, exhale, *bang, bang, bang, bang, bang.*

David watched as each bullet pierced the paper target. The forehead of the diagram was a massive hole once Kevin was done pulling the trigger. "Oh, you meant like *that.*"

Kevin grabbed his phone, snapping a photo as the paper target sped along the rail toward them. "This is going on my Instagram."

The intercom buzzed. "What part of 'Top Secret

Operations' wasn't clear?"

"Ugh," David groaned. "This guy is worst than the teachers at school."

"Dios mío," said their trainer.

* * * * *

"How does she do it?" asked Victor.

"Seriously? She can't even be in the top ten hottest women in this bar?"

Victor grimaced as Lauren stood between two men, grinding to the sounds of a live band butchering the latest pop hits. The former barista had her hands around the neck of one man while the other bumped up against her back.

"She knows we're in a gay bar, right?"

Olivia turned back to the bar and slapped her hand on the counter to get the bartender's attention. "I need bourbon, make it a double."

Victor smiled at the man behind the bar. Olivia followed the marine's gaze. "Him too? Jeez dude, you really are a slut."

"Jealous?"

"Yeah," the moment the man poured a shot, Olivia slammed down the entire drink. "I can not deal with this. Come back form the dead, not the hottest in the room, this is hell on earth."

"We came here to celebrate Lauren's two-week caffeine sobriety, let her have some fun."

"I guess," she said. "Truth--who did you think was going to survive, Lauren or Jessica?"

"All my money was on Jessica," he laughed.

"Ditto."

"So where are these friends of yours?" she asked. "This

your man of the week?"

He rolled his eyes. "They will be here."

The cheerleader pointed behind her to a man waving in their direction. "That him?"

Victor turned to see Miguel as they guy gave him a large bear hug, a phrase fitting the burly man. The top couple buttons Miguel's flannel were open, revealing a chest covered in hair. He leaned in and gave the man a kiss.

"Flavor of the week?" asked Olivia with a condescending smile.

"Actually," Miguel started, "might be a bit longer than that." He held up his hand, showing Olivia a ring on his finger.

Olivia grabbed the man's thick hand and inspected the platinum designer ring. She glanced from the shiny metal to Victor. "You don't..."

Victor pulled a necklace from underneath his shirt. "I didn't want it get damaged in wood shop."

She squealed, hugging both men. Victor laughed, embracing the woman. He paused as a man in tight jeans walked by. He caught his husband staring as well. Olivia laughed, slugging them both in the chest. "Glad to see some things don't change."

"I had him bring his brother," Victor whispered. "I thought you two might hit it off."

"Seriously? You're setting me up? This is a new level of sad."

"Jesus, I've been in this bar five minutes and not a single guy has grabbed my ass," said a man just behind Miguel.

"Meet Hector," Miguel said. "Thought you might have something to talk about. He just signed to be the quarterback--"

Olivia pushed past the Miguel and batted her eyes at Hector. "It's rough when people don't realize we're the hottest people in the bar." The cheerleader pressed her arms together, accentuating her breasts.

"Hi," he said.

"Hi, my name is Olivia..."

* * * * *

It had been weeks since she had last been home. The belt holding a gun at her hip slid off as she tore at the Velcro. Angelica dropped the belt to the floor and started unfastening her leg holsters.

As she moved through the house, she let them land on the floor without consideration. She walked through the living room and paused, imagining her and Renee enjoying a glass of wine in front of the fireplace. Continuing, she worked her way through the dining room and toward the study.

Angelica plopped down in a chair at the end of the table in Renee's study. She pulled off her shoulder holster and set it down on the table. The moment she settled in, the silence swallowed her. In the evenings, Renee could be heard reading, flipping pages and occasionally hawing over a passage in her latest read. Now, the house, her home, held a sense of sadness.

Angelica's fingers ran over the computer. She contemplated opening it and looking through photos, but she couldn't handle anymore sorrow. Tears welled up in her eyes. It was the first time in forever that she had cried. It started with a single tear and within seconds she was wiping streams from her eyes. Angelica started wailing.

"First dad," she wiped the snot from her nose. "Now

mom."

She sniffed, trying to steady herself. "We won mom. We won," she said to the empty room. "You're with dad now."

The tears subsided and Angie was left with her ragged breathing. Reaching across the table to grab a tissue, she noticed an envelope resting near the seat she usually occupied. The cursive letters reminded Angelica of the Christmas cards Renee insisted on mailing every year.

Tentatively, she slid the envelope closer and returned to her seat. Her fingers ran along the pen marks, debating on if she was emotionally prepared for the message from her mom. She imagined it read the traditional, "If I don't return..."

She peeled at the envelope, tearing it open to find a letter inside. With a deep breath, she unfolded the sheet of paper. The woman had a tendency to be long winded in written form, preferring the fine art of scribing over texting. Angelica was shocked to find the paper held almost no writing on it. Midway down, it contained only two words.

No body.

Angelica flipped the paper over, looking for more. She read the two words over and over again, trying to make sense of the mad woman's scribblings. Had she written a secret message only visible under ultraviolet light? She realized in her grief, she was being dense.

Angie laughed, "Till we meet again, mom."

If you enjoyed Suburban Zombie High please leave a review or sign up for Jeremy Flagg's newsletter at www.remyflagg.com.

Suburban Zombie High Series
Suburban Zombie High
Suburban Zombie High: The Reunion
Suburban Zombie High: Final Class

Children of Nostradamus Series
Morning Sun (Book 0)
Nighthawks (Book 1)
Night Shadows (Book 2)

www.ingramcontent.com/pod-product-compliance
Lightning Source LLC
Chambersburg PA
CBHW030656120726
47905CB00001B/238